EMMA

THE CURSE UNLEASHED

*A Gifted Psychic and A Vengeful Spirit -
The Battle between Light and Darkness*

RAVEN A. WOLF

ISBN
Paperback 979-8-89556-263-5
Hardcase 979-8-89724-560-4

Contents

Acknowledgment

This book is a reflection of a journey—one of mystery, transformation, and untold revelations. It is a testament to the hidden forces that shape our lives and to the encounters that bring us closer to who we are meant to be.

To all my spiritual guides and teachers, and to one of the most important teachers—you may never fully know the ways in which you have illuminated my path. In meeting you, I found not just a mirror, but also a guide who helped me see the truest version of myself. Your presence taught me lessons I did not know I needed and gave me the courage to unlearn what no longer served me. For that, I will always be grateful.

To everyone who supported me through this journey—thank you for your belief in me and for holding space when I needed it most.

To you, the reader—thank you for stepping into this world with me. I hope you find the story within these pages as captivating and transformative as the journey that brought it to life.

And to the universe—for its infinite wisdom, synchronicities, and the unseen forces that guide us toward our true paths—thank you for always holding me in your flow.

With love and gratitude,

Raven A. Wolf

Prologue
The Descent into Darkness

Willow's Creek

22nd October 1994

Laura stood hidden behind the thick trunk of an ancient oak tree, her breath shallow as she peered into the small clearing ahead. Though it had only been a year since she first saw him, it felt as if she had known him for lifetimes. Yet, she knew he remained unaware of her presence, oblivious to the ache that consumed her. Each day since had been defined by her obsessive longing, watching him from the shadows, desperately hoping for a fleeting moment when their worlds might finally collide.

The letter clutched tightly in her hand felt heavier with each passing second, its edges worn from the countless times she had unfolded and refolded it. It was filled with confessions, promises, and pleas—words she longed to speak to him but could never bring herself to say. She closed her eyes, clutching the letter tighter, as though it alone could hold the fragile pieces of her resolve together. The wind stirred the branches above her, rustling the leaves and carrying with it the scent of autumn, the same scent that seemed to haunt her every thought of him.

But as she stood there, waiting and watching, her mind drifted back to the ritual she had performed just days earlier, the one that had changed everything...

The flickering candlelight had cast erratic shadows across the walls of the dimly lit room. The air had been thick with the pungent scent of incense and burned herbs, mingling with the earthy odour of damp soil from the freshly dug pit at the centre of the basement in the manor's locked wing. Laura's trembling hands had gripped an ancient, leather-bound book, its pages brittle and yellowed with age. The book had been given to her by a psychic who dabbled in dark forces, promising it would grant her the power to achieve her twisted desires. As she muttered the incantations written in the book, her lips had contorted with the effort, making her expression appear almost grotesque.

For weeks, she had prepared for that night, drawing sigils on the floor with chalk, each line inscribed meticulously according to the instructions in the book. The ritual had demanded exacting precision, and her desperation for its success had driven her to the brink of madness. Her mind, already fragile from years of suffering from depression, unfulfilled longing, and emotional turmoil, had seemed to fracture further with each moment she spent in this dark pursuit.

Her heart had pounded with frantic rhythm as she poured a vial of dark liquid into the pit, watching it bubble and hiss. Her eyes had been wild, darting between the symbols she had drawn on the floor and the book in her hands. Sweat had trickled down her forehead, mingling with the tears that stained her cheeks. She was no longer merely a woman consumed by desire; she had become a vessel for darker forces, pushed to the brink of her sanity by an obsession that eclipsed all reason.

The air had crackled with malevolent energy as Laura raised her arms, her voice rising in a fervent chant that echoed off the walls. The temperature in the room had dropped sharply, and the candles had flickered violently, as though rebelling against her. Shadows had writhed and twisted, casting grotesque shapes on the walls that seemed to mock her resolve.

Laura's mind had spiralled into a maelstrom of chaos. The words she had uttered were not mere spells, but incantations that tore at the very fabric of reality. With each chant, the divide between the physical world and the supernatural had begun to dissolve. A weighty sense of impending doom had settled over her like a suffocating fog, yet she had pressed on, her obsession with him—the man who haunted her thoughts, the one she loved with an intensity that warped her very soul—had consumed every fragment of her sanity.

As the ritual had reached its climax, an icy grip had clutched Laura's heart. Her breath had come in ragged gasps, her hands trembling as she uttered the final incantation. The dark liquid in the pit had erupted into a swirling vortex of shadows, coiling around her like serpents. An unearthly howl had reverberated through the room, filling her ears with a deafening ring. Her vision had blurred as she staggered back, her mind reeling as the dark forces she had summoned had begun to assert their presence.

As the shadows had receded, leaving an eerie stillness, Laura had collapsed to the floor. The book had slipped from her grasp, landing face down amidst the ritual's remnants. Her laboured breaths had echoed in the silence, her body drained of vitality. She had been no longer just a young woman in love—she had become a vessel for an ancient evil far beyond her understanding. An evil that could not be controlled by a mere mortal like herself.

In the days that followed, Laura had withdrawn further from the world, her interactions with family and friends becoming more erratic and unsettling as her descent into madness deepened. Her dreams had been consumed by nightmarish visions, and she had been relentlessly plagued by a sense of impending doom.

But even as the dark forces closed in, Laura felt no regret. Her obsession with him, the man she had loved in silence, demanded this descent into darkness. She embraced it fully, knowing there was no turning back. This was the only path left to her, and she would walk it willingly, no matter the consequences.

And now, standing behind the ancient oak tree, Laura was a shadow of the woman she had once been. Yet despite the darkness that had consumed her, she clung to the hope that he would see and recognise the depth of her feelings. This belief, fragile as it was, sustained her through the darkest hours. With every ounce of strength left, Laura prepared to confess her love, hoping their bond could transcend the darkness and offer a glimmer of salvation.

Watching him now, she had no way of knowing that her obsession, intertwined with the dark forces she had summoned, would ultimately lead her to a fate far worse than she could ever imagine.

CHAPTER 1

The First Vision

Thursday, 6th October 2024

The Yorkshire Dales lay shrouded in a thick fog, the rolling hills barely visible in the dim light of the gloomy October morning. At the heart of this misty landscape sat Hawes, a quaint town nestled in the embrace of the hills, where history whispered through its narrow streets. The town, small but picturesque, clung to its historic buildings and winding pathways. Victorian-style homes and traditional brick storefronts painted a picture of a simpler time.

Towering oak trees lined the streets, swaying gently in the breeze, their leaves rustling softly as if sharing secrets of days gone by. The cobblestone streets were bordered by meticulously kept gardens, vibrant flowers bursting with colour. The town square, with its central fountain and well-worn benches, served as a gathering place, while nearby shops—a charming bookstore with creaky wooden floors, a bakery with the scent of freshly baked bread wafting through the air, and a small antique shop brimming with curiosities—added to the town's unique character. Life in Hawes moved at a relaxed pace, with townspeople exchanging friendly nods and warm smiles as they passed each other.

Just beyond the main square stood the old mill, once a thriving industrial hub. Now a historical site, it had been carefully preserved, its stone walls and wooden structure retaining the character of the past while remaining solid and well-maintained.

Emma Ravenwood had moved to Hawes from London three years ago, after leaving behind a life marred by personal tragedy and loss. Seeking a fresh start, she felt an immediate connection to the place, as if the town itself had been waiting for her. And its residents, intrigued by her mystical ways, had quickly embraced the newcomer.

Standing at an elegant height of 5'6", her slender yet toned frame was a testament to her active lifestyle, exuding both strength and mystery. Her deep green eyes, with a quiet luminescence that seemed to intensify in the fading light, often left people transfixed – as if they could see into the very core of one's being.

Emma walked briskly through the misty streets of Hawes, her long dark hair flowing behind her. Dressed in a black sleeveless dress that clung to her figure beneath a sleek black coat, the hem brushing just above her knee, she exuded both elegance and mystery.

The journey to this point in her life had been anything but easy. Orphaned at a young age, she had been taken in by her father's sister, Aunt Elizabeth, a compassionate widow who had no children of her own. Emma had moved to London to live with her aunt in a grand, historic house nestled in a prestigious neighbourhood. The house's elegant architecture and expansive gardens had provided a beautiful yet sombre backdrop to her adolescence, a time shadowed by the grief of losing her parents.

Growing up in London, Emma attended local schools and excelled academically. Her years there were marked by the challenge of adapting to a new life while finding solace in the city's vibrant cultural environment. Though her aunt was kind in her own way, she struggled with her own emotional demons, often leaving Emma to navigate her teenage years independently. This experience instilled in Emma a sense of self-reliance and strength.

When Aunt Elizabeth passed away a few years ago, Emma inherited her estate, but she never relied solely on that legacy. Instead, it provided her with a foundation to reshape her life and pursue her calling. Her journey to becoming a certified holistic life coach had been transformative. The process demanded not only spiritual insight but also a deep understanding of emotional and mental well-being. She blended her psychic abilities with structured teachings, learning to empower others in meaningful ways. The long nights of studying, personal growth, and countless hours spent honing her skills shaped her both professionally and personally.

One of Emma's most extraordinary gifts was her rare ability to see auras. This heightened perception allowed her to sense the energy fields around people, a skill that set her apart in her profession. While the gift could be overwhelming at times, she had learned to embrace it, using it to guide her clients in powerful and transformative ways. It was both a blessing and a challenge, and over time, it had become an integral part of her work.

Now, at 34, Emma was a compassionate, resilient woman who channelled her personal experiences into a fulfilling career. Her struggles, including managing bipolar disorder, had fostered deep empathy and a unique understanding of the human spirit. By balancing her condition with self-discipline and holistic practices, she not only supported herself but also guided others through their own challenges.

As she approached The Croissant Cottage, the inviting aroma of freshly baked pastries and brewed coffee drifted through the misty air. The bakery's charmingly rustic facade was adorned with flower boxes overflowing with vibrant geraniums, their red and pink petals adding a cheerful splash of colour. A hand-painted wooden sign creaked gently in the breeze, and golden light spilled through large, fogged-up windows, hinting at the cosy warmth inside. Through the glass, she could see rows of perfectly arranged pastries and the gentle glow of pendant lights, creating an irresistible, welcoming allure.

Michael, in his late 30s, had an easy charisma that made him a favourite among the locals. He was tall and had a commanding presence that effortlessly drew attention. His complexion carried a warm, sun-kissed tone that complemented his deep brown eyes and hair. The beard he wore added a rugged charm to his handsome features.

He had shared with Emma his journey from the hustle of city life to the serene pace of Hawes, a transition similar to her own search for a simpler, more meaningful existence. He spoke with quiet passion about the joy he found in baking, the satisfaction of creating something with his hands that brought happiness to others.

As Emma listened, she sensed a positive aura around him – a lightness that seemed to radiate from his very being. It was rare to encounter such genuinely good energy, and she found herself drawn to his sincerity and warmth.

Over the weeks and months that had followed, Emma had become a regular at The Croissant Cottage. With each visit, the comfort between them had grown, and they had begun sharing stories from their past, though never too personal. Michael's bakery had become more than just a place for breakfast; it had become a haven of comfort and budding friendship.

Smiling at the memory, Emma entered the bakery, her footsteps echoing softly on the wooden floor. The warm scent of freshly baked pastries enveloped her.

Michael looked up from behind the counter, his face breaking into a wide, welcoming grin. "Morning, Emma! What can I get you today?" he asked.

Emma's eyes lit up as she returned his smile. "Morning, Michael. I'll have a black coffee and a buttered croissant."

With practiced ease, Michael prepared her order: a steaming cup of black coffee, while warming a perfectly golden croissant in the oven.

"Emma, what are you doing this weekend?" he asked as he handed her the coffee and croissant.

Emma wrapped her hands around the warm cup. "Nothing much, Michael. A bit of gardening if the weather holds, and I'm planning to catch up on some reading," she said with a smile.

"I'm playing at The Obsidian Fog on Saturday night. Would you like to come?" he asked, his smile widening.

Michael was the lead guitarist of the local band Cosmic Echoes, known around town for their captivating psychedelic rock performances.

Emma's eyes lit up with interest. "Yes, I'd love to. What time are you playing?"

Michael leaned forward on the counter, his grin growing. "We start at 9 p.m."

Emma smiled warmly. "I'll be there, Michael."

As Emma took a bite of her croissant, savouring the buttery, flaky layers, Michael moved on to attend to another customer. His easy charisma was evident as he exchanged friendly words. Emma watched, appreciating the warm sense of community that filled The Croissant Cottage.

When she finished her breakfast, she stood, coffee in hand, thanked Michael and stepped out of the bakery.

As she made her way to her studio, Emma reflected on the changes she had experienced since moving to Hawes. Her psychic abilities had become more attuned, and she often felt the town's energy blending with her own. The presence of spirits and the whispers of untold stories had woven themselves into her daily life, becoming an inseparable part of her existence.

One morning, while meditating in the town's park, Emma was enveloped by the serenity of nature—the rustling of autumn leaves and the crisp scent of pine filling the air. As she settled deeper into her meditation, she sensed a subtle shift in the atmosphere—a coolness that stirred her senses, drawing her attention.

When she opened her eyes, her breath caught. At the edge of the park stood a figure—a young woman in old-fashioned attire, her eyes filled with sorrow. Emma immediately recognised that the figure was not of this world. Grounded in the serene surroundings of the park, Emma focused her energy, allowing herself to connect with the spirit.

As she closed her eyes once more, images of the spirit began to emerge – a young woman named Abigail, whose heart had been shattered by unrequited love centuries ago. Emma's heart ached for her, sensing the heavy longing that had tethered her spirit to the earthly plane.

Whispering a prayer into the autumn breeze, Emma sent Abigail love and light, hoping the wind and nature's embrace would offer solace. As her blessing faded into the distance, a deep calm settled within Emma. The spirit's restlessness had eased, and she hoped that Abigail had finally found peace.

Emma's abilities extended beyond merely seeing spirits. She frequently experienced vivid dreams, offering glimpses of the future or deep insights into the lives of those she met. Over time, she had learned to trust these instincts, attuning herself to the subtle whispers of the universe.

Her studio, *The Soul Sanctuary*, was a quiet retreat tucked away on a peaceful street in Hawes. The exterior was modest, with a weathered wooden sign that swayed gently in the breeze, nestled between a cosy café and an old bookstore—*The Oak & Ivy* and *The Enchanted Page*. Emma shared a good relationship with the owners of both places. She often stopped by for a chat or to enjoy a cup of tea with Mrs. Thompson, who owned the café, and Margaret, the owner of the bookstore, had become a good friend.

When Emma had first laid eyes on the empty building, it had been little more than a neglected shell, its potential hidden beneath layers of disrepair. Yet, with determination and a clear vision, she had transformed it into a true sanctuary – a place of healing, peace, and reflection.

Inside, The Soul Sanctuary exuded a calm, welcoming energy. The reception area greeted visitors with soft, comfortable chairs and a low table scattered with magazines on spirituality and wellness. The walls, painted in a warm shade of cream, were adorned with tapestries that depicted scenes from nature and mystical symbols. Shelves lined the walls, filled with books on shamanism, crystals, and spiritual practices, each piece carefully selected by Emma to reflect her own journey and the wisdom she had accumulated over the years.

The space was a reflection of Emma's eclectic taste, with crystals, artefacts, and treasures collected from her travels scattered throughout. In one corner, a small altar stood as the heart of the studio. Adorned with candles, feathers, and crystals, it was a sacred space where Emma often meditated and left offerings, inviting a sense of peace and connection to all who entered.

Emma was also an active member of the town's wellness committee, offering free meditation sessions in the park on select weekends. She also hosted monthly gatherings at *The Soul Sanctuary*, where community members could share their personal journeys— stories of healing, grief, spiritual awakening, or simply navigating everyday challenges. These gatherings had become a cornerstone of the community, fostering connections and promoting a sense of unity.

One of Emma's fondest memories was the first autumn festival she attended in Hawes. The town square had been transformed into a vibrant celebration of the season, with stalls selling homemade crafts, local produce, and delicious treats. Emma had set up a small booth offering tarot readings and aura consultations, and she recalled the long line of people waiting for her guidance. Each interaction deepened her bond with the town.

Through her work and compassion, Emma had become a trusted adviser and friend to many. People came to her not just for her psychic abilities but for her empathetic ear and wise counsel. She had helped mend broken hearts, provided clarity in times of confusion, and offered comfort during moments of grief. Her presence had become a source of solace and strength for the residents of Hawes.

Now, as she opened the door to *The Soul Sanctuary*, the familiar scent of incense filled the air, accompanied by the gentle chime of the doorbell. Rose, her assistant, was already there, arranging a batch of healing crystals on the counter.

Rose Thompson, the granddaughter of Mrs. Thompson, the owner of The Oak & Ivy café, was in her mid-20s and brought a vibrant energy to the studio. With her warm hazel eyes and curly chestnut hair usually pulled into a ponytail, Rose exuded a calming presence that put clients at ease. She was a meticulous and efficient organiser, managing Emma's schedule, handling emails, and keeping track of inventory, including crystals and tarot decks.

Rose's ability to multitask and her compassionate, soothing demeanour made her an invaluable part of *The Soul Sanctuary*. She was often the first point of contact for clients, greeting them with a smile and ensuring they felt comfortable, allowing Emma to focus on their sessions. Rose's unwavering support and positive energy ensured the studio ran smoothly, giving Emma the freedom to concentrate on the healing work that had brought her to Hawes.

"Good morning, Rose," said Emma, her smile warm and affectionate.

"Good morning, Emma," Rose replied, her voice carrying its usual uplifting energy. "I hope you're ready for a full day. Your first appointment is in about fifteen minutes." She glanced at her meticulously organised clipboard. "Do you need anything before we get started? Some coffee?

Emma shook her head with a grateful smile as she set down her bag. "No, I'm good, thank you. And as for the coffee," she lifted her mug with a smile.

Rose returned her smile, "Okay, Emma. I'll make sure everything runs smoothly."

Emma took a final sip of her coffee, savouring the comforting warmth, then nodded. "I'm lucky to have you, Rose. Let's make today a good one."

Rose gave a broad grin. "Thank you, Emma," she said sincerely. "I'm glad to be here and happy to help."

Taking a final sip of her coffee, Emma moved towards her consultation room—a sanctuary within a sanctuary. The space exuded tranquillity, filled with vibrant greenery, well-loved books, and an assortment of crystals thoughtfully arranged to create harmony. She took a moment to breathe in the soothing energy, centreing herself for the work ahead.

Emma took a moment to centre herself. Closing her eyes and drawing in a deep breath, she allowed the calm of the space to envelop her. The familiar scent of sage lingered in the air, while the gentle sound of wind chimes outside the window added to the room's serene atmosphere.

After a few minutes, a soft knock came at the door. Rose stepped in quietly, announcing the first client of the day, a young woman named Lily.

"Welcome, Lily," Emma said kindly, gesturing for her to sit. "Please, make yourself comfortable."

Lily hesitated but then took a seat, her eyes darting around the room. "Thank you," she murmured, her voice barely above a whisper.

Lily appeared nervous; her hands clasped tightly together. She was in her early twenties, with delicate features and wide, anxious eyes. Emma could sense the young woman's emotional turmoil even before she spoke, observing the aura around her—a swirling mix of blues and purples, colours that spoke of sadness and a struggle for inner peace.

Emma leaned forward slightly, her tone gentle and reassuring. "There's no rush, and no need to be nervous. We're here to work through whatever you feel ready to share."

Emma guided Lily through a tarot reading, sensing the young woman's apprehension as she shuffled the cards. As they were laid out on the table, a narrative emerged—a story of heartache, but also one of hope and new beginnings. Emma's voice was gentle and calming, each word chosen with care to provide reassurance.

"Lily," she said softly, her gaze meeting the young woman's with understanding, "I see that you're standing at a delicate point in your journey. You've been through so much pain, but there's also a path unfolding ahead—one filled with the promise of healing and joy."

Tears gathered in Lily's eyes, and she took a shaky breath. "I really needed to hear that," she whispered. "It's been hard to believe there's any light left in my life."

Emma gave her a calm, understanding smile. "It's a big step you've already taken by reaching out for guidance. Trust that you are capable of moving through this."

After a brief moment, Emma's tone shifted to a more practical note, offering Lily advice for the road ahead. She encouraged her to focus on small, daily actions that would nurture her well-being—such as meditation, journaling, or simply carving out time for quiet reflection. Emma reminded Lily that healing wasn't a linear process; it involved taking one step at a time, acknowledging both the progress and the setbacks along the way. She also emphasised the importance of leaning on others for support when needed.

Lily nodded, her expression softening with the weight of Emma's words. As the session ended, Lily left feeling more grounded, her heart a little lighter.

The rest of the morning unfolded in much the same way, with each client sharing their struggles and seeking Emma's guidance. After a brief lunch break, Emma resumed her sessions.

At 4 p.m., her final appointment of the day arrived. Rose showed Mrs. Eleanor Harrington in – a dignified woman in her late 60s. Her sombre demeanour was evident as she moved slowly, her face etched with a lingering sadness. Though lined with the marks of age, her features still held an elegance that suggested an inner resolve. Her weathered skin and deep-set wrinkles spoke of a life rich with experiences.

"Good afternoon, Mrs. Harrington," Emma said, guiding her to a seat.

"Thank you for seeing me, Miss Ravenwood," Mrs. Harrington said, her voice carrying a quiet weariness. "I'm from Willow's Creek, and I've heard about your gifts. I'm hoping you can help me find some peace."

Emma nodded gently. "Of course. Let's start by focusing on the energy you'd like to explore today."

Mrs. Harrington's hands trembled slightly as she spoke, her gaze distant. "I lost my daughter, Laura, around 30 years ago. She'd been struggling with mental health for years. We tried everything we could, but eventually, she was admitted to an asylum. Not long after… she took her own life there. It's been so difficult to make sense of it, and I've never been able to find closure."

With a soft sigh, she reached into her bag and pulled out a faded photograph, her hands lingering on the edges before she passed it to Emma. "This is Laura. She was only eighteen when we lost her."

Her voice was soft, but steady. Emma said, "I'm so sorry, Mrs. Harrington. Losing a child, especially in such painful circumstances, is a heartbreak few can understand. I will do my best to help you find the answers you're seeking."

Emma took the photo; it was old, the edges frayed, and the colours long since faded. Laura appeared young and fragile, with pallid skin and shoulder-length, mousey brown hair. Her eyes, shadowed and sunken, betrayed a sadness that seemed to reach out from the photo itself. Despite her plain appearance, there was a haunting intensity in her gaze, as if something darker lurked beneath the surface. Emma set the photo down carefully on the table.

She closed her eyes, taking a deep breath as she connected with the energy.

As soon as her lids shut, a chilling presence swept over her, heavy and suffocating. The air in the room felt thick, like the oppressive weight of a storm about to break. The energy was dense—cold, hostile, and unyielding. It wasn't the usual sorrow Emma felt when connecting with a lost spirit, but something far more unsettling—an energy that rejected her efforts to reach it, as if the spirit were actively pushing her away.

Emma tried to focus, but the dread surrounding her grew, making it almost impossible to breathe. It was clear that the spirit was not just lost but full of anger and confusion, and it had no intention of communicating.

After a long moment, Emma opened her eyes and turned her gaze to Mrs. Harrington who was looking at her with hope.

"I can sense her presence," Emma began gently, her voice soft yet firm, "but there's something blocking her – an anger, a resistance. She's not ready to reveal herself."

Mrs. Harrington nodded, her expression sombre. "I understand. She had been withdrawing for years before… before her death. I don't know what happened, but I feel as though something is holding her here."

Emma leaned forward, her voice gentle. "Can you tell me more about her? What was she like before her struggles? Any memories that stand out?"

Mrs. Harrington hesitated for a moment, looking down at her hands. "She was a highly intelligent child, but always so quiet and distant. After her father passed, she started withdrawing even more. I thought it was grief at first... but then, things... escalated. I just want to know if she is at peace."

The room grew colder as Emma absorbed the latest information. She knew that understanding Laura's life would hold the key to breaking through the dark energy surrounding her spirit.

Mrs. Harrington's voice trembled as she continued, "The police ruled her death a suicide, but I have always believed there was more to it than the official report."

Emma nodded slowly, her brow furrowing with concern. She closed her eyes for a moment, trying to push through the dense energy in the room, but the oppressive presence remained. She felt a shiver of apprehension as she opened her eyes. "I'm not getting anything more during this session. The energy around Laura is heavy and confused, and it's blocking me from connecting fully. It's as though she's not ready to share the details, or there are unresolved issues that keep her bound to this place."

Mrs. Harrington's face tightened with frustration, but her voice remained steady. "I understand. It's just... I need to know what happened to her, why she became so distant, why she felt she had to end her life. I need closure."

Emma's heart went out to the grieving mother, her words laced with compassion. "I'll do my best to understand more, but right now, all I can sense is that there is a lot of unresolved pain. Sometimes spirits carry those unresolved issues with them, and they resist being understood until they are ready."

Mrs. Harrington's eyes flashed with determination, and she took a deep breath. "I think being in her space will help. It might give you a clearer sense of the energy. Would you come to my home? I feel her presence might be stronger there."

Emma considered it for a moment. The thought of going to the house where Laura had lived made her a little uneasy, but she knew she could not leave Mrs. Harrington without offering whatever help she could. "I'd be happy to visit," Emma said, her voice firm but kind. "We'll see if I can sense more there. I understand how important closure is, for both you and Laura."

She paused, thinking it through. "I'll call you soon to schedule a time that works for both of us."

After Mrs. Harrington left, Emma sat in the consultation room, the lingering chill of the session still hanging in the air. The oppressive energy of the spirit weighed heavily on her, and she felt drained. Lost in thought, she hardly noticed the soft knock at the door until Rose entered, holding the keys to lock up for the day.

Rose paused, her expression softening as she took in Emma's weary look. "You look very tired, Emma. Tough session?" she asked gently.

Emma offered a tired smile, but it didn't quite reach her eyes. "Yes, it was more intense than I expected. I'll need a little time to process everything."

Rose nodded with understanding. "Of course. Take your time. I'll wait for you at my desk."

As Rose left the room, Emma remained where she was, the weight of the session still pressing down on her. The presence of Laura's spirit seemed to linger, and Emma knew she would need to prepare herself for the visit to Mrs. Harrington's home. She hoped that whatever answers awaited her there might offer some relief from the heaviness that clouded her mind.

The First Encounter

Thursday, 6th October 2024

Emma walked home in the evening twilight, her thoughts lingering on her session with Mrs. Harrington. The cool October air carried a crispness, and leaves rustled softly in the breeze. Yet, despite the serene surroundings, a heavy, unsettling feeling gnawed at her. Emma was no stranger to spirits and energies, but this case felt different—darker, more dangerous.

She had encountered countless spirits over the years—some lost and seeking closure, others darker entities that thrived on fear and sorrow. But Laura's presence was unlike any she had felt before. It radiated an intensity, a raw anger and desperation that seemed to seep into her very bones.

As Emma turned onto her lane, her mind replayed the moment when she first sensed Laura's spirit during the session. The room had grown colder, the air thick with tension. Laura's energy had been chaotic, like a storm trapped in a bottle—far removed from the usual calm that surrounded Emma's readings and healings.

She wondered what had driven Laura to such a state of unrest that she had taken her own life, and why her spirit was so troubled. Emma knew there were always hidden truths beneath the surface of these cases, and she would have to dig deeper to understand the root of Laura's anguish if she hoped to help her find peace.

The look in Mrs. Harrington's eyes – fear, sadness, and a silent plea for help – haunted her. It reminded Emma of the responsibility she carried in her work. She had promised to help, but the weight of that promise now felt heavier than ever.

Emma reflected on the delicate balance her work required—connecting deeply with her clients and their spirits while maintaining enough distance to protect her own well-being. It was a constant juggling act, one few could understand.

She thought of the countless nights spent in meditation, grounding herself, seeking guidance from the universe. Those moments of stillness were vital, yet tonight, the idea of finding peace through meditation felt overwhelming. Laura's spirit had left her unsettled, and Emma knew it would take more than her usual practices to regain her equilibrium.

Emma's lane, lined with charming cottages, exuded a quiet, rustic serenity. At the end of the lane stood her cottage, slightly more secluded than the others, nestled in a haven of tranquillity. The rose garden in front—a vibrant splash of colour against the grey—was her sanctuary, a space where she could lose herself in the delicate fragrance of the blooms, finding peace amid the petals.

Beyond the garden stretched a small, shadowy wood, its towering trees forming a natural barrier that separated her home from the rest of the village. The dense canopy, thick with ancient oaks and whispering pines, cast long, eerie shadows in the evening light. The woods seemed to pulse with an energy all their own, a quiet yet undeniable presence that added an air of mystery and seclusion to her property. It was here, in the stillness of the forest, where Emma often found herself drawn for moments of reflection and connection—a perfect retreat for someone like her, whose introspective nature craved both solitude and the unseen currents of the world. The woods, though serene, carried with them a sense of hidden secrets, as though they held more than just flora and fauna within their depths.

Inside, Emma's cottage was a cosy sanctuary, blending modern simplicity with bohemian flair. Sleek, minimalist furniture sat harmoniously alongside vibrant tapestries, eclectic art pieces, and an array of shimmering crystals that caught the soft light. The walls, painted in warm, earthy tones, enveloped the space in a sense of comfort and grounding. Lush plants of various sizes filled the room, their vibrant green leaves bringing life and vitality to every corner, while the subtle scent of sage and lavender lingered in the air, remnants of Emma's daily cleansing rituals.

In a quiet corner of the living room stood her meditation space, a serene haven that invited stillness and reflection. A plush floor cushion rested before a low table adorned with candles, incense, and crystals in various shapes and sizes, each thoughtfully placed to enhance the energy of the space. Shelves surrounding the area held an assortment of carefully arranged crystals, their energies carefully curated for harmony. A small waterfall feature provided a soothing, constant flow of water, adding a peaceful melody to the atmosphere. Soft, ambient lighting illuminated the corner, casting gentle shadows that danced with the flickering candle flames.

Along one wall, a large bookcase housed a varied collection of Emma's favourite reads, spanning several genres. Psychology books, spiritual guides, occult texts, and a few well-worn horror and thriller novels filled the shelves. Her background in psychology, a field she had studied before embracing her path as a psychic healer, was reflected in the depth of the collection. It gave her a unique understanding of the mind and human behaviour, which often complemented her spiritual work. Though her academic past occasionally intertwined with her spiritual practice, Emma kept the two worlds separate, respecting the distinction. Some books were dog-eared and well-loved, their covers frayed from frequent use, while others sat pristine and untouched, waiting for their time to be explored.

A large, comfortable couch dominated one side of the room, adorned with colourful throw pillows and a soft, knitted blanket. It was the perfect spot for Emma to unwind, whether reading, meditating, or simply enjoying a quiet evening of introspection. The coffee table in front of the couch was often scattered with her latest reads, a notebook filled with her thoughts, and the occasional teacup or glass of wine, making the space feel lived-in and personal—an embodiment of Emma's quiet, reflective nature.

The kitchen, though small, was thoughtfully designed for both functionality and style. White cabinets and countertops offered a bright contrast to the darker tones of the living room, and the aroma of herbs and spices often filled the air, reflecting Emma's love for cooking. Fresh flowers from her garden added a splash of colour to the kitchen island, enhancing the space with a touch of natural beauty.

The bedroom, a cosy retreat, was designed for ultimate relaxation. Soft, muted colours set a tranquil tone, with a large, inviting bed dressed in crisp white linens, a plush duvet, and an assortment of pillows. A sheer fabric canopy above gave the room a dreamy quality, while bedside tables with soft-glowing lamps provided the perfect ambiance for late-night reading or unwinding.

In one corner, a vintage vanity table reflected Emma's personal style, its surface adorned with perfumes and lotions. Across the room, a small writing desk held journals, pens, and tarot cards, a space where Emma recorded her thoughts and insights, a daily ritual that grounded her.

The bathroom, with its clawfoot tub and shelves lined with bath salts, essential oils, and handmade soaps, was another sanctuary. Candles often surrounded the tub, and the soothing scents of lavender, eucalyptus, and rose filled the air, creating a spa-like atmosphere to help Emma unwind after a long day.

Each room in the cottage offered a glimpse into Emma's life and personality. The living room and kitchen highlighted her spiritual side and love for knowledge, while the bedroom and bathroom reflected her need for quiet solitude and self-care.

Emma removed her coat and hung it neatly by the door, then slipped off her boots and set them aside. As she passed the hallway mirror, a subtle smudge in her smoky eye makeup caught her attention—a reminder of the long, draining day. She paused, meeting her own gaze, and for a moment, simply stared.

As Emma looked at herself in the mirror, she thought about the peculiar ways her astrological signs guided her life. As a Taurus Sun sign, she found solace in her determination and practical approach to life. Her Cancer moon brought a deep emotional sensitivity and an unspoken connection to her past, shaping her empathy and intuition. And with Aquarius as her rising sign, she embraced her unique perspective on the world, always striving to understand the deeper currents beneath the surface.

The combination of these three astrological signs created a complex tapestry of her identity—grounded yet emotional, introspective yet visionary. She pondered how these astrological influences had subtly shaped her journey through the chaos and courage that marked her struggles throughout her life.

She walked over to the music system and chose her favourite Beethoven playlist. The soothing classical music filled the space with a calming ambiance. Then, she headed to the bathroom, drawing a hot bath to wash away the day's lingering chill. The scent of lavender filled the air as she added bath salts and essential oils, hoping to relax her tense muscles and mind.

While the bath filled, Emma undressed and carefully removed her makeup, using a gentle remover to cleanse her skin. Then, she stepped into the aromatic hot water, allowing herself to sink in as the lavender essential oil and bath salts enveloped her, easing away the stress of the day. As she lay there, her thoughts wandered to the clients she had seen, especially Mrs. Harrington. A shiver ran through her as she recalled the oppressive energy of Laura's spirit, Mrs. Harrington's daughter.

After the bath, Emma stepped out, her skin warm and relaxed from the soothing soak. She wrapped herself in a plush, dark green robe and made her way to her bedroom, which offered a peaceful retreat. Soft, ambient lighting filled the room, mingling with the faint scent of lavender still lingering from the bath. She opened her wardrobe and pulled out a pair of simple white pyjamas, their soft fabric a comfort after a long day.

As she slipped into them, she paused to brush her long, dark hair, smoothing out the tangles with each gentle stroke. She then applied moisturiser to her face, hands, and feet, savouring the familiar motions.

Before heading to the kitchen, Emma took a moment to ground herself. She lit a few candles and some sandalwood incense in her meditation space, letting the calming fragrance fill the room. Sitting on her plush cushion, she closed her eyes and took a few deep breaths, visualising a soft, protective light enveloping her and easing away the day's tension.

When she felt her mind settle, Emma picked up a piece of amethyst, running her fingers over its cool, smooth surface. She whispered a quiet prayer for peace and clarity, savouring the moment of stillness. With a renewed sense of calm, she stood and made her way to the small bar counter in her living room, where she poured herself a vodka on the rocks. The crisp sound of ice clinking in the glass grounded her further.

With her drink in hand, she moved into the kitchen to prepare a meal of chicken breast with fresh vegetables and herbs. She quickly chopped the vegetables, the colours adding a touch of brightness to the space. Seasoning the chicken, she placed it into a hot pan, listening to the satisfying sizzle as it began to cook.

Cooking had always been a source of comfort for Emma. As a Taurean, she found immense pleasure in the simple joys of life, and preparing a meal was no exception. She loved selecting fresh ingredients, savouring their aromas, and experimenting with different flavours. As the chicken browned in the pan, the kitchen filled with the comforting scent of roasting food. She assembled a fresh salad with crisp greens, cherry tomatoes, and a light vinaigrette. Once everything was ready, she set the table, feeling a quiet sense of satisfaction as she sat down to enjoy her meal.

As Emma ate, her thoughts drifted back to her university days. Choosing psychology as her major had been a decision rooted in both curiosity about the human mind and her own personal struggles. Diagnosed with bipolar disorder in her late teens, Emma had experienced the highs of manic energy and the deep lows of depression. Navigating these extremes had been challenging, but it had also sparked a deep desire to understand herself better.

She recalled the countless therapy sessions, medications, and coping strategies she had explored over the years. Her psychology studies had given her a foundation that helped her make sense of her mental health journey, combining knowledge with intuition. This understanding had not only empowered her to manage her condition but had also fuelled her desire to help others facing similar struggles.

Her experiences had shaped her into a compassionate, empathetic healer. As a psychic, she used her academic background and intuitive abilities to guide her clients, blending logic with spirituality in a unique approach to healing.

As she took another sip of her drink, Emma felt a quiet gratitude for the path she had chosen. The challenges had made her stronger, and she appreciated the peaceful life she had created for herself. The sound of the wind rustling through the trees outside brought her back to the present. She finished her meal, tidied up the kitchen, and poured herself another drink.

Then she settled onto the couch, picking up her leather-bound journal. The weight of it felt comforting in her hands, a familiar companion for the reflections she often recorded. Just as she was about to write, her phone buzzed. Glancing at the screen, a smile tugged at her lips. It was Serena, her best friend from university.

Serena had always been a vibrant and outgoing person, a stark contrast to Emma's more introspective nature. With her auburn hair and striking green eyes, Serena had an alluring presence that drew people to her effortlessly. They had met in their first year at Cambridge, thrown together by chance in a psychology class. Serena's vibrant energy and infectious laugh had immediately drawn Emma in, a perfect contrast to her own quieter, more reserved demeanour. They had bonded over late-night study sessions, frustrations with professors, and long walks around the city, delving into everything from psychological theories to personal confessions. Through it all, Serena had been Emma's rock, always providing support, especially during the more tumultuous times when Emma's moods would shift unpredictably.

Serena was a successful child psychologist in London, renowned for her innovative methods and deep compassion for her young patients. Despite the distance, their friendship had only grown stronger. No matter how much time passed, they could pick up right where they left off, sharing their triumphs, struggles, and everything in between.

"Hi, Serena!" Emma answered, her voice lighting up with warmth.

"Emma! How are you? It feels like forever since we last talked!" Serena's cheerful voice came through the phone.

"I'm good, just unwinding after a long day," Emma replied, her tone light. "How are you? How's Ryan?"

"I'm fine. Ryan's good too, busy as always," Serena laughed. "But I miss you! When are you coming to visit me? It's been too long!"

"I miss you too," Emma replied with a smile in her voice. "Let me see if I can plan a weekend trip. How about next month?"

"That sounds perfect!" Serena said eagerly. "I've got so many places I want to take you—new cafes, bookshops, and of course, we need a proper night out. Oh, and there's a new vintage store I want to take you to. You'll love it!"

They talked for a while longer, sharing stories and laughter, the conversation flowing easily, just like it always did between them. Serena's lively spirit and their shared history gave Emma a sense of comfort and excitement for her upcoming visit.

Once the call ended, Emma sat back and let out a contented sigh. She hadn't realised how much she missed Serena's easy laughter and the warmth of their friendship.

As she thought about Serena, her mind naturally drifted to Ryan Ashford. Serena had introduced Emma to him when they first met in Cambridge. He was Serena's childhood sweetheart. Hailing from an aristocratic English family, the Ashfords had long been established in both social circles and business. Ryan had taken on the responsibility of managing the family's construction business, a role he approached with quiet determination and a sense of duty. His reserved nature stood in stark contrast to Serena's vibrant energy, yet there had always been a kind of harmony between them. Serena's liveliness seemed to feed off his steadiness, and Ryan, in turn, appeared to find peace in her exuberance.

Emma smiled as she thought of how far they had come since then. Now, they were married. Serena had once joked about how Ryan was the yang to her yin, and Emma could see it more clearly now. Ryan was grounded, methodical—everything that balanced out Serena's free-spirited nature. She could easily imagine them spending a lifetime together, with Ryan's steady presence calming Serena's occasional storms.

She felt happy for them both, knowing their marriage was built on the same foundation of stability that Ryan brought to everything he did.

With a deep sigh, Emma turned her attention back to her journal. She began to write, the pen gliding smoothly across the page, translating the complexities of her thoughts into words.

Reflecting on her meeting with Mrs. Harrington, she wrote about the palpable grief she had sensed and the lingering, tormented energy of Laura's spirit that had filled the room during their session.

After jotting down her final thoughts, she closed the journal and placed it on the table before settling into the couch.

She turned on the TV and flipped through channels until she found a light-hearted comedy. The familiar characters and humorous dialogue offered a welcome distraction, and she laughed along with the show.

As the night wore on, she turned off the TV and lights, then headed to her bedroom. The cottage was bathed in serene silence, broken only by the occasional creak of the wooden floorboards and the soft rustling of trees outside. She set her phone on the bedside table, slipped under the warm covers, and let out a contented sigh. Though her mind buzzed with the day's events, exhaustion soon pulled her into sleep.

In her dream, Emma found herself walking through a dense, ancient forest. The towering trees, with their gnarled branches and thick canopies, created an almost mystical atmosphere. The air was cool and earthy, tinged with the scent of moss and decaying leaves. Moonlight filtered through the foliage, casting an ethereal glow on the forest floor.

Following a winding path, she ventured deeper into the woods. The silence was broken only by the distant hoot of an owl and the rustling of unseen creatures. Eventually, she came to a clearing bathed in silver moonlight, where an ancient oak tree stood at the centre. Its trunk was so wide it would take several people to encircle it. The tree's roots twisted into natural steps leading down to a hollow.

Compelled by an unseen force, Emma descended into the hollow. Inside, the chamber felt like a sanctuary, filled with symbols of forgotten wisdom. Candles flickered softly, casting dancing shadows on the stone walls.

In the centre stood a stone altar with an ornate mirror framed in silver. Its surface was dark, reflecting only the faint light of the candles. Emma felt a magnetic pull towards it, an irresistible urge to gaze into its depths.

As she stepped closer, the mirror shimmered, revealing an image of herself standing in her cottage's rose garden, surrounded by vibrant blooms. Her reflection smiled, but something was wrong – her eyes were dark and empty, devoid of the warmth she knew so well.

The reflection raised a hand and beckoned Emma closer. Hesitation gripped her, but the pull was too strong. She reached out and touched the mirror. The moment her fingers made contact, a surge of energy coursed through her, and she felt herself being pulled into a void. Fear gripped her as terror surged through her body.

Just as she felt she would be consumed; she was jolted awake at exactly 3 a.m. The room was dark, and a heavy silence filled the air. Her heart pounded as an eerie sensation of being watched crept over her.

A cold draught brushed her skin, raising goosebumps on her arms. Slowly, she turned her head to scan the room, her eyes struggling to adjust to the darkness. The shadows danced around her, deepening the unsettling atmosphere.

Emma reached for the lamp on her bedside table, but before she could turn it on, she saw a silhouette at the edge of her bed. Her breath caught in her throat as she froze in place. The figure was that of a woman, faint and ghostly, her form barely discernible in the dim light from the streetlamp outside, casting long shadows across the room.

The figure flickered, its shape shifting unnaturally, and Emma's psychic senses surged to life. This was no ordinary presence. A cold chill crawled up her spine as her mind raced to make sense of the energy in the room. And then, with sudden, jarring clarity, it hit her—it was Laura. The air grew thick, suffocating with an overwhelming sense of sorrow and fury that seemed to press down on her chest. The weight of her grief was so palpable, Emma could almost feel it in her own bones.

Laura's hollow eyes, dark with pain and regret, locked onto Emma's. In that instant, the temperature in the room dropped sharply, and Emma saw her own breath misting in the icy air. A wave of emotions crashed over her – fear, anger, and an all-encompassing sorrow. She felt Laura's torment, her lingering suffering, and the darkness that had followed her even in death.

The room seemed to pulse with a menacing energy, growing colder and darker with each passing second. Emma lay still, her heart hammering in her chest, her mind scrambling for a way to protect herself. Instinctively, her lips parted, and without thinking, the words of a familiar mantra began to form silently in her mind. She focused on the rhythm of the chant, the ancient words flowing through her thoughts like a protective shield. The energy in the room began to shift as the chant grew stronger, her intent sharpening.

The temperature plummeted further, but Emma's chanting continued, steady and unwavering, as she visualised the light expanding, pushing the shadows back. Her breath became shallow, her pulse quickening, but she held her ground. Slowly, she felt the weight in the room lift—though it was a struggle, as though something unseen clawed at her, unwilling to let go.

Laura's form remained, flickering at the edge of the bed, shifting like a flame caught in the wind.

With one final, forceful surge of energy, Emma pushed the darkness back. The air cleared, the cold receded, and the heavy presence dissipated. Laura's figure flickered one last time before vanishing into the shadows. The room warmed, and the sensation of being watched slowly ebbed away.

Emma lay in the stillness, her heart still racing, knowing this encounter was only the beginning. Laura's spirit was far from peaceful; it was a force of pure anguish and wrath. Emma understood that in order to find peace, she would need to uncover the root of Laura's torment—before it consumed her.

CHAPTER 3

The Awakening

Friday, 7ᵗʰ October 2024

Gloomy clouds hung low over the village as rain pattered steadily against the windows, casting a grey, melancholic light across Emma's bedroom. She had drifted off to sleep in the early hours of dawn but woke abruptly at 6 a.m., her heart still racing from the unsettling events of the night. The room was quiet, yet the heavy weight of her encounter lingered, clinging to her like a thick fog.

Emma sat up in bed, rubbing her eyes, trying to shake off the remnants of a restless sleep. The image of Laura's shadowy silhouette by the edge of her bed was still vivid in her mind, a haunting figure in the dimness that felt almost tangible. She wondered if it had been a dream, or if something more sinister had happened. Her pulse quickened at the thought. Spirits did not typically invade her space so directly—why had Laura chosen to?

The unease from the night heightened her senses, leaving her hyper-aware of the quiet around her. The air felt heavier than usual, as if it carried the echoes of something unseen. Emma took a deep breath, grounding herself, trying to calm the swirl of questions and concerns racing through her mind. It was clear the encounter had not been a random occurrence; there was something more at play here. But what?

Determined not to let the unsettling encounter take hold of her day, Emma decided to follow her usual routine. She needed normalcy, something to anchor herself to.

In the kitchen, she reached for her favourite coffee beans, the ritual of brewing a cup offering a small sense of comfort. The rich, earthy aroma filled the room, the sound of the coffee machine humming steadily grounding her as the dark liquid slowly filled the pot. The first warm sip was a small but necessary balm, spreading a sense of comfort through her body.

With her cup in hand, she moved to her meditation space. The soft glow of candles flickered in the quiet room, and the scent of sandalwood incense filled the air. As she settled onto her cushion, Emma closed her eyes, exhaling deeply, trying to quiet the buzzing thoughts in her mind. The meditation would help—she needed clarity and some peace of mind after what had happened. She focused on her breath, letting each inhale and exhale calm the storm within. But even as she sat there, she could not shake the feeling that this was just the beginning of something she was not fully prepared for.

Following her meditation, Emma moved effortlessly into her yoga routine, flowing through each pose with grace. The stretches eased the tension in her muscles, calming her mind and grounding her energy. Yoga had become an essential practice for maintaining balance, especially given her heightened sensitivity.

With her yoga session complete, Emma settled onto her cushion, surrounded by crystals—amethyst for protection, rose quartz for self-love, and clear quartz for clarity. She opened her journal to a fresh page and began writing her affirmations: "I am strong and resilient. I trust in the universe's guidance." The words felt grounding, reinforcing her inner strength and aligning her energy with her intentions for the day.

Next, she wrote down specific goals: "I am committed to expanding my knowledge and skills to better serve others, and I will take time each day to nurture my own well-being." This practice of affirmations and intention-setting helped her stay grounded and aligned with her goals, filling her with a quiet sense of confidence.

After a few minutes, she gently extinguished the candles in her meditation space, the faint wisps of smoke curling into the air. The serene atmosphere lingered, wrapping around her as she concluded her practice.

Feeling a renewed sense of calm, Emma stepped into the shower. Warm water cascaded over her, easing the last of her muscle tension and rinsing away the lingering weight of the previous night. As the steam swirled around her, a memory surfaced—one from her early days of practising in London.

A client had reached out to her about disturbances in their home. The house was a grand, yet eerie, Victorian townhouse in an old part of the city, its once majestic facade now worn with time. The client spoke of flickering lights, doors slamming shut on their own, and a pervasive feeling of being watched. There was something undeniably oppressive about the place. The disturbances had grown stronger over time, pushing the family to the brink of fear and frustration.

When Emma visited the client's house, she felt it at once — the air was thick, heavy with unresolved energy. She soon discovered the source: the spirit of an angry man, a former tenant named Richard, who had died there years earlier under violent circumstances. His presence was unmistakable — dark, swirling, and full of unspent rage. His anger had kept him trapped in the house, unable to move on, and it clung to every room.

Richard's spirit was angry and violent, his fury stemming from his untimely death in the house. He had been murdered during a robbery, and his unresolved emotions had left him bound to the place, his bitterness manifesting as the disturbances in the home. Emma connected with his spirit over several days, carefully unravelling the layers of his grief and anger. It was no easy task, but with patience and compassion, she helped him understand that his unresolved rage was keeping him tethered to the earthly realm.

In the end, after a long and emotionally taxing session, Emma was able to guide Richard to the light. She helped him release his anger, and in doing so, freed him from the house that had been both his prison and his torment. It was an intense experience— one that left her feeling drained but also reaffirmed in her work as a psychic healer. The power to help a lost soul find peace, to help them cross over, was a gift she would never take for granted.

Returning to the present, Emma finished her shower and moved to her wardrobe, where she selected an outfit that blended contemporary elegance with her signature bohemian flair. She chose a pair of dark skinny jeans that hugged her figure perfectly, offering both comfort and sophistication. These jeans were a versatile staple in her wardrobe, easily adaptable to any occasion.

For her top, she picked a fitted, sleeveless blouse in soft, earthy beige. The subtle V-neckline and lightweight fabric draped gracefully over her frame, creating a simple yet elegant look that matched her preference for clean lines and understated style.

To add a touch of colour, Emma chose a light, patterned scarf in shades of turquoise and gold. She draped it loosely around her neck, allowing it to fall naturally and frame her outfit; the scarf's vibrant hues offering a striking contrast against the neutral tones.

For accessories, she opted for one of her favourite pieces: a pendant necklace featuring a polished amethyst crystal, known to enhance intuition and spiritual awareness. On her wrists, she stacked beaded bracelets adorned with various crystals – rose quartz, citrine, and turquoise – each one contributing its grounding energy and boho charm.

Her earrings were small but distinctive – simple silver hoops that caught the light as they glinted softly. She finished the look with a pair of comfortable yet stylish ankle boots in warm tan, their slight heel adding just the right amount of height and completing the effortlessly chic ensemble.

Emma stepped outside, the cool air brushing against her skin as she made her way toward *The Croissant Cottage*. As she walked, she spotted her neighbours, Sophie and Mark, a couple around her age. They were standing outside their house, exchanging a few words before heading out. Sophie waved in Emma's direction, her smile warm despite the overcast morning. Emma gave a small nod in return, acknowledging the gesture as she passed by.

The brief interaction was enough to remind her of the quiet rhythm of a small town life. As she walked, the sound of her boots on the cobblestone path was a steady rhythm, grounding her as she moved forward.

She noticed the vibrant colours of the blooming flowers in neighbouring gardens, their petals glistening with raindrops like jewels. She paused to inhale the fragrant blooms, allowing their sweetness to momentarily distract her from the weight of the previous night's events.

Suddenly a fleeting movement caught her eye—a shadow darting behind a tree. Emma's heart raced, but as she focused, she realised it was just a cat, its fur slick from the rain, darting off into the underbrush. With a nervous chuckle, she reminded herself to stay grounded and embrace the ordinary sights around her.

Her thoughts drifted to the protective techniques and rituals she had learned over the years to guard against harmful spirits. Then she thought of the previous night; Laura's presence had felt almost personal, as if trying to convey a message just for her. Determined to find answers, Emma resolved to learn more about Laura Harrington, hoping that understanding her life and untimely death might reveal what the spirit was trying to communicate.

Emma reached The Croissant Cottage, the familiar sight of the quaint bakery offering a welcome distraction. As she pushed open the door, the cosy warmth wrapped around her like a soft embrace, and the aroma of freshly baked bread and brewing coffee soothed her frayed nerves. The bell above the door chimed, catching Michael's attention as he worked behind the counter.

"Morning, Emma!" Michael greeted with a bright smile. "What can I get you today?"

"Morning, Michael," Emma greeted him back with a smile.

Then, taking a moment to glance at the array of pastries displayed in the case. Each one looked more tempting than the last. She paused, allowing herself to savour the sight of the warm, golden-brown cinnamon rolls and delicate fruit tarts, before making her decision.

"I'll have a black coffee and a cinnamon roll," she said.

"Coming right up," Michael said, moving swiftly to prepare her order. "How is everything? You look a bit... preoccupied."

Emma hesitated for a moment, not wanting to delve into the details of her night. "Nothing. Just work-related things," she said lightly.

Michael nodded sympathetically as he poured her coffee. "I hear you. Some days just start off on the wrong foot. But hey, you are still coming to the gig, right?"

"Of course I am," Emma replied with a smile. "It'll be nice to unwind and listen to some great music."

Michael grinned, handing her the coffee and muffin. "Awesome! I am playing a couple of new songs that I think you will love."

Emma took the bag and her coffee, savouring the rich aroma. She replied warmly. "Looking forward to it!"

As she stepped back outside, she felt relaxed. Her conversation with Michael had been a welcome distraction, grounding her in the present moment and giving her something positive to look forward to. She took a sip of her coffee, the warmth spreading through her, and continued her walk to work, feeling a little more at ease.

As Emma stepped into her office, she was greeted by the sight of Rose bustling around, organising files and setting up the day's schedule. Rose looked up and smiled warmly.

"Good morning, Emma!" Rose greeted her.

"Morning, Rose," Emma replied, her spirits lifted by the familiar comfort of her workspace.

Rose glanced at the schedule on her tablet. "We have a busy day. Your first client, Clarissa, is at 9 am. Then James at eleven. Lunch break after that, followed by Elena at 1 pm and Mark at three."

Emma nodded, preparing herself mentally. "Anything specific I should know?"

Rose scrolled through her notes. "Clarissa is new, dealing with a tough breakup. James is anxious about his career. Elena has family issues, and Mark wants clarity on a personal decision."

"Got it," Emma said. Rose added, "Oh, and I ordered some new crystals and sage. They should be here by the end of the week."

"Perfect. Thanks, Rose," Emma felt grateful for Rose's efficiency. Heading into her consultation room, she settled in before her first appointment.

A moment later, Rose announced Clarissa, a young woman with hunched shoulders and sadness clouding her eyes. Emma took a deep breath, centreing herself, as she noticed the heaviness in Clarissa's aura, a reflection of the emotional burden she carried. Emma prepared to provide the support and guidance Clarissa needed.

"Hello, Clarissa," Emma greeted, her voice calm and soothing. "Please, come in and have a seat." She waited until Clarissa settled into the chair, then gently asked, "How can I help you today?"

Clarissa sighed, her eyes filling with tears. "I've been going through a tough breakup. It has been... unbearable."

Emma nodded empathetically and closed her eyes to better sense Clarissa's aura. A cold sensation swept over her, a sharp echo of recent trauma. "Let's begin with a tarot reading," Emma suggested, shuffling her deck with practiced ease. As she did, three cards flew out, almost eager to be read.

Emma gently turned over the first card: *Three of Swords.* Her heart ached in tandem with Clarissa's as she explained, "This card represents deep heartbreak, betrayal, and emotional pain. It mirrors the anguish you're feeling."

She drew the second card, revealing *The Star.* Emma's voice softened with reassurance. "The Star is a beacon of hope and healing. It promises that, despite your current suffering, a path to renewal and brighter days lies ahead."

Finally, she turned over the third card: *Ace of Cups.* Warmth flowed through her, a gentle energy full of promise. "The Ace of Cups signifies a new beginning in love and emotional fulfilment. Once you've allowed yourself to heal, new and meaningful connections will blossom."

Emma placed the cards down and reached for Clarissa's hands, her touch grounding and compassionate. "Healing takes time," she said tenderly. "Focus on nurturing self-love and surrounding yourself with those who uplift you. A cleansing ritual with sage and healing crystals could also help release the negative energy."

Clarissa's eyes shimmered with unshed tears, but she managed a small, hopeful smile. "Thank you, Emma. This gives me hope."

Once she left, Emma prepared her space for her next client, James, who entered with an air of anxiety and uncertainty. She immediately sensed the heaviness in his aura, a reflection of his inner turmoil and the weight of being at a career crossroads. Emma attuned herself to his unease, recognising the deep conflict and desire for purposeful growth within him.

As she shuffled her tarot deck, the cards painted a story of James's current struggle. The reading emphasised the need for introspection, encouraging him to step back and reflect on what truly mattered in his career and life. There was an indication of impending disruptive change – a moment of upheaval that, while daunting, had the potential to transform his path and bring newfound clarity.

Despite the looming challenges, the cards also pointed to a reservoir of inner strength and the promise of triumph through determination and focus. Emma sensed that James needed to channel his energy into decisive action, setting clear intentions for his future. The reading offered him a blueprint for navigating his anxiety, with a reminder that even the most unsettling changes could serve as catalysts for growth.

After a morning of intense sessions, Emma took a break for lunch, grateful for the respite. Rose had brought back a meal from the café next door: a fresh, crisp tuna salad with the bright aroma of dill and lemon, alongside a small bowl of creamy tomato soup—perfect for the cool, overcast afternoon. Rose had also added a special treat: a buttery almond croissant that made Emma smile.

As she ate, the gentle patter of rain began to fall against the windows, casting a soothing rhythm over the cosy studio. The food and Rose's quiet presence offered Emma a sense of calm, a welcome moment of comfort before the afternoon's demanding appointments.

Refreshed, Emma prepared herself for the afternoon's clients. Elena was first, bringing with her the tangled complexities of family issues that needed Emma's deep empathy and intuitive guidance. Emma listened intently, using her skills to untangle the emotional knots woven through Elena's aura.

Next was Mark, who needed clarity on a significant personal decision. Emma drew on her insights to guide him towards a path that felt right, helping him find both direction and confidence. Each session demanded Emma's complete focus, but she navigated them with her usual grace. As the final client departed, early evening had descended, casting the studio in a soft twilight.

Emma waited for Rose to finish locking up, and they exchanged goodbyes before parting ways. The rain had stopped, leaving the air fresh and cool. Heading home, Emma felt the satisfying weight of a day well spent.

Stepping into the warmth of her cottage, Emma was greeted by the familiar cosiness that always made her feel at home. The rain had paused, leaving behind a damp, misty atmosphere that clung to the cool evening air. Soft light from her living room lamps cast a gentle glow, warding off the lingering gloom of the overcast day. Emma set down her bag and slipped off her boots, relishing the plush feel of the carpet beneath her tired feet.

She poured herself a glass of water in the kitchen and carried it to the living room, where she took a moment to jot down some notes about the day's sessions. Reflecting on each client, she carefully recorded her insights, organising her thoughts while the experiences remained fresh in her mind.

By 7 p.m., hunger had set in, and she returned to the kitchen to prepare a simple yet satisfying meal. She toasted slices of bread, layered them with creamy avocado and juicy tomato slices, and sprinkled everything with salt, pepper, and a drizzle of olive oil. Fresh basil leaves completed the dish. With her plate in hand, she poured a glass of white wine and sat at the table, allowing herself to relax and enjoy the soothing quiet of the evening.

After dinner, Emma cleaned up, rinsing her plate and glass before placing them in the dishwasher. She wiped down the counters, enjoying the small ritual of tidying her space. With the kitchen in order, she returned to the living room, settling into her favourite armchair with her wine. She picked up a thick, leather-bound book: *Spirits and Hauntings: A Guide to the Unseen*, a volume she had been meaning to delve into for months.

Outside, the rain began again, a gentle patter against the windows that created a soothing rhythm. The renewed hum of the rain and the soft glow of her cottage's lights created a peaceful ambiance. As Emma finally opened the book and began to read, she felt the day's remaining tension melt away, ready to lose herself in the mysteries of the unseen world.

As she opened the book, the musty scent of old paper wafted up, mingling with the aroma of her wine. She flipped through the pages, stopping at a chapter titled "Encounters with Malevolent Spirits." Her eyes scanned the text, absorbing the detailed accounts of people who had experienced encounters similar to her own.

The author described various signs of a malevolent presence: cold drafts, shadows moving in the periphery of vision, a sense of being watched, and physical manifestations such as objects moving or unexplained noises. Emma's fingers traced the lines of text as she read, comparing the experiences to her own encounter the previous night. The shadowy silhouette, the oppressive atmosphere—it all matched.

The book also discussed methods for dealing with such spirits. Protective rituals, cleansing techniques, and the importance of maintaining a strong, positive energy field were emphasised. Emma found herself nodding in agreement as she read about the significance of inner strength and emotional resilience. These were qualities she had cultivated over the years, knowing they were essential for her work as a psychic healer.

A section on ancestral spirits caught her attention, but she decided to keep it for later. The next chapter detailed protective symbols and charms that could be used to ward off negative entities. Emma recognised many of them: the evil eye, protective crystals like black tourmaline and obsidian, and various herbs used in smudging rituals.

Feeling reassured by the detailed descriptions and practical advice she had absorbed; Emma closed the book and placed it gently on the small table beside the couch. She took one last sip of her wine, savouring the rich flavour, then stood up. She carried the empty glass to the kitchen, rinsed it, and set it in the sink.

With that done, she made her way to the bedroom. She undressed and walked into the shower. The warm water, along with the wine she had at dinner, added a pleasant warmth, and she felt the tension of the day melting away.

After drying off, she changed into a soft pink nightdress and slipped into bed. She put on her EarPods and selected her favourite playlist of soft, soothing meditation music. She rested her head on her pillows and closed her eyes. The tranquil meditation music, the quiet of her cottage, the comfort of her surroundings, and the contentment of a peaceful evening all combined to create a perfect sense of calm. She felt grateful for this moment of serenity, knowing it was these small, simple pleasures that made life truly meaningful.

Eventually, Emma decided to call it a night. She set her EarPods and phone aside on the bedside table, her mind drifting to thoughts of Saturday night with Michael at The Obsidian Fog. With a quiet sense of anticipation, she let sleep gently overtake her.

CHAPTER 4

The Witching Hour

Saturday, 8ᵗʰ October 2024

Emma opened her eyes to the dim morning light filtering through the curtains, the rhythm of raindrops tapping against the windowpane. The world beyond lay hushed, wrapped in a misty grey that brought a sense of stillness and peace. She stretched lazily, embracing the calm of the morning, thankful for a full night's sleep and the promise of a quiet weekend.

Rising from bed, she moved through her familiar morning routine. She brewed a pot of coffee, letting the rich aroma fill the room, and took a moment to freshen up. By the time she returned to the kitchen, the drizzle had stopped, though the sky remained overcast. With a quiet sense of anticipation, Emma knew it was the perfect time to connect with nature and ground herself after a busy week.

Slipping into a cosy, oversized sweater, comfortable shorts, and sturdy boots, she grabbed a lightweight scarf to ward off the chill. A soft blanket tucked under her arm, she stepped outside, ready to embrace the fresh, earthy air of the rain-soaked woods.

As Emma entered the woods, the canopy above offered natural shelter, with only occasional droplets of rain filtering through the leaves. The air was alive with the sounds of rustling foliage, distant bird calls, and the gentle trickle of leftover droplets. She walked along the familiar path, her steps soft against the damp earth.

With each stride, she felt the tension in her body ease. The towering trees, their trunks draped in moss, stood as silent sentinels, offering a sense of peace and stability. Emma paused before a grand oak, its ancient presence calling to her. As a healer, she understood the power of nature's energy, and she knew that to connect with the tree, she needed to first acknowledge its spirit. Closing her eyes, she took a deep breath, silently attuning herself to the tree's essence. When she felt its quiet acceptance in her heart, she placed her hands gently against its weathered trunk. The moment her palms made contact, a surge of energy flowed through her, grounding her further into the earth's embrace.

After a few minutes, Emma opened her eyes and resumed her walk, feeling deeply grounded by the energy she had drawn from the tree. As she made her way towards her usual meditation spot—a quiet clearing nestled deeper in the woods—her thoughts drifted back to the shadowy figure she had encountered that night. Was it truly Laura? Even though her intuition had offered some clarity, a part of her still sought more answers.

Reaching the clearing, Emma spread out the small blanket she had brought with her. She slipped off her shoes, sat down, and crossed her legs. Closing her eyes, she took several deep breaths, centreing herself. With each inhale, she imagined drawing in pure, positive energy, and with each exhale, she released any unwanted thoughts.

Emma's mind began to clear, and a deep sense of peace washed over her. She visualised herself surrounded by a protective light, forming a shield against any negative energy. In this state of calm, she silently set her intentions for the day: to find clarity, remain grounded, and face her fears with unwavering courage.

Rejuvenated, she gathered her blanket and began the walk back home, the woods providing a therapeutic journey that left her feeling balanced and centred. As she approached her cottage, she noticed the earlier drizzle had left a delicate mist lingering in the air, enveloping everything in a gentle, ethereal haze.

Once inside, Emma changed out of her damp clothes and into something more comfortable: pastel pink shorts paired with a loose, white sleeveless top. She tied her hair back and made her way to the kitchen to prepare a hearty breakfast.

She toasted two pieces of bread and prepared a spinach, mushroom, and cheese omelette. The aroma filled the kitchen, wrapping her in a sense of warmth and comfort. Emma sat down and enjoyed her meal, appreciating the flavours and the moment of stillness.

With breakfast complete, she felt ready to tackle her household chores. She put on some upbeat music, starting in the living room where she dusted the shelves and vacuumed the floor. The rhythm of the music kept her energised as she moved from room to room, cleaning and organising.

In the bedroom, she made the bed, fluffing the pillows and straightening the covers until everything looked perfectly neat. The order of the room gave her a sense of control and tranquillity. She then moved on to the bathroom, scrubbing the tiles and polishing the fixtures until they gleamed.

Finally, she turned her attention to the kitchen. Emma wiped down the counters, cleaned the stove, and organised the pantry. The methodical process of cleaning felt almost meditative, allowing her to focus entirely on the task at hand and clear her mind.

When she was done, the cottage was spotless, and Emma felt a satisfying sense of accomplishment. The physical activity had channelled her energy effectively, and the organised, serene environment around her mirrored the inner clarity she had been striving for.

Once her morning chores were done, Emma headed to the bathroom for a quick shower. Feeling fresh and renewed, she decided to take a moment for herself before preparing lunch. She went to the living room, where a closed shelf along the wall held her prized saxophone—an instrument she hadn't played in quite some time. It had been a part of her life since her school days in London, and though not many people knew, Emma played with the skill of a seasoned musician. It was a passion she'd kept to herself, a private escape.

She carefully removed the saxophone from its case and, as she held it in her hands, noticed the slight dissonance in the tone. She took a moment to tune it, gently adjusting the mouthpiece and testing each note. The process felt familiar and soothing, like reconnecting with an old friend. When it was in tune, Emma closed her eyes for a brief moment, steadying her breath before she began.

She started with *"Dance Me to the End of Love"* by Leonard Cohen, her fingers flowing fluidly over the keys, coaxing a haunting, soulful melody from the instrument. The sound seemed to fill the room, the warm, rich notes rising and falling with an ease that surprised her, as if the music had been waiting to return. Each note resonated with a quiet intensity, and Emma's body swayed with the rhythm, lost in the music as the world outside her living room faded away.

Then she moved on to a few more classics, each one evoking its own sense of nostalgia and depth. The melodies washed over her, each song a familiar companion, grounding her in the moment.

When the last note drifted into the silence, Emma exhaled slowly, a smile curving her lips, flushed with the satisfaction of the music. She placed the instrument back on the shelf, the room still echoing with the resonance of the piece, before moving on to prepare lunch.

In the kitchen, Emma deftly chopped carrots, celery, and potatoes before sautéing onions and garlic in olive oil. She added the chicken breast, seasoning it with salt, pepper, and thyme, and browned it to perfection. Combining everything in a baking dish, she poured over chicken broth and a splash of white wine, then sprinkled cheddar cheese and breadcrumbs on top. Once the casserole was in the oven, she tidied up the kitchen, savouring the rich, savoury aroma that filled the space.

When the dish was ready, golden and bubbling at the edges, Emma served herself a generous portion. She savoured each comforting bite, the flavours and textures bringing a sense of contentment. After lunch, feeling pleasantly full and relaxed, she decided to take a short nap. Pulling a soft blanket over herself on the couch, she let the warmth of her home, and the satisfaction of a hearty meal lull her into a restful sleep.

When she woke up from her nap, Emma glanced at the clock and saw that it was half past three. After a gentle stretch, she made her way to the kitchen sink and splashed some cool water on her face, shaking off the remnants of sleep. Feeling energised, she slipped into her sturdy gardening boots and stepped outside. Making her way to the side of her cottage, she opened the small enclosure where she stored her gardening tools. With everything she needed in hand, she set off towards the garden, eager to immerse herself in the simple, grounding work awaiting her.

The morning's drizzle had left the garden looking lush and vibrant. Emma spent the afternoon tending to her plants, weeding, pruning, and planting some new plants. The earthy scent of the soil and the pleasure of working with her hands further grounded her, providing a peaceful escape from the stress of her work and recent events. She focused on the present moment, finding joy in the simple, rhythmic tasks of gardening.

Suddenly, she heard the soft patter of paws approaching and looked up to see Mrs Penelope Whitaker, her elderly neighbour, walking her dog, a beautiful Golden Retriever named Max. Penelope was a sprightly woman in her late sixties, with a head of silver curls and a perpetual twinkle in her eyes. Max bounded ahead, sniffing eagerly at every patch of grass.

"Good evening, Emma!" Penelope called out cheerfully, waving as she approached the garden gate.

Emma stood up, wiping her hands on her gardening apron. "Good evening, Mrs. Whitaker. How are you today?"

"Oh, I'm fine, dear. And you? How's the gardening coming along?" Penelope asked, her eyes twinkling as she glanced at Emma's handiwork.

"It's coming along nicely," Emma replied with a small smile. "I always find gardening so therapeutic."

Penelope nodded as she approached, a gentle smile on her lips. "There is something about working with the earth that calms the soul, isn't it?"

Emma nodded and asked, "Isn't it a bit early for your walk?"

"Yes. With the day feeling so cool and peaceful, Max and I just couldn't resist taking an extra stroll."

Max wagged his tail enthusiastically, his nose twitching as he sniffed around Emma's flower beds.

Emma reached out to pet him, enjoying the softness of his fur beneath her fingers. "What have you been up to, Max?" she asked, her voice warm with affection.

"He's as mischievous as ever," Penelope replied with a chuckle, her eyes sparkling. "Keeps me on my toes, that's for sure. But I wouldn't have it any other way."

Emma laughed softly, feeling a sense of bonding with the familiar banter. "It is good to have a companion like Max. He must bring you so much joy,"

Penelope looked at Emma with a kind, knowing expression. "And how are you, dear? You look a bit tired."

Emma hesitated for a moment, then sighed. "I didn't sleep well last night. Just...restless, I suppose."

Penelope's gaze softened. "Oh, Emma, if you ever need to talk or just some company, you know where to find me."

"Thank you, Mrs. Whitaker. That means a lot," Emma said sincerely.

Penelope smiled warmly. "You are a strong woman, Emma. Remember that. But with the nature of your work, sometimes it is okay to lean on others. We are a community, after all."

Emma nodded, feeling a sense of gratitude. "I appreciate that, really."

"Now, don't let me keep you from your gardening," Penelope said, giving Max's leash a gentle tug. "Come along, Max."

Max gave a final sniff at the flowers before trotting after Penelope. Emma watched them walk away, a small smile playing on her lips. The brief interaction had lifted her spirits, reminding her that she was not alone.

By the time she finished, the garden looked well-tended and full of life. Emma washed up and headed back inside, feeling a deep sense of satisfaction from the day's work.

At around 7 pm, Emma took a long and luxurious shower and prepared for Michael's gig at The Obsidian Fog. She slipped into a sleeveless red mini dress that accentuated her figure, paired with sleek black Giuseppe Zanotti stilettos that added a touch of glamour. Her makeup was bold and striking: smoky black eyes that framed her gaze with an intense allure and red lipstick that completed the look with a classic touch. She finished by spraying her favourite Jo Malone perfume. With her outfit and makeup in place, Emma felt confident and ready for the night ahead.

She called for an Uber, and as she settled into the back seat, the town's lights blurred past, creating a soft glow that heightened her excitement for the night.

Once she arrived at The Obsidian Fog, she stepped out into the lively atmosphere of the pub, which featured dark wooden interiors and plush velvet drapes, filled with an intriguing mix of locals. The air was thick with the scent of incense and the rich notes of psychedelic rock music.

Spotting the bartender, Kyle, whom she knew from her frequent visits, she greeted him with a warm smile. Kyle was in his early thirties, with a friendly demeanour and an easy-going smile.

He welcomed her with a warm smile. "Evening, Emma. What will you have?" he asked.

"Hello, Kyle. Bourbon on the rocks, please," Emma replied, as she smiled and slid onto a stool. "And how's your night been so far?"

"Busy, as always. But it's been good. Always lively when the band plays," Ryan responded, placing her drink on the counter.

The bourbon warmed her as it slid down, the rich flavour settling comfortably within her. It was the perfect start to her evening. She glanced around the pub, noticing the familiar faces scattered throughout the room.

The pub was dimly lit, with a cosy, almost mystical atmosphere. Candles flickered on the tables, casting shadows that danced along the walls. The air was filled with the low hum of conversation and occasional bursts of laughter. One of the best pubs in the area, it attracted people from neighbouring towns, all drawn to its welcoming vibe.

When Michael's band, *Cosmic Echoes*, took the stage, the atmosphere in The Obsidian Fog shifted instantly. The dim lights seemed to lower even further as the first strum of the guitar rang out, and the crowd's anticipation grew. The psychedelic rock music they played was a mesmerising blend of swirling guitar riffs, hypnotic drumbeats, and rich, layered vocals. Michael's intricate guitar solos were always the highlight of the evening, his fingers moving with a fluidity that made it look effortless.

Emma watched as Michael's energy transformed. Offstage, he was friendly and grounded, a warm presence at the bakery, but here, under the stage lights, he was a different person entirely.

There was a wildness to him, an almost untamed energy that pulsed through every note he played. It was as though the music brought him to life in a way nothing else did, and Emma couldn't help but be drawn to it.

The crowd responded enthusiastically, swaying and dancing to the entrancing rhythms. The music created an almost otherworldly ambiance, the sound rich and immersive. It was as if the entire room had fallen under the spell of the band's performance, lost in the world of Cosmic Echoes.

Emma found herself immersed in the music, each intricate melody and pulsing beat weaving a rich tapestry around her. As someone who understood the language of music, she could appreciate the subtle nuances and the way each instrument complemented the others—how the guitar's riffs seemed to spiral and stretch, how the drums grounded the sound, and how the bass anchored the whole experience, vibrating through her chest. The music wasn't just heard; it was felt, and Emma could sense the skill and intention behind every note.

She closed her eyes, a smile tugging at her lips, as the rhythms filled her entire being. The deep bass notes thrummed through her, syncing perfectly with the steady beat of her heart, and for a moment, she felt completely in tune with the world around her. The vibrant, swirling lights overhead danced in time with the music, casting a mesmerising glow that enhanced the surreal, almost ethereal atmosphere.

When she opened her eyes, Emma glanced around the dimly lit pub, the sound of the band still enveloping her. It was as if the music had created a world of its own—one she was fully a part of. Her spirit soared with every beat, lost in the magic of the performance.

When the band took a break between sets, Emma found herself at the bar again, nursing her drink and chatting with a few familiar faces. She enjoyed the sense of community and the camaraderie of the crowd, where she could let down her guard and simply be.

Suddenly, Emma felt a tap on her shoulder. She turned to see Michael, grinning and slightly breathless from the performance. "Hey, Emma. Hope you're having a good time?" He pulled her into a quick hug, and as he did, the combined scent of his cologne and the faint musk of sweat from the stage clung to him. There was something deep and intoxicating about the mixture—a warmth, a rawness that seemed to echo the energy he had just poured into his performance. His embrace was brief, but Emma could still feel the heat radiating from him, the pulse of his energy still humming in her veins.

"Yes, Michael. The way you play, it's just captivating. It feels like the music takes over, and you're right there with it," Emma said, her eyes reflecting the truth of her words.

"Thanks, Emma," Michael said, his grin widening, eyes glowing with the same intensity he had on stage. "When I'm up there, it's like I'm completely in the moment. The music takes over, and everything else just falls away." His voice softened, but the intensity remained. "I'm glad you can feel it too."

They shared a brief pause, letting the music fill the air between them. Michael finished the glass of water Ryan had given him and spoke to a few others in the crowd before heading back to play the next set.

As the night wore on, Emma joined the crowd, losing herself in the music. It felt freeing, a release of all the tension she had been holding, as the melodies eased her nerves and enveloped her in a sense of peace.

When Michael finished his set, Emma was waiting for him at the bar. He joined her with a grin, his face flushed from the performance. They shared a drink together, and their conversation flowed easily as they discussed the performance and the music. Emma felt a sense of comfort and ease with Michael that she had not felt with anyone else in a long while.

By the time Emma left The Obsidian Fog, it was well past midnight. She thanked Michael and said goodbye before calling an Uber for the ride home. The crisp night air greeted her as she stepped outside; she shivered slightly and wished she had carried a jacket with her. When the Uber arrived, she got in and closed her eyes. The drive was quiet, and the rhythmic hum of the cab's engine lulled her into a contemplative mood.

When she reached her cottage, Emma locked the front door and headed straight to the kitchen where she drank a glass of water. Then she headed to her bedroom, where she slipped off her stilettos and carefully hung her red dress in the closet. She changed into comfortable loungewear and removed her makeup with practiced ease.

Settling into bed, she felt the calm of her bedroom providing a soothing retreat from the night's excitement. As her eyes grew heavy, memories of the evening's highlights floated through her mind, and she soon drifted off into a restful sleep.

At some point in the dead of night, Emma was jolted awake by an unsettling sensation. The room was dark and eerily silent. She felt a heavy, sinister presence and a chilling cold that seemed to seep through the walls. As she tried to orient herself, she noticed a shadowy figure at the edge of her bed. Though the figure was indistinct and shifting, its shape barely discernible, Emma felt an overwhelming sense of dread and familiarity.

Her heart pounded as she tried to make sense of what was happening. The air in the room had grown thick, almost tangible, pressing down on her chest and making it difficult to breathe. A faint, rancid odour permeated the room, like something decayed and forgotten. Emma strained her eyes, trying to discern the features of the apparition, but it remained an amorphous shadow, dark and menacing.

As the figure moved closer, a cold sweat broke out on Emma's skin. The shadow seemed to ripple and writhe, its edges flickering as if caught in an invisible wind. With every step it took, the temperature in the room seemed to drop further, until Emma could see her breath misting in the frigid air.

The oppressive presence brought with it a cacophony of whispers, barely audible but unmistakably spiteful. They seemed to emanate from the shadow itself, filling Emma's mind with a chorus of hissing, spiteful voices. She could not make out the words, but the tone was unmistakable: anger, sorrow, and a desperate yearning for something just out of reach.

Emma's instincts screamed at her to move, to run, but she found herself paralysed, her body refusing to obey. The shadow loomed over her, and she could feel the weight of its gaze, heavy and invasive. It felt as if it was peering into her very soul, probing for weaknesses and secrets.

Just as she thought she could endure no more, the shadow began to take shape, coalescing into Laura's image. Emma felt an intense, burning hatred radiating from it as the whispers grew louder, more insistent, filling her ears with their venomous chorus.

Suddenly, Laura's spirit lunged forward, and Emma felt a cold, clammy hand clamp around her wrist. The touch was both icy and searing, sending jolts of pain shooting up her arm. She gasped, the sound swallowed by the oppressive darkness surrounding her.

With a surge of adrenaline, Emma managed to wrench her hand free and scrambled out of bed. Her breath came in ragged gasps as she backed away from the figure, her mind racing to find some way to fight back. She reached for the bedside lamp, fumbling in the dark until her fingers closed around the switch. With trembling hands, she turned it on.

The sudden burst of light flooded the room, banishing the shadows to the corners. The spirit recoiled, its form flickering like a candle flame caught in a gust of wind. For a moment, Emma thought it might disappear entirely, but instead, it seemed to solidify, its outline becoming sharper and more defined.

Laura's face was twisted in an expression of anguish and fury. Her eyes were hollow, empty voids, and her mouth opened, and the whispers swelled into a deafening roar.

Emma backed away further, her whole body trembling with fear. She knew she had to do something, anything, to drive the spirit away. The presence was overwhelming, suffocating, and she could feel her own fear feeding it, making it stronger.

Summoning every ounce of courage, Emma began to recite a protective chant she had learned from Kai, her mentor. Her voice was shaky at first, barely audible over the din of the whispers, but she forced herself to continue, her words gaining strength and conviction with each repetition.

The spirit's reaction was immediate. It writhed and twisted, as if in agony, its form becoming less distinct. Laura's spirit, filled with rage and sorrow, seemed to resist the power of the chant, fighting against its calming influence.

Emma closed her eyes and focused harder, channelling all her energy into the chant. She could feel the presence of Laura's spirit pushing against her, trying to break her concentration. The room grew colder still, and the whispers reached a fever pitch, but Emma held firm, refusing to let fear overwhelm her.

The spirit let out an agonising scream, its form distorting and contorting in a display of otherworldly rage. Emma could see Laura's face more clearly now, twisted in pain and anger, her eyes burning with a desperate, haunting intensity.

Suddenly, the spirit lunged at Emma again, and she felt an icy grip around her throat, squeezing the air out of her lungs. Panic surged through her, but she forced herself to keep chanting. She could feel her voice growing hoarse with the effort, but with a final, desperate push, Emma summoned all her strength and let out a powerful cry, the chant reaching its crescendo. The room was flooded with a brilliant, blinding light, and the oppressive presence began to recede, the whispers fading into the background.

The spirit let out one last anguished wail before dissolving into the darkness, leaving Emma gasping for breath. The room was still and silent once more, but the sense of foreboding lingered, hanging in the air like a thick fog.

Emma collapsed onto the bed, her body trembling from the encounter. The aftermath of the attack by Laura's spirit was nothing short of harrowing. The disturbance had left physical and emotional scars that would linger far beyond the night. The temperature in the cottage had plummeted, and a bone-chilling cold permeated every room, leaving Emma shivering. The once-comforting glow of her lamps was replaced by flickering, erratic lights that seemed to dance to a rhythm of evil intent.

Her heart pounded in her chest as she could still feel the oppressive weight in the air.

The emotional toll was profound, and Emma felt a deep, visceral fear that left her numb and disoriented. She struggled to make sense of what had happened, her mind racing with a mix of dread and disbelief. The sheer intensity of the haunting had left her physically and mentally exhausted.

Unable to shake the feeling of being watched, Emma stumbled from the bedroom, her breath coming in ragged gasps, making every step feel laboured. She reached the kitchen and filled a glass with cold water. Her hands trembling, she lifted it to her lips and drank. The chilly water was a small comfort, but it did little to ease the shivering that had taken hold of her.

With her glass emptied, Emma made her way to the living room. The familiar surroundings offered no solace; the shadows cast by the dim lighting seemed to dance menacingly on the walls. She sank into the couch, her body curling up instinctively as though to protect itself from the invisible threats lurking in the darkness. Her mind was a whirlwind of fear and confusion, and the terror she felt was as palpable as the cold that seemed to linger around her.

After some time, as the initial intensity of the encounter began to recede, Emma reached for the remote, seeking some form of comfort in the familiar hum of the television. The screen flickered to life, casting a muted glow across the room, a feeble attempt at filling the unsettling silence left behind. She hoped the soft background noise might ground her but found herself unable to focus on any of the images or sounds. The channels flashed by in a blur of colour and noise, her eyes glazed over, unable to settle on anything.

Finally, the exhaustion from the day's events and her encounter with Laura's spirit overcame her. The night's ordeal was not just a fleeting disturbance; it was a grim reminder of the dark force that had now invaded her life. The haunting had left an indelible mark on her psyche, foreshadowing a gruelling journey ahead as she sought answers and a way to free herself from Laura's vengeful grip. Despite her efforts to stay alert, fatigue set in, and she slumped further into the couch. As the TV droned on in the background, her eyes grew heavy, and eventually, Emma succumbed to sleep, her mind still haunted by lingering fear.

CHAPTER 5

Echoes of the Night

Sunday, 9th October 2024

Emma's eyes snapped open to the grey, gloomy dawn light filtering through the windows, her body feeling as though it hadn't truly rested. The haunting encounter with Laura's spirit the night before had left her deeply unsettled, and the dim room seemed to carry the weight of her unease. Her heart pounded, and a cold sweat clung to her brow. Every creak in the house felt like an echo of the previous night's terror.

Lying on the couch, Emma replayed the encounter in her mind. The image of Laura's ghostly figure—hollow eyes, twisted face—was burned into her memory. The resonance of Laura's voice left Emma feeling as if she had been dragged through a nightmarish abyss. Even in the safety of her own home, she felt exposed, vulnerable.

The encounter was more than just a chilling apparition; it was as if Laura's grief and rage had seeped into Emma's very core. The emotions Laura had projected – fear, sadness, anger – were so intense, they felt almost tangible. Emma could still feel the icy grip of dread around her heart and the lingering despair that had settled over her, reverberating through every corner of her mind.

At 6 a.m., Emma staggered off the couch and shuffled to the kitchen, her movements heavy and sluggish. Moving through her dimly lit cottage, each familiar sound—the drip of the coffee machine, the hiss of steam—felt strangely foreign, amplifying her unease.

As she tidied up absentmindedly, her mind churned with fear and confusion. Laura's anguished wailing echoed in her memory, and Emma couldn't shake the image of the spirit reaching out, bound in torment. She wondered what had driven Laura to such desperation and why her spirit seemed fixated on her.

Once she finished her coffee and sat down to meditate, hoping to find calm amid the chaos. But as she closed her eyes and tried to focus on her breath, the images of Laura's apparition invaded her mind with an insidious persistence. Her heart raced, and her breath became shallow as she tried to escape the haunting memories. The meditation, instead of providing peace, left her more agitated, a stark reminder of how deeply the night's events had unsettled her.

The haunting had left her drained, an exhaustion that settled into her bones. Her body felt heavy, her mind dulled by a fog of unease that even a warm shower couldn't quite clear. The water offered a brief comfort, but as soon as she stepped out, the weight of the night's terror returned, clinging to her like a shadow.

As Emma sat down for breakfast, the bowl of yogurt and fruit in front of her seemed bland, offering none of its usual comfort. Her mind was still tangled in the events of the night before, and she struggled to focus on anything other than the relentless churn of her thoughts.

Afterwards, she sat at her computer, diving into research about Laura Harrington. As she sifted through online records and news articles, her heart quickened with each new revelation about Laura's final moments and the circumstances surrounding her death. The details of Laura's leap from the asylum rooftop deepened Emma's sorrow and intensified her determination to uncover the truth.

But the more Emma uncovered, the more questions arose. What had driven Laura to such desperation? What had fostered her despair? With each discovery, Emma felt a growing determination to understand Laura's tragic end and its connection to the haunting she had experienced. Her sense of unease shifted into a fierce resolve to uncover the truth and bring some semblance of peace to the troubled spirit that had so profoundly affected her.

The haunting and the findings about Laura's death left Emma feeling both unsettled and driven. To find answers, she knew she needed to delve deeper into Laura's life and the circumstances surrounding her death.

As she continued her research online, Emma discovered that the chief doctor at Ravensbrook Asylum during Laura's stay was Dr. Evelyn Hartley, a well-regarded psychiatrist known for her work in mental health. Hoping that Dr. Hartley could offer valuable insights into Laura's state of mind and the events leading to her death, Emma spent the rest of the morning and early afternoon searching for information about the retired psychiatrist. She learned that Dr. Hartley had retired several years ago and now lived in Willow's Creek.

With the information in hand, Emma decided to take a break. She prepared a light lunch – a chicken sandwich and a salad – and ate while reflecting on her research. The weight of the previous night's events and her morning research began to settle heavily on her, so after finishing her meal, Emma allowed herself a short nap to recharge.

Emma felt a bit more refreshed when she woke up from her nap, though a sense of unease still lingered. Determined to make the most of the rest of the day, she decided to head to the local farmers' market. The market was a weekly ritual for her, offering a chance to connect with the community and stock up on fresh produce for the week ahead. Before leaving, Emma took a warm shower, letting the hot water invigorate her and ease the tightness in her shoulders. Wrapped in a soft towel, she chose a simple yet stylish dress in a soft, muted colour, complemented by a light jacket for warmth. Comfortable shoes rounded out her look, making it perfect for a leisurely stroll through the market.

As she stepped outside, though it was still gloomy, the cool autumn air greeted her, adding a refreshing contrast to the warmth of her home. She walked to the garage that was on one side of the cottage and opened its shutters. She opened the door of her black Jeep Grand Cherokee. It was a rugged yet refined SUV, perfect for someone like Emma who lived in a rural area but did not want to sacrifice comfort. The Grand Cherokee was known for its off-road capabilities, which were useful for Emma's explorations of the countryside and for when she needed to visit clients who lived in neighbouring towns and villages. Its spacious, well-appointed interior provided comfort during long drives. The vehicle's strong, confident presence aligned with Emma's independent spirit. She drove to the market, parked her vehicle in the parking lot, and got out.

The market was alive with colour and activity. The stalls were lined with vibrant fruits and vegetables, homemade baked goods, and handcrafted items. Emma made her way through the market, stopping to chat with familiar vendors and admire the seasonal offerings. She picked up a variety of fresh vegetables, including crisp lettuce, juicy tomatoes, and fragrant herbs. A visit to the bakery stall resulted in a selection of freshly baked bread and pastries, adding a touch of indulgence to her haul. She also picked up a few jars of homemade preserves and locally sourced honey.

As she wandered through the market, Emma felt a sense of calm begin to settle over her. The lively atmosphere and the simple pleasure of choosing her groceries provided a welcome distraction from the shadowy events of the past night.

She was carefully selecting a bunch of fresh basil when she spotted Rose across the market. Rose was examining a display of heirloom tomatoes, her basket already filled with a variety of fresh produce.

"Hey, Rose!" Emma called out with a wave.

Rose looked up, her face breaking into a warm smile. "Emma! It's quite the market today, isn't it?"

Emma nodded, joining Rose at the tomato stand. "Yes, it is! The selection is amazing," she replied, glancing around at the bustling crowd.

They continued browsing through the stalls together, chatting about their favourite produce and picking out a few items along the way.

After some time, Rose said, "Well, I'll let you finish up here, Emma. And I'll see you tomorrow at the studio."

Emma smiled and said, "See you tomorrow, Rose."

She waved as Rose headed off to another stall. The brief interaction had been refreshing, adding a touch of normalcy and connection to her day. After finishing her shopping, Emma placed her fresh produce into the back of her Jeep, feeling the earlier unease beginning to creep back in.

Determined to find some peace, Emma climbed into the driver's seat and drove to the local church, a comforting sanctuary she often turned to in times of distress. Though she was not ritualistically religious, the church's timeless presence offered a sense of tranquillity amidst the chaos of daily life.

Arriving at the church, Emma was greeted by the calm and stillness of the surroundings. The classic stone facade, adorned with intricate carvings, rose majestically against the backdrop of a clear sky. Gracefully arching spires framed the entrance, while manicured gardens flanked the pathway, their vibrant flowers swaying gently in the breeze.

Emma entered and took a seat near the back of the empty church, opting for a corner where the light was softer. The stillness of the space enveloped her, providing a momentary escape from the chaos swirling in her mind. She closed her eyes, focusing on her breath, seeking to ground herself in the tranquillity of the sanctuary.

Though the weight of the previous night's encounter lingered, here, in the quiet, Emma let the fear slowly unravel. The church's silence was more than the absence of people; it was a steady presence, easing the tension she had been holding. Gradually, she felt her nerves settle, finding comfort in the simple act of being still.

As she sat there with her eyes closed, she could feel the church's energy coursing through her entire being. She suddenly remembered the first time she discovered she could see auras with her naked eyes. It was a few years ago, on a tranquil winter evening in London. The entire city had been covered by a soft blanket of snow.

She had been curled up in her cosy apartment, in her reading nook by the fireplace, savouring the warmth of the crackling flames. The room had been filled with the comforting aroma of cinnamon and pine from a few scented candles. As she immersed herself in the book that she had been reading, a curious sensation had begun to stir within her.

Looking up from the pages, her attention was drawn to a single snowflake resting on the windowsill. Its delicate, intricate patterns sparkled in the firelight, creating a picturesque scene. Suddenly, she noticed something extraordinary. The snowflake began to emit a soft, iridescent glow. At first, it was barely perceptible, but soon it expanded into a cascade of colours—gentle pastels of pink, blue, and violet—that radiated outward from the snowflake.

She had risen from her seat, her heart racing with a blend of astonishment and wonder. The light had seemed to envelop the snowflake in a halo, casting an ethereal mist that had spread gently through the room. The beauty of that spectacle had been both mesmerising and surreal, as if the snowflake had become a portal to a hidden layer of reality.

Reaching out to touch it, she felt a cool, tingling sensation. The glow was not merely an optical illusion but a manifestation of the snowflake's energy. It was a profound revelation, a glimpse into the vibrant energies that infused the world around us.

That day had marked the beginning of her ability to see auras. It opened her eyes to a new dimension of perception that allowed her to connect with the unseen energies of both objects and people. As she embraced this newfound gift, she felt a deep sense of gratitude and awe, knowing that this experience had forever transformed her understanding of the world.

Opening her eyes, Emma felt a sense of calm and determination. The empty church had provided her with a brief respite from her worries and a moment to reconnect with her inner peace. As she stood to leave, she felt a subtle shift within herself—a gentle reminder of her resilience and the strength she had to face the challenges ahead.

Emma exited the church with a final, appreciative glance at the peaceful surroundings. The experience had been a balm for her troubled spirit, and she walked towards her Jeep feeling lighter.

Returning home, Emma unloaded her bags and put the groceries away, taking care to organise her refrigerator and pantry.

Then she sat down to write her client reports. Sarah, struggling with anxiety from her demanding job, had made noticeable progress, so Emma detailed her recent achievements and suggested daily mindfulness exercises and scheduled relaxation times. Next, she worked on Mark's report, focusing on his efforts to improve communication with his partner. Emma highlighted their active listening exercises and encouraged Mark to continue fostering open dialogue. Finally, Emma turned to Julia's report, noting her networking and skills development progress as she pursued a new career path. Emma summarised the action plans for all her clients, offering constructive feedback and additional resources where needed.

With that done, she turned her attention to dinner. Emma chose a comforting, easy meal for tonight: hearty tomato basil soup with a grilled cheese sandwich. The aroma of simmering tomatoes and fresh basil filled the kitchen.

Once dinner was ready, Emma set the table and sat down to eat. As she savoured her meal, her mind drifted to the Sundays she had spent in London with her friend Serena, especially their cherished shopping trips. She recalled a particular afternoon at a boutique in Covent Garden, where they had spent hours laughing and exploring the racks, with Serena eagerly picking out outfits for her to try. Emma could still hear Serena's laughter as they debated the best finds and celebrated their discoveries.

Another memory that stood out was a visit to a vintage store, where Serena, with her uncanny eye, had unearthed a beautiful 1950s dress. Emma remembered the thrill of trying it on, their laughter filling the small shop as they admired the unique treasure. Those carefree days were a testament to their bond, filled with joy and a mutual love for fashion.

Emma felt a quiet warmth from these memories as she finished her dinner. She realised how much she missed having someone like Serena here in Hawes—a friend to share laughter, adventures, and the small joys of everyday moments.

Afterwards, she cleaned up the kitchen, feeling a renewed sense of calm. Then she retreated to her living room, deciding to watch "The Bridges of Madison County," one of her favourite films.

She settled into her couch, wrapped in a soft blanket, and pressed play. As the film began, the familiar scenes and characters drew her in. Meryl Streep's portrayal of Francesca Johnson and Clint Eastwood's Robert Kincaid brought to life a poignant and introspective love story that never failed to move Emma.

With its warm, golden hues, the beautiful cinematography enveloped her in the film's atmosphere. She lost herself in the narrative, where the quiet moments of connection between the characters resonated deeply. The themes of love, sacrifice, and the passage of time captivated her as the movie unfolded.

As the film progressed, Emma was tearing up at the tender moments, the raw emotion of the characters' experiences mirroring her longing for understanding and connection. As she watched a particularly poignant scene, her thoughts turned to Michael. It wasn't just his gentle demeanour that drew her in; something deeper about him intrigued her.

During one of their conversations, Emma had learned that Michael was a Cancerian, a sun sign associated with nurturing and deep emotional understanding. She knew this well, not only because of her research into astrology but also because she herself had a Cancer moon. This insight had made her realise why she felt so at ease around him. His caring nature had become especially evident several months ago when Emma had come down with the flu. Not wanting to compromise her clients' energy, she had stayed home and kept to herself. Michael, noticing she hadn't visited the bakery in a few days, had called to check on her. When she explained that she was unwell, he immediately showed up at her door with a thermos of homemade soup and sandwiches. For the next couple of days, he had called regularly, ensuring she had everything she needed and was resting.

Even at the bakery, Emma had noticed Michael's kindness extended beyond her. He was warm and friendly with all his customers, but he went a step further—always opening the door for older patrons and remembering nearly everyone's favourite order. These small gestures, both at the bakery and beyond, made Emma realise how deeply caring he was, and it only deepened her respect for him.

By the time the credits rolled, Emma felt a sense of calm wash over her. The film had provided an emotional release, allowing her to process the recent events gently. She turned off the TV, set her blanket aside, and headed to her bedroom, hoping for a peaceful night's sleep. As she settled into bed, her mind began to drift, the comforting images of the movie melding with her thoughts, and soon, she was enveloped in a deep, dream-filled slumber.

In her dream, Emma stood in the living room of her childhood home in Maplewood. The room was bathed in a warm, golden light emanating from the walls themselves. Everything looked just as it had years ago, with her mother's favourite floral curtains swaying gently in an unseen breeze and the smell of freshly baked cookies wafting through the air.

She absorbed the familiar surroundings and noticed her parents standing in the doorway. Her heart leapt at the sight of them. Her mother, Catherine, looked as vibrant as ever, her eyes sparkling with love and wisdom. Her father, Adrian, stood tall and reassuring beside her, his presence exuding strength and warmth.

Emma rushed forward, enveloping them in a tight embrace. The sensation was so real and tangible that tears welled in her eyes. She could almost hear their voices in her mind, soothing and familiar. They conveyed their unwavering love, reminding her that they were always with her, watching over her.

Emma felt her mother's soothing touch, her cool hands gently stroking her hair, while her father's calming presence enveloped her. A sense of peace washed over Emma, the warmth of her parents' love surrounding her like a comforting embrace. They reminded her of the cherished memories they shared, guiding her through life.

As her parents communicated without words, the room began to change. The golden light dimmed, replaced by a soft, silvery glow. Emma clung to the warmth of their love, savouring the memory of their touch and presence.

But then her mother's expression turned serious, her eyes locking onto Emma's with an intensity that sent a shiver down her spine. There was something important her mother was trying to convey, a message Emma needed to understand. Her heart quickened as a sense of urgency built within her. Just as she tried to grasp her mother's words, a sudden rushing sound drowned them out.

The room began to blur and fade, and Emma felt herself being pulled away into the waking world. Desperately, she reached out, trying to hold on to the dream and her connection with her parents. But it was too late. The dream dissolved into darkness, and Emma woke with a start, feeling a heaviness in her heart.

A Taste of Normalcy

Monday, 10ᵗʰ October 2024

She rubbed her eyes and glanced at the clock – it was almost 6:00 am. The soft patter of rain against her bedroom window filled the silence, its soothing rhythm momentarily cocooning her from the outside world. The sky was a muted grey, casting a gentle, diffused light into the room, creating a calm, almost dreamlike atmosphere. Taking a deep breath, Emma inhaled the cool, fresh scent of rain that lingered in the air.

Determined, she resolved to uncover what her mother had been trying to convey. The answers were within her reach, and she was ready to seek the truth, no matter what it took.

She slid out of bed, ready to face the day ahead. Her first task was a routine of somatic exercises—mindful movements designed to foster a connection between the mind and body, promoting both physical and emotional well-being. As she moved through gentle neck rolls, shoulder shrugs, and spinal twists, Emma felt the tension in her muscles release, leaving her body awake and energised, grounded for whatever the day would bring.

After completing her workout, Emma gently rolled up her mat and made her way to the bathroom for a shower. She turned on the water, and as the steam began to fill the room, she stepped under the warm cascade.

The soothing water flowed over her, and Emma closed her eyes, allowing the warmth to envelop her. As she lathered up with lavender body wash, the calming scent filled the air, wrapping her in tranquillity. After shampooing her hair with rosemary and mint, she rinsed thoroughly and applied conditioner, savouring the refreshing aroma. Once she rinsed out the conditioner, she lingered under the water for a moment longer, relishing the sensation before turning off the shower. Wrapping herself in a towel, she enjoyed the cool air against her skin, a refreshing contrast to the warmth she had just experienced.

She padded back to her bedroom, where she slipped into a flowing emerald-green skirt paired with a matching sleeveless top, the rich hues complementing her complexion beautifully. Black ankle boots grounded the outfit, adding a touch of sophistication. She accessorised her look with layered necklaces, statement earrings, and a colourful beaded bracelet that echoed her vibrant style. Her long dark hair cascaded in loose, soft waves, imparting an air of effortless elegance. With a touch of light makeup and a spritz of her favourite perfume, she completed her ensemble, ready to embrace the day.

After enjoying a comforting cup of coffee, Emma grabbed her umbrella and stepped out into the fresh morning air. The gentle drizzle created a reflective mood as she made her way to The Croissant Cottage. With each step, her thoughts drifted back to the early days when she first started practising as a professional psychic. The rhythmic sound of raindrops hitting her umbrella reminded her of the emotions she had felt during those initial experiences.

After mastering her abilities under Kai's guidance, Emma had felt a deep calling to use her gifts to help others. Her decision to become a professional psychic was not easy; it came with its own set of challenges and uncertainties. She remembered the first time she set up her practice in London, feeling both excitement and trepidation. The small, cosy studio had been a haven for her—a place where she could offer solace and insight to those in need.

In the beginning, clients had come mostly through word of mouth, often sceptical but curious. Emma's first reading was with Kathleen, who had unexpectedly lost her husband. The session had been intense, with emotions running high. Emma recalled the moment she connected with Kathleen's husband's spirit, feeling the surge of love and the deep sadness, he carried. Communicating his messages to Kathleen had brought her closure and peace, and the gratitude in her eyes was something Emma would never forget.

Each client had brought a unique story and set of challenges. There were times when Emma questioned her path, especially when faced with sceptics or clients whose pain was overwhelming. But she persevered, driven by the difference she made in people's lives. Her reputation had grown, and with it, her confidence. She had found a rhythm in her work, developing a deep sense of empathy and understanding for the human experience.

Emma had also learned to establish personal boundaries with her clients. Balancing her psychic work with her emotional well-being was a learning process. There had been moments when the energy from her readings lingered, affecting her deeply. She had to learn to cleanse her space and herself, often turning to meditation, nature walks, and somatic exercises to ground her energy.

Despite the challenges, there had always been immense fulfilment in her work. Emma cherished the connections she made, the lives she touched, and the healing she facilitated. Her practice in London had been formative, intertwining with her personal growth and spiritual journey.

As Emma arrived at *The Croissant Cottage*, the warm, inviting aroma of freshly baked pastries greeted her, instantly putting her in a good mood. She stepped inside, her eyes scanning the cosy space until they landed on Michael behind the counter. She smiled and approached him, feeling a sense of ease.

After ordering a freshly baked muffin for breakfast, they caught up on his recent gig at *The Obsidian Fog*. Emma shared her experience of the night, describing the electric atmosphere of the show and the way the music had transported her. Michael responded with stories of the band's antics and the energy of the crowd, laughing as he recounted some of the lighter moments with his bandmates. Their conversation was easy and comfortable, each exchange filled with a shared appreciation for the night's music.

Finally, with a smile of gratitude, Emma thanked him for the muffin and made her way to her studio.

Once inside, she stopped by Rose's desk to go over the latest crystal orders, taking a moment to ensure everything was in order.

"Good morning, Rose," Emma greeted, her voice warm.

"Morning, Emma," Rose replied, looking up from her computer with a smile. "I need to update you on the new crystal inventory."

"Perfect timing," Emma said, leaning against the counter. "What do we have coming in?"

Rose pulled up the order details on her screen. "We have some beautiful pieces arriving. A new batch of amethyst clusters and a few large pieces of black tourmaline."

Emma's eyes lit up at the mention of the crystals. "That sounds wonderful. The amethyst clusters always go quickly. Let's make sure we display them prominently."

Rose nodded, making a note. "Absolutely. I was thinking we could put them near the front, by the window. The natural light will really make them sparkle."

"Great idea," Emma agreed. "And the black tourmaline—it is such a powerful stone. It is perfect for grounding and protection. It is one of my personal favourites. We should highlight its protective properties."

"Okay, Emma," Rose said.

Emma walked over to the display area, picturing the layout in her mind. She said, "Let's create a small section dedicated to protection stones. We can include black tourmaline, hematite, and smoky quartz."

"That sounds perfect," Rose said, following her.

Emma and Rose continued to discuss the crystal inventory, making plans for the new arrivals and brainstorming ideas to enhance the store's displays. As their conversation drew to a close, Emma left Rose to finish her tasks and stepped into her consultation room. The anticipation of the new crystals and the prospect of sharing their benefits with others filled her with a surge of energy and a deep sense of contentment.

Emma picked up the phone and dialled Mrs. Harrington's number, eager to finalise the details for her upcoming visit—a request made by Mrs. Harrington during their earlier appointment. As the call connected, Emma focused on confirming the time and date for their meeting.

Mrs Harrington answered, and after exchanging pleasantries, the conversation quickly shifted to arranging the visit. Emma asked for a suitable time, considering both Mrs Harrington's availability and her own schedule. They fixed the appointment for the next afternoon.

As Emma ended the call, a mix of anxiety and determination washed over her. The thought of delving into Laura's past weighed heavily on her, yet she recognised the importance of this visit in piecing together the mystery surrounding Laura's tragic end and her encounters with her spirit.

Determined to keep everything organised, Emma decided to inform Rose about her upcoming absence. She found her at her desk, focused on her tasks. "Rose, I just scheduled an appointment with Mrs. Harrington for tomorrow afternoon, so I'll need to leave the studio around that time. Could you please clear my schedule?"

Rose looked up and nodded. "No problem, Emma. I'll make sure everything's handled. Just let me know if there is anything specific you need me to do."

"Thanks, Rose," Emma said. "I appreciate it."

As the afternoon wore on and Emma was finishing some paperwork, she heard a soft knock at her consultation room door. "Emma, Michael is here," Rose announced, her tone cheerful.

Emma looked up, her eyebrows raised in surprise. "Really? Please send him in!" she replied, curious about the unexpected visit. A moment later, Michael stepped through the door, his expression brightening the room as he greeted her with a friendly smile.

"Hey, Emma," he said, stepping closer. She quickly got up from her chair, walked over to him, and they embraced in a warm hug. "I was just passing by and thought I would see if you wanted to join me for dinner tonight. There's a new Italian restaurant called La Bella Vita. What do you say?"

Emma's face lit up with a genuine smile. "That sounds wonderful, Michael! I'd love to join you."

"Awesome!" he replied, his eyes sparkling with enthusiasm. "How about I swing by to pick you up around seven?"

"Perfect! I'm looking forward to it. It'll be nice to catch up over dinner," Emma said, feeling a warm sense of anticipation.

"Great! I'll see you then." With a friendly wave, Michael headed out, leaving Emma uplifted by the unexpected invitation.

As she returned to work, Emma noticed a new email notification on her screen. She opened it, and her heart sank as she read the subject line marked "Urgent." It was from one of her long time clients, Patricia. The message described an escalating personal crisis involving family tensions and recurring unsettling dreams that were deeply affecting her well-being. Patricia was a high-profile client who had struggled with chronic anxiety for years, and their sessions had always provided her with a much-needed sense of stability and insight.

Emma knew she needed to address the issue at once. She began by reviewing Patricia's past sessions and notes to refresh her memory on the ongoing themes and concerns. Reading through them made it increasingly clear that Patricia's situation had taken a darker turn.

Emma spent the next hour preparing for an emergency virtual session with Patricia. She gathered her notes, arranged a quiet, calming space in her studio, and ensured her laptop, headset, and video setup were working perfectly. As she prepared, her mind focused on providing the reassurance and support Patricia needed during this challenging time. Every detail mattered, and Emma approached the session with a sense of purpose, ready to help Patricia find clarity and comfort.

As the video call connected, Patricia's face appeared on Emma's screen. Her eyes were red-rimmed and weary, evidence of recent tears. She looked visibly distressed, her expression etched with exhaustion and worry. Emma's heart went out to her as she gently greeted Patricia, offering a warm, grounding presence.

During the session, Emma listened intently as Patricia shared her mounting fears, describing vivid nightmares and a growing sense of impending doom that had begun to overshadow her waking hours. Emma responded with calm empathy, guiding Patricia through grounding techniques and offering practical strategies to help her navigate the surge of anxiety.

As the session ended, Emma offered Patricia a reassuring smile. "Remember, you are not alone in this. Take it one step at a time, and reach out if you need support between sessions," she said gently.

Patricia nodded, her expression softened slightly, as if a weight had been lifted. After exchanging goodbyes, Emma ended the video call, taking a deep breath as the screen went dark. She felt a mix of relief and exhaustion settle over her. While she was thankful to have guided Patricia through her immediate crisis, the intensity of the session had left her a little drained. Taking a moment to centre herself, Emma closed her eyes, reminding herself to ground her energy before moving forward with the rest of her day.

When she opened her eyes and glanced at her watch, she realised it was almost time for Michael to pick her up for dinner. Emma quickly put away her video equipment and tidied up her workspace before heading into the bathroom. She freshened up, brushing her hair, adding a touch of makeup, and checking that her outfit was still in place. Just then, her phone buzzed with a text from Michael, letting her know he was waiting for her outside. She walked to the front of the studio, said goodbye to Rose, and then headed to the front door.

As Emma stepped outside, her gaze fell on Michael, who was waiting by his car. He looked effortlessly charming in a casual yet stylish outfit that struck a balance between relaxed and polished. He wore a crisp, navy-blue button-down shirt that complemented his dark, slim-fit jeans. Over the shirt, he had a lightweight, charcoal-grey blazer that added a touch of sophistication without being overly formal. His look was completed with polished brown leather loafers that gleamed softly in the evening light. Michael's overall appearance reflected his easy-going personality while still showing that he had made an effort for their evening out.

"Hi, Emma," Michael greeted, his warm smile illuminating the early evening as he stood by the car.

"Hello, Michael!" Emma replied, returning his smile as she approached. "Thank you for picking me up."

As he opened the car door for her, she settled into the passenger seat, feeling the weight of the day begin to dissipate.

Once they were on the road, their conversation flowed effortlessly. Emma found herself captivated by Michael's animated discussion about his band's preparations for an upcoming gig.

"We've put together a new setlist that I think you'll find truly engaging," he remarked, glancing at her with enthusiasm. "I can hardly wait for you to hear the new pieces we've been crafting. We are aiming to create an immersive experience that resonates with the audience."

Emma leaned forward, genuinely intrigued. "Sounds fantastic! I'm eager to listen to them."

The drive to La Bella Vita was filled with moments like these, where their laughter intertwined with the gentle hum of the car and the soft glow of the setting sun, creating an ideal ambiance for the evening ahead.

Upon arrival, the restaurant welcomed them with the comforting aroma of freshly baked bread and simmering sauces. Soft Italian music played in the background, enhancing the ambiance. The hostess led them to a table by the window, where they could enjoy a view of the town lights twinkling as the evening set in.

"This place is beautiful," Emma remarked, taking in the warm, rustic decor. The walls were adorned with vintage Italian posters and photographs, and the tables were elegantly set with crimson and ivory gingham cloths.

Michael nodded. "Though they opened recently, I've heard their food is amazing."

Once they were seated, they were handed menus, and Emma's eyes widened at the array of choices. "Everything looks so good," she said, glancing over the selections. "I'm having a hard time deciding."

Michael chuckled. "I know what you mean. How about we start with a bottle of Chianti and some appetisers while we make up our minds?"

Emma agreed, and Michael ordered the wine and a bruschetta plate. As they waited, their conversation flowed effortlessly. They talked about their favourite foods, childhood memories, and travel experiences. Emma found herself laughing more than she had in days, feeling a genuine connection with Michael.

When the wine and bruschetta arrived, Emma picked up her glass. "Cheers, Michael," she said.

"Cheers," Michael replied, clinking his glass against hers. They both took a sip, and Emma smiled at the delightful flavour. "This wine is delicious!" she exclaimed.

The bruschetta was a delightful start to their meal, featuring crispy bread topped with ripe tomatoes, fragrant basil, and a drizzle of balsamic glaze that elevated the dish. They each took a bite, and Emma closed her eyes, savouring the burst of flavours that danced on her palate.

Emma opted for the seafood pasta for the main course, while Michael chose the risotto, which the restaurant proudly touted as one of their specialties. As they placed their orders, the conversation flowed effortlessly. Michael shared anecdotes from his university days, recounting the late-night study sessions that often turned into impromptu jam sessions with friends and the camaraderie that made those years unforgettable. Emma found herself captivated by his stories, laughing at the mischief they got into, and the lessons learned along the way. She shared her excitement about an upcoming trip to London to visit her best friend, Serena, reminiscing about their past adventures and the new places they planned to explore together.

When their main courses arrived, Emma's seafood pasta was a vibrant medley of succulent shrimp, tender mussels, and calamari, all tossed in a rich, aromatic tomato sauce. The colours were as inviting as the aroma, which wafted enticingly from the plate. Michael's risotto was equally impressive, creamy, and fragrant, enriched with earthy mushrooms and finished with a generous sprinkle of Parmesan cheese that added depth to each bite.

As they enjoyed their meals, the restaurant buzzed with the murmur of other diners and the clinking of glasses, creating an atmosphere that felt lively yet intimate. Emma was enveloped in a sense of peace and contentment that had eluded her for some time. The delicious food, engaging conversation, and cosy ambiance combined seamlessly, transforming their dinner into a perfect evening.

The waiter approached with the dessert menu as they finished their main courses. He suggested the classic tiramisu and Emma's eyes lit up with enthusiasm. "Let's share one," she replied eagerly.

Once their orders were placed, Emma excused herself, stepping into the washroom to touch up her makeup. As she looked in the mirror, she couldn't help but smile at how much she was enjoying the evening. The ambiance of La Bella Vita, the delightful company of Michael, and the delicious food all contributed to a sense of warmth and joy she hadn't felt in a long time.

Yet, amidst this pleasant moment, her thoughts flickered to the protection rituals and mantras she had been practising. Perhaps they were working, keeping Laura's spirit at bay and allowing her to fully immerse herself in this night without the weight of lingering shadows. With a deep breath, she straightened her hair and made her way back to the table, feeling lighter and more at ease.

When she returned, the tiramisu had just arrived, beautifully presented and inviting them to indulge. They each took a spoonful, savouring the combination of espresso-soaked ladyfingers, creamy mascarpone, and a delicate dusting of cocoa powder. The dessert was heavenly, striking the perfect balance of flavours and textures, and Emma couldn't help but smile at the delightful experience they were sharing.

"This is divine," Emma said, closing her eyes to fully appreciate the taste.

"I'm glad you're enjoying it," Michael replied, watching her with a satisfied smile.

As they finished their dessert, Emma felt a sense of contentment settling over her.

When the bill arrived, Michael insisted on treating her, refusing to allow her to share the bill. They walked slowly to his car, the crisp night air was refreshing. The drive back was quiet and pleasant, filled with a comfortable silence that spoke volumes. When they arrived at Emma's cottage, they opened the doors and stepped out of the car, the stars twinkling above them.

"Thank you for tonight, Michael," Emma said, her voice genuine. "I truly needed this."

"Me too, Emma," he replied. "We should definitely do this again."

As they stood at her doorstep, Emma turned to him, a warm smile gracing her lips. "I had a wonderful time. Thank you again."

Michael returned her smile, his eyes reflecting his enjoyment. "So did I. Good night, Emma." He gave her a hug, stepped back, and got into the car, his gaze lingering on her.

"Good night, Michael," she replied, watching as he drove away, the taillights of his car fading into the night.

She paused at her doorstep, gazing at the darkened woods bordering her property. The trees stood tall and silent, their silhouettes ghostly against the dim light of the street lamps. A slight breeze rustled the leaves, carrying with it the earthy scent of damp soil and decaying leaves, and the air felt cool and crisp against her skin.

A fleeting sense of intuition brushed against her awareness as she stood there – a subtle nudge, like a whisper from the woods themselves. The way the trees seemed to lean in, their branches swaying slightly, suggested they held secrets waiting to be revealed.

Emma's gaze lingered on the shadows weaving intricate patterns on the ground, and she felt a vague but persistent sensation that the woods would play a role in her future.

With each heartbeat, the feeling deepened, a gentle reminder of the connection she shared with the natural world—a bond that often provided insight into the mysteries surrounding her. This intuition was not fully formed or understood, but it echoed in her thoughts as she turned and entered her home, closing the door behind her.

Stepping into the cosy warmth of her cottage, Emma took a moment to breathe deeply, grounding herself in the familiar scents of lavender and cedar wood. The woods remained on her mind, leaving her with a sense of quiet anticipation. She knew that whatever lay hidden in those shadows might hold vital clues to the haunting she was unravelling.

Heading to the bathroom, Emma drew a warm bath. As the tub filled, she added a few drops of lavender oil and lit some candles, their gentle glow casting soft shadows on the walls. Once the water reached the perfect temperature, she slipped in, allowing the warmth to envelop her and ease the tension from her day. The soothing scent of lavender mingled with the heat, wrapping her in a calming embrace.

After a long, relaxing soak in the bathtub, Emma dried off, applied a rich moisturiser, and slipped into her soft cotton pyjamas. The simple ritual left her feeling rejuvenated and at peace, ready to embrace the quiet of the night.

She picked up the book she had started reading the week before and settled into bed. It was titled *The Mystic's Path: Journeys Through the Unknown*, a collection of accounts from various mystics and spiritual seekers sharing their profound experiences with the mystical and the unknown. The cover featured a mesmerising image of a winding path through an ancient forest, illuminated by an ethereal, otherworldly light.

Emma flipped through the pages until she found the chapter that she wanted to read. It was called "Crystals and the Astral Realm." As she read about the experiences of others who had used crystals to enhance their spiritual journeys, her mind drifted back to one of her own mystical encounters.

It was during her early years as a professional psychic in London before she moved to Hawes. Emma had been gifted a unique crystal by a fellow practitioner – a vibrant piece of fluorite known for its ability to clear negative energies and enhance spiritual insight. She remembered how she had felt an immediate connection to the crystal, its energy resonating with her own in a profound way.

One evening, Emma decided to meditate with the fluorite, hoping to deepen her connection to her intuition. A wave of calm washed over her as she held the crystal in her hand and closed her eyes. The room around her faded away, and she found herself transported to a different realm.

In this astral landscape, Emma walked through a vast, luminescent forest. The trees glowed with an inner light, and the air hummed with a sense of ancient wisdom and tranquillity. She felt a presence guiding her, leading her deeper into the forest until she reached a clearing.

At the centre of the clearing stood a towering crystal formation, radiating a brilliant, multicoloured light. The hues of the fluorite shifted and danced, casting a serene, ethereal glow over the surroundings. As Emma approached, she experienced an overwhelming sense of peace and understanding. The crystal seemed to communicate with her, imparting knowledge and insights that felt just beyond her grasp. It was as if the fluorite had unlocked a doorway to a higher consciousness, allowing her to see the world differently.

This transformative experience deepened her connection to the spiritual realm and affirmed her path as a psychic and healer. The essence of that moment lingered with her, serving as a reminder of the profound insights that meditation could offer.

As Emma finished reading the chapter, she closed the book and placed it on her bedside table. The memories of her mystical journey with the fluorite crystal filled her with wonder and gratitude. She turned off the light and snuggled under the covers, her mind still lingering on the vivid images of the luminescent forest and the powerful crystal formation.

Before drifting off to sleep, Emma whispered a silent thank you to the universe for guiding her on her path and for the incredible experiences she had been blessed with.

CHAPTER 7

Echoes of the Past

Tuesday, 11ᵗʰ October 2024

The next morning, Emma woke up feeling refreshed and grateful for the wonderful evening she had shared with Michael. The sky outside her window was overcast and grey, casting a muted light over her cottage and creating a cosy atmosphere indoors.

Once she got out of bed, Emma went to the kitchen, the rich aroma of brewing coffee filling the air as it percolated. While it brewed, she slipped into the bathroom to freshen up. When she returned, she sat at the kitchen table, wrapping her hands around the warm mug, savouring the first sip as it grounded her for the day ahead.

With a sense of calm settling in, she turned on soft meditation music, the gentle sounds filling the room. Moving to her meditation corner, she closed her eyes and allowed herself to sink into stillness. After a few moments of peace, she transitioned smoothly into her yoga routine, flowing through the poses with fluidity, stretching, and releasing the tension in her body.

After half an hour, she completed her session and stepped into the shower. The warm water cascading over her eased the last traces of tension from her muscles.

Feeling refreshed, she stepped into her room and selected her outfit for the day. She chose a knee-length forest green skirt, paired with a cream-coloured sweater and brown leather boots. She applied her makeup with practiced ease and completed the look with a soft swipe of light brown lipstick. Her hair fell loose in natural waves, adding a touch of effortless elegance. Delicate crystal jewellery shimmered softly, perfectly complementing the ensemble.

After a light breakfast of oatmeal topped with sliced bananas and a drizzle of honey, Emma left the warmth of her cottage. The morning sky was overcast, casting a muted grey light, but the cosy ambiance of her home lingered as she slid into her Jeep. She decided to drive to work, knowing she would need to make her way to Willow's Creek later for her appointment with Mrs. Harrington.

At The Soul Sanctuary, she settled into her routine, checking inventory, discussing updates with Rose, and preparing for upcoming client appointments. Despite the busyness, a quiet unease began to settle over her, the thought of her visit to Mrs. Harrington weighing heavier with each passing minute.

A little after 10:00 am, Emma called Mrs. Harrington to confirm their appointment. During the conversation, Mrs. Harrington gave her directions to her home in Willow's Creek. As they spoke, Emma couldn't shake the feeling that something significant awaited her later that day.

After a light lunch that Rose had picked up from the café next door, Emma set out for Willow's Creek. The hour-long drive took her through rolling hills and quaint villages, transforming the familiar landscapes of Hawes into the broader, more expansive views that awaited her. The overcast sky loomed overhead, and a chilly breeze rustled the trees, amplifying the sense of unease that had settled in during the morning.

As she drove, Emma turned on soothing music, allowing the gentle melodies to fill her Jeep. The familiar tunes wrapped around her like a warm embrace, helping to calm her racing thoughts. With each passing mile, she reflected on the mysteries surrounding her clients. What challenges lay ahead with Mrs. Harrington? What more would she face with Laura's spirit? Would this visit bring her the answers she needed?

The landscape changed as she approached Willow's Creek, the trees giving way to open fields and gently rolling hills.

The village itself was quaint, with picturesque cottages and neatly tended gardens. Yet, even here, the overcast sky cast a pall over everything, muting the colours and lending an air of melancholy to the scene.

Emma drove slowly through the village, scanning the quaint cottages and neatly tended gardens as she focused on finding the address. She followed Mrs. Harrington's directions, noting the street names as they appeared on the signs.

She suddenly spotted the turn-off for Mrs Harrington's home. The narrow road wound through a patch of dense woodland, its towering trees creating a natural archway that filtered the muted light overhead. As she drove, the scent of damp earth and fallen leaves filled the air, heightening her awareness of the serene yet eerie atmosphere surrounding her. The road gradually opened to reveal an imposing wrought-iron gate adorned with intricate, curling patterns hinting at a bygone era.

Emma parked her car and stepped out, feeling a chill in the air that sent a shiver down her spine. The gate creaked as she pushed it open, the sound echoing in the stillness. She hesitated for a moment, taking in the manor ahead of her. Its vastness was daunting, and the lack of character in its design amplified her sense of foreboding. The building loomed before her, a monolith of muted grey stone, its grandeur overshadowed by an air of dreariness that felt almost oppressive.

As she walked up the path to the front door, Emma noted the overgrown gardens, the flowers wilted and browned, adding to the home's unwelcoming air. Each step felt heavy, the anticipation of what awaited her weighing on her heart. With a deep breath, she reached for the doorbell, her pulse quickening as she prepared to enter the place that had once been Laura Harrington's home!

She was greeted by the housekeeper at the front door with a polite but distant smile. She ushered Emma inside and directed her to the living room while she went to inform Mrs Harrington of Emma's arrival.

Emma stepped into the living room, where the atmosphere felt as solemn as the house's exterior. The room was vast, with high ceilings and an expansive floor space that was only partially occupied by sparse, heavy furniture. The walls were adorned with dark wood panelling and an array of old portraits that seemed to watch her with indifferent eyes. The carpet beneath her feet was a deep, muted brown, and several antique rugs scattered across it added little warmth to the otherwise chilly room.

A grand fireplace dominated one wall, though it had long been cold. Above the mantelpiece, an ornate mirror framed in gold added a touch of elegance, but its reflective surface merely amplified the dim, grey light filtering through the tall, arched windows. The windows were covered with heavy, dark drapes that were drawn tight, allowing only a faint, filtered light to illuminate the room.

Large, overstuffed armchairs and a dark, polished wooden coffee table were arranged in the centre, while several bookshelves lined the walls, filled with a mix of old volumes and decorative objects. A few potted plants sat in the corners; they looked dull and did not seem to thrive in the dim environment.

Emma sat in one of the armchairs, the room's silence amplifying her anticipation. She glanced around, noting an opulence that felt more oppressive than inviting; the grandeur of the space did little to ease her unease about the meeting. She looked up as Mrs. Harrington entered, exuding the same quiet dignity as the first time they had met. The older woman wore a smart, albeit slightly outdated, navy blue dress with a string of pearls adding a touch of formality. Emma rose to her feet and smiled politely.

"Ms. Ravenwood, thank you for coming," Mrs. Harrington said warmly, her voice a soothing contrast to the sombre atmosphere of the room. "Please, make yourself comfortable. I have had some coffee prepared for us."

Emma returned her smile with a nod. "Thank you, Mrs. Harrington. I appreciate the invitation," she replied, settling into the armchair as Mrs. Harrington poured coffee into the delicate china cups the housekeeper had brought in.

They exchanged a few polite remarks about the weather and the village, creating a moment of normalcy before turning to the purpose of Emma's visit.

As they sipped their coffee, Mrs. Harrington's tone shifted, growing more contemplative. "I've always wondered if there was something more to Laura's story, something I missed," she said softly, her eyes clouded with regret.

Mrs. Harrington began to share more about her daughter's struggles. Laura's journey through the harrowing maze of her psyche had been marked by profound highs and devastating lows. From an early age, Laura displayed a sensitivity that bordered on the preternatural, often withdrawing from others in favour of books and nature. Those around her saw her intense emotions and vivid imagination as quirks of a gifted mind, but as she grew older, these traits morphed into signs of something more troubling.

By her teenage years, Laura's behaviour had become increasingly erratic. Mrs Harrington recounted nights when she would find Laura pacing her room, muttering to herself, or scribbling furiously in her journals, her eyes wild with a mix of fear and anger. "Her mood swings became more extreme, and she fell into deep, paralysing depression," Mrs Harrington said softly.

"I took her to therapists and psychiatrists, but the treatments were often invasive and ineffective, leaving Laura feeling more isolated and misunderstood. Medications dulled her mind and spirit but did little to quell the tormenting voices or the shadows that seemed to follow her," said Mrs. Harrington, her voice filled with sadness.

"Then there was this one particular incident. Laura had come home from school one afternoon, and something seemed to have set her off. She was studying at Willow's Creek High School here in town. She had been showing signs of distress for weeks, but this episode was unlike anything we had seen before. It happened right here, in this very room."

Emma's mind stirred at the mention of Willow's Creek High School, where Laura had studied. Her father had taught there for years. The connection was subtle, but the realisation lingered in her thoughts.

"It was then that I had no choice but to admit her to Ravensbrook Asylum," continued Mrs. Harrington, her expression bleak. "Despite treatments, her condition didn't improve. Her time there was filled with turmoil, and nothing seemed to help."

"Do you think something at the school might have contributed to Laura's state?" Emma asked, her voice tinged with curiosity.

Mrs. Harrington shook her head. "There's no concrete evidence. By the time she was at Willow's Creek, Laura was already battling severe mental health issues. This particular incident was sudden."

Emma nodded, sensing the depth of Mrs. Harrington's pain. "Is there anything else you remember - anything that might have happened before... before she passed?"

Mrs Harrington leaned in, her voice growing quiet and urgent. "It was just before her death, every time I visited her at the asylum, I found her more distant, darker."

Emma felt a chill settle in the air as she listened. There was something more to Laura's story—something unsettling—that tugged at Emma's instincts.

Mrs. Harrington continued, her voice heavy with sorrow, "When I got the call about her death, I was devastated. They told me she had taken her own life, jumped from the roof of the asylum," Mrs. Harrington said, her voice strained.

"The details were sparse, and I had many questions. The circumstances surrounding her death were unclear."

As Mrs. Harrington spoke, Emma's psychic senses stirred, a deep foreboding settling in her chest. The anguish Laura had endured was undeniable, but Emma's intuition whispered that there was far more lurking beneath the surface. It wasn't just the torment of a troubled mind—something darker, more insidious, seemed to cling to Laura's story. Her death, and the circumstances surrounding it, felt like a fragment of a much larger, more enigmatic puzzle. Emma couldn't shake the feeling that the answers she sought lay hidden, waiting to be unearthed.

As Emma mulled over the unsettling details, Mrs. Harrington broke the silence, rising from her seat. "Let me take you to Laura's bedroom, I think you may find something that could shed light on all this," she said, her voice steady but tinged with an air of mystery. She led Emma through the dimly lit corridors of the manor, the faint creak of old wood beneath their feet the only sound. At the end of the hall, Mrs. Harrington stopped before a heavy door. She unlocked it with a brass key, its worn surface gleaming faintly in the low light, and motioned for Emma to enter.

Emma stepped inside, sensing the gravity of the moment. Mrs. Harrington gave her one last, lingering glance before she turned and headed back to the living room, leaving Emma to continue her exploration.

The room was grand but heavy with an oppressive atmosphere. High ceilings loomed over faded, ornate wallpaper. A massive, dark wood bed dominated the space, its canopy draped in thick, dusty fabric. Antique furniture—an intricately carved desk and a large, empty bookshelf—added to the room's sombre grandeur. Heavy, dark curtains obscured the windows, allowing only a sliver of muted light to filter through.

Emma stepped inside, her senses alert. She closed her eyes and took a deep breath, trying to connect with any residual energy that Laura might have left behind. As she focused, she felt the weight of the room's melancholy and the echoes of past distress. But after 25 years since the occupant's death, nothing concrete or specific lingered.

She wandered around the room, lightly touching surfaces and searching for lingering impressions. The feeling was profound emptiness—Laura's presence was there, but there was no direct contact or clear messages. The room seemed to hold its secrets tightly, offering little more than a deep, unsettling quiet.

Her gaze drifted to the bed. The heavy, dark wood frame felt almost oppressive, and the canopy, once luxurious, now hung like a shroud. She could almost imagine Laura lying there during one of her hysterical episodes, her emotional turmoil pressing down on her as the bed seemed to press down on the room. The neatly made linens were faded and thin, a ghost of their former richness.

Emma moved to the desk next. The intricate carvings on its surface spoke of a time when craftsmanship was cherished. Now, it stood as a repository of forgotten memories. She ran her fingers over the smooth, cold wood, pausing at a small drawer. Opening it, she found it empty except for a few yellowed papers that crumbled at her touch. The scent of aged paper and dust filled the air, a reminder of time's passing and the weight of history contained in the room.

The vanity table, positioned near the window, caught Emma's eye. The oval mirror reflected her image, but as she studied it, she could almost see Laura standing behind her— a shadowy figure filled with sorrow. The glass, clouded with age and secrets, seemed to hold its own memories. Emma reached out and touched it, feeling a cold chill run through her fingers.

She then turned her attention to the small armchair in the room's far corner. The upholstery, worn and faded with time, seemed to hold an air of significance. Emma could almost picture Laura sitting there, perhaps reading or staring out of the window, lost in her own thoughts. She felt deep empathy as she imagined the young woman's struggles within these walls. With renewed determination, Emma vowed to uncover the truth about Laura's life and death.

After a long pause, Emma finally turned and walked towards the door. Her footsteps echoed in the silent room as she closed the door gently behind her, the weight of the space still lingering with her. She returned to the living room, where Mrs. Harrington sat, waiting patiently. Emma settled into a chair across from her, her expression thoughtful.

"I didn't sense much in the room," she said quietly. "There was a feeling of emptiness, but no clear messages or impressions."

Mrs. Harrington's face fell slightly at the news, her disappointment evident. She folded her hands in her lap and sighed before speaking again. "I had hoped that you might uncover something more, something that would help explain Laura's suffering... But perhaps, it was too much to expect."

Emma sat momentarily, absorbing Mrs. Harrington's words, the heaviness of the conversation settling over her. She then stood up slowly, her thoughts still lingering on Laura's tragic story. She glanced at Mrs. Harrington, her expression softening with empathy.

"I'll keep looking," Emma said, her voice gentle but firm. "If I uncover anything that might help explain what happened to Laura, I'll be sure to let you know."

Mrs Harrington nodded, her eyes filled with a mixture of hope and sorrow. "Thank you, Emma. I appreciate your help."

Emma got up from her chair and gave her a reassuring smile. Mrs. Harrington stood as well, and together they made their way out of the room, the air between them heavy with unspoken understanding. As they reached the door, Emma paused, giving Mrs. Harrington a final nod before stepping outside.

As Emma drove back from Willow's Creek, the heavy atmosphere of Laura's room lingered in her mind. The winding roads and overcast sky mirrored her contemplative mood, amplifying the image of Laura's anguish and the isolation she had endured within the manor's oppressive walls. The long drive offered Emma ample time to reflect on her own struggles.

She knew all too well the torment of a mind at war with itself. Diagnosed with bipolar disorder in her late teens, Emma had felt both terrified and relieved by the diagnosis. Finally, there was a name for the tumultuous mood swings—the exhilarating highs and crushing lows—that had dominated her life.

Her thoughts drifted to the darker times when even getting out of bed felt insurmountable. There were nights when the weight of her existence was so suffocating she could barely breathe. She remembered the sleepless hours, lying awake as intrusive thoughts raced through her mind and the moments when she teetered on the edge, questioning whether the struggle was worth it.

When Emma's psychic abilities began to manifest, they added another layer of complexity to her condition. The sensitivity that allowed her to connect with otherworldly energies also made her vulnerable to the chaotic emotions of those around her. It was a double-edged sword—giving her unique insights while leaving her susceptible to overwhelming emotional turbulence. Over the years, Emma had learned to balance her abilities with her mental health, meditating for hours to quiet her mind and find a centre of calm.

Reflecting on Laura's life, Emma felt a deep empathy for her. Despite receiving all the help available at the time, Laura was still lost in a world that misunderstood her, trapped in a mind that betrayed her at every turn. Emma wondered how different Laura's life might have been if the support she had received had been more effective.

By the time Emma reached her home, the overcast sky had begun to lighten, with a hint of the setting sun breaking through the clouds. The drive had been long, but it also gave her ample time for reflection and to process the day's events.

She parked in her driveway and made her way to the front door of her cottage. Once inside, she took a deep breath, appreciating the warmth and familiarity of her home. She hung her coat on the rack and slipped off her boots, savouring the feel of the soft rug beneath her feet. She poured herself a glass of water in the kitchen and leaned against the counter. Her mind drifted back to Mrs. Harrington's words—her father had taught at the same school Laura had attended. The connection had unsettled her then, and now, as she thought about it more, a nagging intuition told her it might be more than just a coincidence.

Setting the glass down, Emma walked into her bedroom to wash up and change into a comfortable pair of soft pastel shorts and a t-shirt. After a few quiet moments, she returned to the kitchen to prepare dinner.

Emma felt the day's tension still clinging to her after dinner, a simple yet comforting meal of roasted chicken with steamed vegetables and a small glass of red wine. She cleared the table, washed the dishes, and tidied up the kitchen, her movements automatic as she processed the day's events.

She then settled on the couch, flicking on the TV for a few moments of distraction. The soft hum of the television provided a welcome break, allowing her to shift her focus before her nightly routine.

Once the credits rolled, she turned off the TV and meditated for a few moments to clear her mind.

As Emma settled into her meditation, the soft glow of the candlelight flickered gently around her, casting dancing shadows on the walls of her cosy living room. She took a few deep breaths, allowing her chest's rhythmic rise and fall to anchor her in the present moment. Her mind began to quieten, and she slipped into the tranquil state she had grown accustomed to.

Emma sensed a gentle shift in the energy around her in this meditative state, like a delicate ripple passing through a still pond. An almost imperceptible sensation accompanied her usual calm that something was subtly off—an intangible feeling she could not quite grasp but was undeniably present.

A faint chill brushed against her skin as she focused on breathing like a breeze carrying coldness. Her inner vision began to reveal fleeting, fragmented images: a dimly lit corridor in the manor, dark wood panelling, and heavy curtains. Though blurry, the images carried an eerie sense of familiarity.

She felt a presence—neither threatening nor comforting, just there. It was like standing at the edge of a foggy precipice, the mist obscuring clear sight but suggesting something significant just beyond.

Then, a fleeting image of Laura's room flashed before her. The room's oppressive atmosphere returned, now laced with a vague urgency. The walls seemed to pulse, and the light took on an unnatural, spectral hue.

The psychic impressions were brief, slipping away before she could fully grasp them. She tried to hold on, but they faded like sand slipping through her fingers.

She opened her eyes, realising the calm she sought had eluded her.

With a sigh, she rose and made her way to the bedroom. The soft sheets seemed inviting, and she slid into bed, seeking comfort. She spent a few moments scrolling through social media on her phone before finally drifting off to sleep, the whispers of her intuition still lingering in her thoughts, hinting at revelations yet to come.

CHAPTER 8

Echoes of the Past

Wednesday, 12th October 2024

Emma woke up with an unsettling heaviness, the world around her feeling distorted—colours too bright, sounds too loud. Her bipolar disorder was already taking its toll, pulling her from a restless sleep into a state of agitation. Her heart raced, and her mind swirled with racing thoughts and fears, each more intrusive than the last.

She sat up slowly, the bed spinning beneath her. Her breathing was erratic, and focusing on her coping techniques felt impossible. Deep, controlled breaths, which usually anchored her, seemed too difficult today.

Emma started her morning with a calming cup of herbal tea, the blend of chamomile, valerian root, and lemon balm soothing her from the first sip. As she drank, she settled into her meditation space, surrounded by the gentle energy of her crystals. Holding an amethyst, rose quartz, and black tourmaline, she focused on her breath—deep inhales, a pause, then slow, controlled exhales. The combination of the tea, the calming stones, and the rhythmic breathing usually helped ease the tension, but today, the storm inside her still felt relentless. She stepped into a hot shower, hoping the steam would offer some relief, but the chaos within lingered. After a quick shower, she dressed for work, steeling herself for the day ahead.

In the kitchen, Emma prepared a pot of strong coffee, another one of her coping strategies. The ritual of brewing it and the comforting aroma helped, but today, even the simple pleasure of a warm cup was overshadowed by her overwhelming anxiety. She sipped the coffee slowly, trying to steady her nerves, but the familiar comfort offered little relief. Once she finished, she grabbed her bag and headed out the door.

Arriving at the studio, Emma felt the weight of the turbulent energy within her. This bipolar episode, combined with the lingering encounters with Laura's spirit, had drained her. She felt fragmented and unsteady, knowing she was not in the right mind to provide the focused, empathetic service her clients deserved. Always mindful of how her own energy could affect her work, Emma decided to cancel her appointments for the day. She asked Rose to handle the cancellations, understanding that ensuring her clients received clear and compassionate guidance was far more important than pushing through a session when she was not fully aligned. Aware of Emma's struggles, Rose nodded and left to take care of it.

She settled into the consultation room, her mind still buzzing with unease, and focused her energy on research. Opening her laptop, she began digging into the history of Ravensbrook Asylum. She discovered that it had been established in 1825 as a pioneering institution for mental health care. Its founders had envisioned a compassionate and humane environment, aiming to set a new standard in psychiatric treatment. Unlike the grim conditions common in such facilities at the time, Ravensbrook had committed to "moral treatment," emphasising structured routines and therapeutic activities like gardening and crafting. Today, the facility continued this legacy of excellence, offering a comprehensive range of mental health services—from inpatient and outpatient care to specialised programmes.

While ample information was available on the asylum's history and innovative practices, Emma found the specifics about Laura Harrington's tragic end frustratingly sparse. The few details she uncovered hinted at a dark conclusion: Laura had taken her own life, jumping from the terrace on the asylum's roof. It felt as if something was missing. Emma's intuition told her that Laura's death held secrets no one had dared to reveal.

Shifting her focus, Emma began researching Dr. Evelyn Hartley, the chief psychiatrist during Laura's time at the asylum. She discovered that Dr. Hartley, now retired, had been a respected figure in her field, known for her progressive and compassionate approach to mental health care. Since her retirement, Dr. Hartley had kept a low profile and was currently living in Willow's Creek. Emma wondered if she held any insights into Laura's story that had yet to be uncovered.

Around midday, a soft knock on the door interrupted her focus. Rose entered with a warm smile, carrying a steaming bowl of soup. The comforting aroma of chicken and herbs filled the room.

"Hey, Emma," Rose said gently, placing a bowl of soup on the desk. "Thought you might need a little break. How are you holding up?"

Emma looked up, her gaze softening. "Thanks, Rose. I needed this. It's a rather rough episode today, but I'm managing."

Rose nodded, offering a sympathetic smile. "I figured something light might be easier to eat—and might make you feel a little better." Emma nodded gratefully, her eyes reflecting both exhaustion and appreciation. "Thank you, Rose."

"Any time. Just let me know if you need anything else." With a reassuring nod, Rose headed back to the front of the studio to tend to her tasks.

Emma picked up the spoon and took a small sip, allowing the warmth of the soup to offer a brief moment of comfort. The soft, familiar taste provided a small distraction from the chaos in her mind. After finishing her lunch, she set the bowl aside and returned to her research, hoping to uncover more details.

She looked into the high school where Laura had been studying when the troubling episode led to her admission to the asylum. Willow's Creek High School, a well-regarded public institution established in the early 1900s, was known for its academic excellence. As Emma dug deeper, she discovered that her father had indeed been a professor there during the same period Laura attended, realising that he would have still been teaching when Laura's hysterical episode occurred.

This connection lingered in her mind, drawing her thoughts back to Maplewood, where she grew up. Her father's daily commute to Willow's Creek High School had been a constant part of their routine. The discovery of his presence during Laura's breakdown left Emma with a nagging feeling she could not quite shake.

By late afternoon, the effects of her bipolar episode grew more pronounced. The emotional turmoil weighed heavily on her, leaving her feeling scattered and exhausted. Her body felt leaden and slow, the exhaustion from hours of research only amplifying the tension in her muscles. She rubbed her tired eyes, trying to clear the fog clouding her thoughts. Her legs were stiff from sitting too long, and she stretched them out, flexing her toes to shake off the numbness. The sense of overwhelm was becoming too much, and she realised that pushing through any longer would only make things worse.

Emma stood up from the desk with a heavy sigh, her movements slow and deliberate, as though each step took more energy than she had to give. She found Rose at the front of the studio, handling the last few tasks of the day. 'I'm heading home for the rest of the day,' Emma said softly. 'Can you take care of things here?'

Rose looked up, concern flickering in her eyes. 'Of course, Emma. Take care of yourself. Call me if you need anything, okay?'

Emma offered her a small, grateful smile before turning to leave.

Returning home, Emma found herself unable to rest. She tried to lie down for a nap, but sleep eluded her, her mind racing with unrelenting thoughts. She turned on the TV to distract herself, but the images on the screen felt distant and unfocused. Time seemed to pass slowly, each minute stretching longer than the last.

Eventually, as evening set in, she prepared a simple dinner—vegetable soup with warm, crusty bread rolls. The comforting meal provided a temporary sense of solace but did little to lift her spirits. As she sat at the table, the room's stillness only seemed to amplify the restlessness within her.

After dinner, seeking a way to calm her racing thoughts, she turned to her crystals. She arranged them in a circle on the floor, hoping their soothing energy would bring her some peace. Closing her eyes, she focused on her breath, allowing the stillness to settle around her. A brief calm enveloped her for a few moments, but it quickly slipped away, leaving her feeling just as unsettled as before.

Finally, feeling drained, Emma decided to retire early, hoping for some rest. She went to her bedroom, turned off the lights, and lay down. But even in the quiet darkness, sleep remained elusive. She tossed and turned, eventually drifting into a fitful sleep. In the middle of the night, she woke with a start, her thoughts still tangled in unrest. She immediately reached for the bedside lamp and turned it on, the soft glow casting a warm light that did little to dispel the chill she felt.

Then, without warning, an inexplicable urgency gripped her, an overwhelming pull that urged her to leave her bed. She did not fully understand why but felt an undeniable compulsion to get up, as though something—or someone—was calling her. She swung her legs over the side of the bed, her feet touching the cool wooden floor. Her mind raced as she stepped out of the bedroom.

The cottage was eerily silent, except for the soft creaks and groans of the ageing structure. The quiet seemed almost oppressive, amplifying her sense of urgency. She glanced at the clock in the living room—it was 12:00 a.m. The late hour only deepened the mystery of her restless awakening. Emma felt compelled to leave without understanding why as if the night was calling her.

As Emma opened the front door and stepped outside, she was met by a thick blanket of fog that had settled over the fields and trees surrounding her cottage. Moonlight filtered through, casting ghostly hues across the mist, transforming the familiar scenery into something surreal. Each breath she took was visible in the freezing air, her exhalations mingling with the fog. The world outside her cottage appeared altered, blurred between the known and the unknown.

Emma's steps were hesitant at first, but the magnetic pull grew stronger, urging her deeper into the night. She moved slowly, her senses heightened by the chill and the dense fog. As she ventured further, the mist swirled around her, shifting into fleeting forms and shadows. A strange sensation prickled at the back of her mind, as though an unseen presence were guiding—or perhaps watching—her.

Before she fully realised it, Emma found herself in the woods near her cottage. Shadows cloaked the trees, and silence hung heavy in the air. Her heart pounded as she stepped cautiously through the underbrush. A chill suddenly washed over her, and the temperature dropped, blanketing the forest in an unnatural cold. In the corner of her vision, movement flickered.

At first, it was just a shadow shifting between the trees, indistinct and elusive, but it soon began to take shape. Emma's breath caught as the figure grew clearer—a twisted, distorted form hovering at the edge of darkness. Her heart raced as she recognised the piercing gaze, eyes that seemed to burn through the fog: Laura. Her spectral form faded in and out of view, each glimpse more menacing than the last.

Emma was gripped by an overwhelming wave of terror, freezing her in place as Laura's spirit drew closer. The air grew thick with a hostile energy, and Emma sensed the full extent of Laura's malevolent intent. This was more than a haunting; Laura's spirit was consumed by anger and a desire to inflict harm. A chilling realisation struck her: Laura wasn't simply restless—she sought revenge, her spirit driven by an intense, unrelenting hatred.

Desperate to escape the suffocating malice radiating from Laura's spirit, Emma stumbled blindly through the forest, her senses overwhelmed by the malignant energy that seemed to shadow her every step. The oppressive darkness deepened as if the forest was conspiring to keep her trapped. Shadows closed in, the trees stretching their twisted branches towards her like skeletal hands while the underbrush grabbed at her feet, tripping her at every turn.

A bone-deep chill seeped through her clothes, turning her breath into small clouds of fog that dissolved into the dense, icy air. The silence was punctuated only by her own ragged breathing and the occasional crack of a twig underfoot, each sound amplified in the foreboding quiet. As she pressed forward, her vision blurred with fleeting images of Laura's twisted, vengeful face, those eyes filled with an unnatural rage that haunted the periphery of her vision.

Suddenly, faint flickering lights appeared in the distance, like ghostly lanterns hovering in the mist. Desperate for a way out, she staggered toward them, but each time she got close, the lights would vanish, reappearing just beyond her reach, luring her deeper into the forest. A prickling sense of dread crept over her—she was being led into a trap.

The temperature plummeted further, her shivers turning to violent tremors. She strained to hear, but the only sounds were faint, hissing whispers voices sharp and taunting as they breathed her name, *"Emma..."* The sound lingered, chilling her to the core with every repetition, each utterance colder and more menacing than the last. She felt unseen eyes on her—watching, stalking.

Suddenly, the faint lights she'd been following vanished, plunging the forest into an oppressive, suffocating darkness. Emma froze, her pulse roaring as she peered into the shadows. The whispers intensified, and a low growl reverberated from somewhere closer, deeper, the sound thick with malice. *"Emma..."* the voice growled again, closer now, its venomous tone crawling over her skin like ice.

Heart hammering, she took a shaky step backward, the instinct to flee rising within her. But as she turned to escape, her foot snagged on a root, sending her sprawling to the ground. She lay there, breathless and trembling, as the shadows seemed to coil around her like smoke. A chilling breath brushed the back of her neck, and she sensed something just inches away, a presence emanating pure malice.

Scrambling to her feet, Emma forced herself forward, fighting her way through the tangled underbrush. Her frantic movements were wild and erratic as branches clawed at her arms and face, leaving stinging scratches in their wake. Every snap and rustle seemed to echo with sinister intent as if the forest itself were alive and hungry.

In her panic, Emma did not see the headlights piercing the darkness until they flooded the woods, briefly illuminating her path and breaking the hold of the shadows.

The car abruptly stopped, the engine's hum cutting off almost immediately. Emma's breath came in ragged gasps as she stumbled toward the vehicle, her body trembling with fear. She saw a man step out of the car. In her terror, she did not recognise him at first. But as she drew closer, the dim light revealed his face— Michael. He had been on his way to his house, situated beyond the end of Emma's lane, nestled further along the winding road that meandered through the countryside.

"Emma! What are you doing out here at this time?" Michael asked, his voice thick with alarm as he caught her. Emma, barely able to stand, leaned heavily on him for support.

"I—I don't know," she stammered, her voice trembling with fear. "I was just… in the woods. Something… something made me go there. I need to get home."

With a worried glance, Michael helped her into the car, gently shutting the door behind her. He hurried to his side, started the engine, and quickly reversed towards her house, which was only a few metres away.

When they reached her gate, Michael stopped the car and got out. Still trembling, Emma leaned heavily on him as she slowly exited the car. With his arm around her, he guided her to the front door. Once inside, she collapsed onto the couch, her hands shaking uncontrollably. Michael went into the kitchen and returned with a glass of water. He sat beside her, offering the glass, his brow furrowed with concern and curiosity. Emma took a few sips before setting the glass down on the table.

"Emma, you look shaken. What happened out there?" Michael asked gently, his voice filled with concern.

"I saw Laura," Emma whispered, her voice trembling. "Her spirit... it's consumed with anger and malice. It was trying to hurt me."

Michael's brow furrowed, his concern deepening. "Laura? Who is she?"

Emma struggled to steady herself, the fear still evident in her eyes. "Her spirit is... dark. Hostile. It's unlike anything I've ever encountered."

Michael listened, his confusion and worry clear on his face. "Emma, I don't understand. Who is Laura? How can I help you? Please, just tell me what happened."

Emma closed her eyes briefly, gathering her thoughts as she fought to regain control. She could feel her emotions pulling at her, but she did not want to drag him into this. "I just… I need to think things through. Figure out what to do next," she said, her voice soft but firm. "Thank you for helping me tonight. But you should go home now, Michael. I'll be okay."

Michael hesitated, his concern still evident in his eyes. "Are you sure?" he asked gently. "I don't feel right leaving you alone, especially after what happened." He lingered momentarily, but Emma's steady gaze told him she was determined.

"I'll be fine," she reassured him, though her voice wavered slightly. "I just need some sleep."

He stood up slowly, reluctant to leave, but after a long moment, he nodded. "Okay," he said softly. "Lock the door behind me." At the threshold, he hesitated, casting one last concerned glance her way before stepping out. He lingered for a beat, waiting for her to close and lock the door.

Emma walked back to the living room, the house's quiet settling around her. Alone now, the weight of her encounter with Laura's spirit pressed down on her, suffocating, as if the fear had taken root inside her. She heard the sound of Michael's car fade into the distance as she sat in the dim light of her living room, her thoughts scattered and frantic. She struggled to make sense of the night's events, trying desperately to steady her racing mind, but it felt like the darkness still lingered in the corners of the room, just as it had in the woods.

She glanced nervously around the room, half-expecting something to appear.

Determined to regain control, Emma went to her altar and picked up her protective crystals – a black tourmaline, amethyst, and clear quartz. She sat on the couch, placing them on the table before her. Still trembling slightly, she took a deep breath and closed her eyes, reciting a simple mantra – a small comfort against the heavy tension.

A few moments later, she opened her eyes, the air feeling slightly lighter. It wasn't much, but it was enough to dull the sharp edge of her fear.

Knowing sleep would elude her, Emma grabbed her laptop and sank deeper into the couch. Despite the exhaustion weighing on her, she focused on her research, jotting down her thoughts and findings, trying to make sense of the tangled web of events.

Somewhere close to dawn, Emma's body finally succumbed to the overwhelming fatigue, and she drifted into a restless sleep on the couch. Her dreams quickly pulled her into a shadowy, labyrinthine forest, where the mist swirled with an almost palpable malevolence. The forest felt familiar and foreign, its darkness hiding more than it revealed.

Amidst the shifting shadows, Emma glimpsed Laura's distorted form, her eyes burning with a fierce, ominous glow. The spirit's rage saturated the air, creating a heavy atmosphere of dread.

As Emma went through the fog, the dream morphed into an unexpected scene: her father appeared in the mist, distressed, reaching out to her. His presence in the dream felt disquieting, as if he, too, were trapped in the same ethereal torment that haunted the forest.

Unravelling Threads

Thursday, 13th October 2024

At dawn, Emma woke up, her body heavy with exhaustion. She sat up and rubbed her temples, still feeling the weight of the night. The image of her father from the dream lingered in her mind, unsettling her. Why had he appeared? She had always believed that dreams were more than mere reflections of the subconscious – they often held deeper meanings, revealing hidden truths. Was the dream a cryptic message, hinting at a possible connection between him and Laura?

With a sigh, she swung her legs over the side of the bed, her feet meeting the cool wooden floor. Her small cottage was quiet. Moving slowly, she made her way to the kitchen. As the rich aroma of freshly brewed coffee filled the air, she felt a momentary sense of calm. Wrapping her hands around the warm mug, she leaned against the kitchen counter, staring out the window at the mist-shrouded landscape.

Her thoughts remained a whirlwind of the night's encounter in the woods and the unsettling dream. Seeking a brief distraction, Emma carried her coffee to the couch and switched on the TV, letting the familiar cadence of the morning news wash over her. But the anxiety lingered, and she knew she couldn't face the day's obligations.

At around 7.30 am, she picked up her phone and dialed Rose's number. The line rang twice before Rose's familiar voice answered, cheerful despite the early hour.

"Good morning, Emma. How are you? Feeling better?" Rose asked, her tone warm and caring.

"Morning, Rose," Emma replied, trying to muster some energy into her voice. "I'm feeling drained. I wanted to let you know I won't be coming today. Could you cancel my appointments and tell everyone I am not feeling well?"

There was a brief pause on the other end before Rose responded. "I figured you might be feeling like this after yesterday. That's why I rescheduled your appointments for today and yesterday to Saturday. I hope that's okay."

Emma felt a wave of relief wash over her. "Thank you, Rose. I appreciate it more than you know."

"Of course, Emma. I know how tough these episodes can be for you," Rose said gently. "You need to rest and take care of yourself. If you need anything at all, just let me know."

Emma sighed, feeling a bit more at ease. "I will. Thanks again, Rose. You are a lifesaver."

Rose, her voice soft, said, "Take care, Emma. I'll see you tomorrow."

After ending the call with Rose, Emma felt a surge of gratitude for her assistant's foresight and support. Setting her phone aside, she realised she needed to find some inner peace. She began a meditation session, breathing deeply and visualising herself walking through a tranquil forest. With each breath, the stress of the past few days melted away, and her muscles relaxed.

After twenty minutes, Emma opened her eyes, feeling calmer. She stretched, then retrieved a small wooden box from her bedroom, selecting amethyst, rose quartz, and clear quartz. Arranging the crystals on a table, she added drops of a soothing essential oil blend to her diffuser. As the calming scent filled the room, Emma sat with her journal, pouring her thoughts onto the pages. Writing eased her mind, grounding her in a renewed calm and determination.

The combination of meditation, crystals, aromatherapy, and journaling helped to a great extent, leaving her feeling better than before.

Afterward, she went to the kitchen to prepare a simple breakfast of scrambled eggs and toast. As she cooked, her thoughts turned to the research from the previous day. Dr. Evelyn Hartley had emerged as a key figure in her search for answers. Emma knew that speaking with her could provide crucial insight into Laura's time at the asylum and the events that led to her suicide. She decided to reach out later in the morning.

As she was finishing her breakfast, her phone rang again. It was Michael, and Emma knew he must be calling to check on her after the previous night's incident.

"Emma," came Michael's voice on the phone. "I just wanted to see how you were doing after last night," he said, his voice filled with concern.

"Thank you, Michael. I'm okay, just taking it easy today," she replied, trying to sound reassuring.

"Are you sure you're alright? You seemed really shaken up," Michael said, his concern evident in his tone.

Emma reassured him that she was feeling better today, but Michael did not seem convinced.

"Who is Laura?" he asked.

Emma hesitated for a moment. "Just someone from a case I'm working on. It's nothing to worry about," she said, avoiding further explanation.

Sensing her reluctance, Michael didn't press. "Alright, just take care of yourself. Let me know if you need anything."

"Thanks, Michael. I will," Emma replied.

Once the call with Michael ended, Emma knew she needed to clear her mind. She tidied up the kitchen and went to the bathroom, where she turned on the tap, watching the tub slowly fill with steaming water. She added a generous amount of lavender bath salts and essential oil, the scent quickly filling the room and soothing her senses. When the tub was ready, she undressed and sank into the warm water, letting its heat envelop her. Resting her head against the edge, she closed her eyes, allowing her thoughts to drift back to the past—particularly to Christian.

Christian Moors was a charismatic and mysterious figure at the University of Cambridge. With a magnetic presence and an intense drive, he was known for his academic excellence and the charm that drew people to him. Christian was a senior when Emma began her undergraduate studies, and their paths crossed in a way that would change both of their lives.

He was pursuing a degree in literature, and his reputation had already preceded him. Christian was involved in numerous student organisations and had a reputation for being both brilliant and elusive. His lectures were filled with passionate insights, making literary analysis feel like an adventure. His piercing blue eyes and thoughtful demeanour made everyone feel he was truly listening to them, drawing them into his orbit.

Emma first encountered Christian in a seminar class at the university. Though she was a psychology major, her interests extended beyond her field of study. She often attended various seminars and lectures that piqued her curiosity. In one of these seminars on modernist literature, an elective she had chosen out of a love for reading and exploring different perspectives, she met Christian.

It was a small, intimate setting, and Christian was known for his incisive comments and deep understanding of the material. Emma, eager to make a mark in her new academic environment, was drawn to his discussions. She admired his ability to dissect complex texts with ease and began seeking opportunities to engage in conversations with him.

Their initial interactions were friendly but charged with a palpable undercurrent of attraction. Christian had noticed Emma's keen intellect and enthusiasm, and he began including her in his academic circles. He invited her to study groups and discussions, and they soon spent hours discussing literature and philosophy over coffee or dinner.

As the semester progressed, their connection deepened. They began to spend more time together outside of academic settings. They attended university events and explored the historic city of Cambridge together. Christian's genuine interest in Emma's thoughts and ideas matched his charisma, making their conversations both stimulating and intimate.

One evening, after a particularly engaging discussion on a literary theory, Christian invited Emma to his apartment. It was a cosy, book-filled space, with shelves overflowing with well-worn novels and vintage editions, each one a testament to his intellectual depth. The walls were adorned with framed black-and-white photographs, some abstract, other portraits of authors and thinkers he admired. A large, worn leather armchair sat in the corner, next to a dimly lit desk cluttered with notebooks and papers filled with his scribbles and ideas. The room smelled faintly of aged paper and cedar wood, a space that seemed to hold his every thought and influence. They spent the night talking about their dreams, aspirations, and the future. It was during this evening that their relationship took a more personal turn. The night had been filled with their vibrant connection, and as they entered his bedroom, the air was thick with anticipation. Their passion was overwhelming, their physical connection intense and consuming. Emma had felt a sense of completeness and ecstasy she had never known before, every touch and kiss deepening their bond. The connection they had felt in intellectual conversations became a passionate romance.

But that night also marked the beginning of something dark. The lingering euphoria was soon overshadowed by an unsettling feeling in Emma's heart. She recalled lying in bed afterward, her head resting on Christian's chest, feeling the warmth of their shared intimacy. The joy and connection she felt were palpable, but so was a creeping sense of unease.

Their relationship was intense from the start, characterised by a deep emotional and physical connection. They shared many moments of joy and intimacy, each experience reinforcing their bond. Christian's presence in Emma's life was a whirlwind of excitement and discovery. Emma felt she had found someone who understood her, and their relationship became a central part of her university experience.

However, as their relationship deepened, so did the challenges. Christian's charisma and charm came with a complexity that Emma struggled to navigate. Despite the joy and passion they shared, there were moments of tension and misunderstanding. Christian's commitment to his own pursuits and his mysterious nature often left Emma feeling uncertain and insecure.

Their relationship reached a breaking point one rainy evening when Emma, newly accepted into a prestigious graduate programme, arrived at Christian's apartment with the excitement of sharing her news. Instead of the celebration she had envisioned, she was confronted with a scene that shattered her heart: Christian entwined with another woman, their laughter echoing through the apartment.

"Emma, it's not what it looks like," Christian had pleaded, but the betrayal was already a searing wound in her heart. She had fled from his apartment, the fragments of their shared dreams and the pain of his deceit collapsing around her.

Drenched and numb, Emma wandered through the rain-soaked streets of Cambridge, her thoughts a whirlwind of pain and disbelief. The steady rhythm of the rain against the pavement was no comfort—only a cold backdrop to the storm inside her.

When she finally returned to her dorm room at the university, the emptiness swallowed her whole. She sat in the dark, her body trembling, as she struggled to process the heartache that had just shattered her world.

The following weeks blurred into a haze of sorrow and isolation. Emma's emotional state grew increasingly unstable; she struggled to focus on her studies and withdrew from social interactions.

Christian had never tried to contact her after that, and it felt like another betrayal, reopening old wounds from her past.

Growing up, Emma had often felt the sting of loss and loneliness, the absence of her parents a constant ache. Her aunt had done her best to provide a stable home, but the shadows of the past always lingered, resurfacing with every new hardship.

During this time, Serena had been away in Edinburgh, caring for her mother, who was in the final stages of Cancer. Not wanting to add to her friend's burden, Emma kept the news of the breakup to herself, retreating further into solitude. With no one to talk to and the weight of her emotions pressing down, Emma sank into a deeper abyss. Her nights were restless, filled with vivid, unsettling dreams that left her feeling more unsettled with each passing day. It was the dark night of the soul, a period of deep emotional turmoil she could not escape.

In the brief time they were together, Christian had become her beacon. But when he betrayed her, the devastation was more than she could bear. The pain from his betrayal, compounded by the trauma of losing her parents, drove her to the brink. Her heartache was so profound that it pushed her into a dark place. One desperate night, alone in her room, her sorrow became unbearable. In a moment of utter despair, she took a razor blade from her drawer and made a deep cut across her wrist. The sharp edge sliced through her skin, and the blood began to flow, mixing with her tears as she felt her life slipping away.

But something unexpected happened just as she teetered on the edge of darkness. The sharpness of her pain seemed to shatter the thin veil between this world and another. A surge of energy - a psychic force - swept over her, flooding her senses with an overwhelming intensity. As if her very soul had been touched by something beyond her understanding, the boundaries between her physical reality and other realms began to dissolve, leaving her in a state of profound awareness.

Emma felt herself floating above her body in this altered state, observing herself from a new perspective. The pain and sorrow, once overwhelming, now seemed to guide her into a deeper understanding of herself and the universe. She saw flashes of energy—vivid, swirling patterns of light and colour—interwoven with her emotional turmoil. These patterns felt alive, almost sentient, and communicated with her in ways that defied explanation. It was as though the universe itself was offering her an unspoken message, revealing layers of reality that had previously been hidden.

But even as she lingered in this heightened state, still bleeding and on the brink of death, her friend found her. The stark contrast between her profound spiritual experience and the harsh reality of her physical state was jarring, and at that moment, her friend rushed her to the hospital. Though she recovered from the physical wounds, the memory of Christian's betrayal remained a raw scar, but it became the catalyst for her journey towards self-discovery and healing.

Her journey was far from over, but the awakening had given her a profound understanding of herself and the world around her. It had set her on a path of personal and spiritual growth, guiding her towards a deeper sense of purpose and resilience.

Now, lying in the bathtub, Emma felt a familiar ache in her chest. She closed her eyes, letting the tears mingle with the bathwater, her mind replaying the moments that had shattered her trust and changed her forever.

As the water cooled, Emma took a deep breath and wiped her eyes. Determined to find answers to the lingering questions about Laura, she climbed out of the tub, dried off, and wrapped herself in a robe.

She walked into her bedroom, picked up her phone from the bedside table, and dialled Dr. Evelyn Hartley's home number, her heart racing with a mix of hope and apprehension. After a few rings, a soft, professional voice answered.

"Hello?"

"Hello, is this Dr. Evelyn Hartley?" Emma asked, her voice steady despite the nerves.

"Yes, this is she. May I ask who is calling?"

"This is Emma Ravenwood," Emma began, taking a deep breath. "I'm a holistic life coach and psychic. I specialise in reading energy. I'm reaching out because Mrs. Harrington, Laura Harrington's mother, recently contacted me. She came to me seeking closure regarding her daughter's untimely death, and I believe that Laura's case may hold some answers I need. I understand that you were the chief at Ravensbrook Asylum when Laura was a patient there, and I'm hoping you might be able to shed some light on her time there."

Dr Hartley's voice softened, and she briefly paused before responding. "I see. Laura was a very delicate case. Although I am retired, I may still be able to offer some guidance or insights into her situation."

Emma felt a glimmer of hope. "I would be grateful for any information you could share. It is important for me to understand more about her and what happened."

"Please let me know a convenient time to meet you," Emma said.

"Let me check my schedule," Dr. Hartley replied. After a brief pause, she continued, "Would tomorrow afternoon at 2 p.m. be suitable for you?"

"That would be perfect," Emma replied, relieved. "Thank you so much."

Before ending the call, Dr. Hartley's tone turned thoughtful. "Can you repeat your full name once more?"

"Certainly," Emma said. "It's Emma Ravenwood."

"Thank you, Emma. I will see you tomorrow afternoon," Dr. Hartley confirmed.

After ending her call with Dr. Hartley, Emma felt a flicker of hope stir within her. She needed a break—a moment of peace away from the whirlwind of emotions and the haunting presence of Laura's spirit that had consumed her lately. Determined to clear her mind, she decided to treat herself to a relaxing day out.

She headed to her closet and chose her outfit with care. She slipped into a white sleeveless blouse, its delicate lace and intricate embroidery adding a soft, feminine touch. The outfit exuded effortless elegance, paired with a high-waisted, flowy white skirt that fell just above her knees. Keeping her makeup minimal, she allowed her hair to cascade naturally down her back, the dark strands shimmering in the light. Her tan ankle boots, made of soft suede, were stylish and comfortable—perfect for a day spent outdoors. She layered necklaces, stacked bangles, and rings to complete the look, adding a touch of personality and charm. With her look perfected, she was ready for her day of respite.

Emma picked up her bag and Jeep keys and left the cottage. She drove to *The Hearthstone Bistro*, a charming spot tucked away in a quiet corner of town. Known for its cosy ambiance, warm lighting, and delectable seasonal dishes, it also offered a carefully curated wine list, making it the perfect place for Emma to unwind. The staff greeted her with familiar smiles as she was led to a table by the window. Outside, the mist hung thick in the air, casting a soft, muted glow over the bistro, adding to the intimate, quiet atmosphere inside.

Emma chose Chicken Marsala, steamed rice, and a salad with a glass of Pinot Grigio. The delicious aromas filled the air when the food arrived, and each bite was a treat. She sipped her wine, savouring the crisp, light notes of the Pinot Grigio, which perfectly complemented the rich, savoury taste of the dish.

After finishing her meal, Emma lingered for a moment, enjoying the peaceful atmosphere of the restaurant. She then decided to take a leisurely drive. She walked to her car, inhaled the cool, misty air, and slid into the driver's seat. The soothing rhythms of her favourite music filled the car as she drove through the streets of Hawes, heading out into the quiet of the countryside.

The road wound through picturesque landscapes of rolling hills and vibrant autumn foliage. Golden leaves drifted from the trees, and the soft, muted light of the mist cast a serene glow over the fields. Emma took deep breaths, letting the stillness of the drive wash over her.

Without a specific destination, she embraced the freedom of the open road. The journey offered a much-needed escape from her routine, allowing her to peacefully reflect on her thoughts.

As the landscape shifted, the town gave way to sprawling meadows, wildflowers swaying in the breeze. The serenity of nature calmed her mind, and she felt a deep sense of gratitude for the beauty surrounding her.

Her thoughts turned inward. Her psychic abilities, once a source of confusion and fear, had become integral to her identity. She had learned to embrace them, using her gifts to help others and connect with the unseen world. Despite the challenges, they had given her purpose and strength she never thought possible.

She also thought about Michael—his genuine concern for her well-being was comforting. While hesitant to share the details of her work with him, she valued his support and wondered if their friendship might evolve into something more.

Her mind then drifted to Christian. The pain of his betrayal still stung, but she recognised how it had ultimately led to her psychic awakening. That dark period had shaped her growth, transforming pain into power and reminding her of her resilience.

As the evening approached, Emma decided it was time to head home. The drive had been a much-needed escape, and she felt refreshed and more centred. Around 6 o'clock, she pulled into her driveway, the soft mist of the day giving way to the cool calm of twilight. The quiet of the evening seemed to match her mood—peaceful and introspective.

Emma took a deep breath, feeling a sense of calm settle over her as the day's peaceful moments lingered. She smiled, appreciating the quiet of the evening. Slipping off her boots, she entered her small, charming garden. The cool air and the gentle rustle of the leaves created the perfect atmosphere to unwind.

As she strolled through the garden, admiring the colourful blooms and lush greenery, Emma took her time watering each plant. The rhythmic task was soothing, grounding her and adding a sense of balance to the moment.

When she finished, a sense of quiet satisfaction washed over her. She returned inside, washed her hands, and changed into comfortable loungewear—cosy leggings and an oversized sweater. A light dinner seemed like the perfect way to end her peaceful day.

Emma decided on a hearty vegetable soup, filled with fresh carrots, celery, tomatoes, and a handful of kale. As it simmered on the stove, the rich aroma began to fill the kitchen, creating a welcoming atmosphere.

While the soup cooked, Emma poured herself a glass of white wine and set the table, arranging a bowl, spoon, and a small plate of crusty bread. When the soup was ready, she ladled a generous portion into her bowl and sat at the table. She enjoyed each spoonful, the warmth of the meal spreading through her.

After finishing dinner, Emma tidied the kitchen and went to the living room. She selected a light-hearted romantic comedy from her streaming service and settled onto the couch with a soft blanket as the movie began.

Wrapped in the blanket's warmth, Emma relaxed into the film, enjoying the witty dialogue and upbeat soundtrack. She laughed at the funny moments on-screen, the cheerful energy filling the room. But suddenly, during a particularly humorous scene, the TV screen went dark, and the music cut off abruptly. Emma blinked in confusion, reaching for the remote and pressing buttons, but the TV remained stubbornly off.

Emma rose to check the TV's power cord, but everything seemed in order. The cord was securely plugged in, and nothing appeared out of place. As she sat back down, a sudden chill seemed to fill the room, the warmth from earlier slipping away.

She tried to shake off the unease, but the air in the room felt different now, heavier, as if something was watching. The lights flickered, dimmed, and went out completely, plunging the room into darkness. Emma's heart pounded as she rushed to the kitchen, fumbling for a flashlight. When she finally switched it on, the beam cast a cold, uneven glow across the room, only heightening the strange atmosphere.

Then, without warning, the lights flickered back on, and the TV sprang to life. But the screen was filled with grainy static instead of the movie, flashing with brief, distorted images. A shadowy shape darted across the screen before everything went black again, leaving the room eerily quiet.

Emma sat in stunned silence, her mind racing. The contrast between the cheerful movie she had been watching and the strange occurrences was jarring.

Then once again the cottage lights came to life, and the TV resumed playing the movie she had been watching. Emma stared at the TV in silence. She knew, with unsettling certainty, what—or rather, who—was causing this.

After a moment, she stood, her thoughts swirling. With a steadying breath, she switched off the TV and went to her bedroom, her heart still thudding in her chest. Once there, she recited a brief protection prayer under her breath before climbing into bed, pulling the covers up and sinking into the pillows.

As sleep began to claim her, her mind wandered to the following day. Meeting with Dr. Hartley and discussing Laura's case was a significant step in her search for answers. She sighed, closing her eyes and allowed the quiet to envelop her.

Chasing Shadows

Friday, 14ᵗʰ October 2024

In her dream, Emma found herself running through an ethereal forest bathed in a mystical glow. It felt like a journey to another realm, one filled with enchantment and ancient magic.

The forest was alive with bioluminescent plants glowing in shades of blue and green, casting a soft, otherworldly light on the path. Tall, majestic trees with shimmering silver leaves stood overhead, and the air was filled with the intoxicating scent of night-blooming flowers mixed with the freshness of recent rain. The moss-covered ground cushioned her steps, making her movements effortless.

Tiny fireflies danced around her, their lights flickering like fallen stars. The shadows of the trees weren't menacing but instead moved in harmony with her, guiding her deeper into the woods. Her breath fell into a rhythmic pattern, perfectly synchronised with the pulse of the forest.

The path suddenly opened into a clearing bathed in golden light. At the centre stood a grand, ancient oak tree, its wide branches embracing the space protectively. Delicate, glowing flowers adorned its limbs, pulsing gently and illuminating the area with warmth.

Emma slowed as she approached, awe replacing her earlier apprehension. She reached out to touch the smooth bark, and a surge of energy flowed through her. The tree felt vividly alive, its essence merging with hers. The leaves rustled as if sharing ancient secrets.

From behind the tree emerged a shimmering figure. Draped in flowing, light-infused robes, the figure moved gracefully.

Emma's breath caught—her mother, Catherine, stood before her, looking radiant and serene. Her presence filled the clearing with warmth and love, and though she didn't speak, her gaze conveyed everything: reassurance, love, and a bond that defied time.

Tears welled in Emma's eyes. She reached out, and Catherine extended a hand. As their fingers touched, a wave of light and warmth enveloped Emma. The connection was fleeting but deeply comforting, a reminder of their unbreakable bond.

The dream began to fade, the clearing dimming as the forest melted away. Catherine's image lingered, glowing softly before dissolving into the darkness. Emma woke with a start, her heart lighter and a small smile on her face. The memory of her mother lingered, and though brief, the encounter filled her with a quiet peace.

She pushed the sheets aside and got out of bed, moving through her morning routine with a newfound calm. In the kitchen, she began brewing coffee, the familiar ritual grounding her as the rich aroma filled the air. With a steaming cup in hand, Emma stepped into her living room and settled onto her yoga mat.

Starting with gentle stretches, she eased into her yoga practice, feeling tension from the dream melt away. The flowing movements reconnected her to the present, while her breath guided her to a place of quiet focus. Afterwards, she sat in meditation, letting her mind settle. Thoughts of her mother drifted in, but she allowed them to pass, cherishing the subtle sense of connection that lingered.

Once she finished, she sipped the last of her coffee, feeling centred. Emma showered and dressed in dark blue jeans, a white sleeveless top, and her sturdy boots, adding a jacket to complete the look. She made herself another cup of coffee and prepared a simple breakfast of toast and scrambled eggs.

As she ate breakfast and sipped her coffee, Emma's mind shifted to the day ahead. She had a meeting that afternoon in Willow's Creek with Dr. Evelyn Hartley, who might hold answers about Laura's case. It wasn't just the dream of her mother that made her feel this way; her intuition told her the meeting would be significant. An unshakeable anticipation settled in her chest, making her wonder what truths would be revealed today.

Finishing her breakfast, Emma grabbed her bag and Jeep keys, locking the door behind her as she stepped outside. The fog hung heavy in the air, casting a muted veil over the cottage. She slid into her Jeep, started the engine, and made her way towards her studio.

The morning passed quickly, with Emma diving into her work at the studio. Her first client of the day arrived promptly at nine: Claire, a middle-aged woman who had been referred by a friend in London. She sought guidance on her tumultuous family issues. Emma could sense the heavy burden Claire carried—the weight of strained relationships, unspoken resentments, and the longing for harmony. Through her intuitive insights and gentle counsel, Emma helped Claire navigate the emotional labyrinth of her family dynamics, offering tools to foster understanding and reconciliation.

Her second client was a familiar face: Julia, a regular at Emma's studio who had been struggling with persistent mental health challenges for years. Julia's visits were a crucial part of her ongoing journey toward inner peace and stability. Emma had worked with her through the highs and lows, helping her manage anxiety, depression, and the residual trauma from past experiences.

Today, Julia seemed particularly weary. Emma guided her through a series of grounding exercises, utilising healing techniques to soothe Julia's troubled mind. The session blended meditation, energy work, and empathetic listening. By the end, Julia appeared centred and calmer, a soft glow of gratitude in her eyes.

As Julia left, Emma felt a deep sense of purpose in her work. The familiar satisfaction of having made a positive impact settled in her chest.

At lunchtime, Rose brought in sandwiches and salads from a nearby café. Emma ate quickly, eager to get on the road to Willow's Creek.

Once she finished her meal, Emma said goodbye to Rose and left the studio, the weight of the upcoming meeting pressing on her mind. The misty air outside matched her mood—cool and damp, with an undercurrent of anticipation.

She started the car, the engine's steady hum offering a small comfort as she navigated through the empty streets of Hawes. The village soon gave way to the winding, quiet roads, the small cottages and shops fading into the backdrop as the landscape stretched out before her. Emma's thoughts drifted back to the morning's clients, especially Julia. Helping them had provided a brief escape from her own worries, but it was only temporary.

Her mind wandered again, this time to her mother, Catherine. Memories of her were scattered and fragmented, obscured by time and the pain of losing her too soon. Yet the dream had brought Catherine's presence back to her, vivid and close. Emma's heart tightened with a mix of sorrow and longing. She wondered what advice Catherine might have given her about the challenges she now faced.

As the road narrowed, dense woods began to line both sides. The trees loomed overhead, their branches forming a dark canopy that blocked out the sky. The mist thickened, swirling around the car as it cut through the quiet, almost desolate countryside.

As Emma neared the outskirts of Willow's Creek, her eyes caught sight of a sign for Ravensbrook Hospital & Asylum. The sign, crisp and modern, directed to the facility in clear, bold lettering. A shiver ran down Emma's spine as she passed it, the weight of its significance suddenly pressing on her. She had not noticed it on her drive to meet Mrs. Harrington earlier, but now, with the knowledge of Laura's admission and tragic death here, a deep sense of foreboding settled over her. The grim reality of what had happened within those walls made her pulse quicken, and an uneasy knot formed in her stomach.

Emma continued her drive towards Dr. Hartley's house, glancing at her phone to confirm the directions. The map guided her down a winding, narrow road, flanked by towering trees whose branches arched overhead like a natural tunnel. The mist clung to the trunks, and the fading light from the overcast sky gave the surroundings a soft, eerie glow. The shadows of the trees stretched long across the road, their movement almost hypnotic as they swayed gently in the breeze.

As she followed the path, the scenery grew quieter, the trees giving way to a small, secluded clearing. Soon, Emma spotted Dr. Hartley's home – a large Victorian house that stood in stark contrast to its surroundings. The house, with its high, pointed roof and intricate details, was set back from the road, surrounded by a well-maintained garden. A cobblestone path wound through lush greenery, leading to the front door. The exterior of the house was painted a muted shade of blue, and ivy crept up one side of the building, lending it an air of faded elegance. The setting felt timeless, almost as if the house had been there for centuries, watching over the land.

As Emma approached the front door of Dr. Hartley's home, an unexpected sense of warmth washed over her, a comforting familiarity she could not quite place. It was as if the house itself recognised her, or perhaps there was some deep, unspoken connection that made her feel she had been here before. The feeling was subtle but undeniable, a quiet reassurance that eased some of the tension in her chest. She exhaled slowly, her nerves settling just enough as she rang the doorbell.

Standing on the doorstep, Emma took a deep breath and waited. When the door swung open, there stood a woman who exuded a quiet but unmistakable authority. Emma immediately knew this was the doctor. In her late sixties, Dr. Hartley was tall and slender, her posture upright and dignified. Her silver hair was pulled neatly into a low bun, revealing sharp, intelligent grey eyes that seemed to take in every detail with a practiced ease. Her gaze was steady, thoughtful, and immediately made Emma feel as though she was under scrutiny, yet there was no judgement in it— only a sense of calm observation.

"Emma?" Dr Hartley asked with a warm smile.

"Yes. Hello, Dr. Hartley. Thank you for meeting with me," Emma replied, returning the smile, though her voice betrayed a hint of nervousness.

"Come in, let's get comfortable and talk," Dr. Hartley gestured, leading Emma inside. The door closed softly behind her, and Emma immediately noticed the scent of old wood and fresh flowers filling the space.

The interior was a blend of old-world charm and modern comfort. The foyer opened into a spacious sitting room adorned with antique furniture, rich wooden floors, and walls lined with bookshelves filled with an eclectic variety of books. A large, ornate rug in deep red and gold covered the floor, and a stone fireplace dominated one wall, its mantel adorned with family photos and delicate decorative items. The room was bathed in soft, natural light streaming through tall sash windows, their white curtains fluttering slightly in the breeze. Plush armchairs and a well-worn leather sofa were arranged around a low, polished coffee table, creating a cosy, intimate setting.

Every corner of the room spoke of a life well-lived, filled with history and a distinctive touch, making it feel both comforting and nostalgic. As Emma settled into one of the armchairs, a housekeeper entered quietly, carrying a tray with a pot of tea, cups, and a plate of freshly baked scones. She set it down on the coffee table with a polite nod before discreetly retreating, leaving Emma and Dr. Hartley to their conversation.

As Dr. Hartley handed Emma a cup of tea, she studied her closely, her expression thoughtful. "Emma, I'm going to ask you this first. Are you related to Catherine Ravenwood?"

Emma's heart skipped a beat. She hadn't expected such a direct question. "Yes, she was my mother."

Dr. Hartley's eyes widened with recognition, a mixture of sadness and warmth filling her gaze. "I thought so. When you first called, I wanted to ask, but I decided it would be better to wait until we met. Your name... it brought back memories."

A wave of nostalgia and sorrow washed over Emma. "I didn't know you knew my mother."

"Catherine," Dr. Hartley said softly, her voice laced with emotion. "Catherine and I were very close. I remember her fondly... and I remember you too. You were just a child, but I have vivid memories of you visiting this very house."

Emma's throat tightened as she listened, her heart heavy. Dr. Hartley continued, her expression filled with compassion. "Catherine was a remarkable woman. I had hoped to reconnect with you after you left, but I lost track of you."

"After my parents died, I went to live with my aunt in London. So, that's why we…," Emma said, her voice breaking.

The weight of the revelation settled heavily on Emma's chest, and tears started welling up in her eyes.

Dr Hartley reached out, placing a comforting hand on Emma's. "I am glad you're here now. I hope I can offer the answers that you are seeking."

Emma nodded; her voice choked with emotion. "Thank you. I hope so too."

Emma started by telling Dr. Hartley everything she knew about Laura – the bits of information she had gathered from Mrs. Harrington, her visit to the manor, and her research. As she spoke, the conversation bridged the gap between the past and present, deepening their connection and adding emotional weight to their meeting.

Finally, after a quiet pause, Emma asked, her voice steady, "Dr. Hartley, I need to understand more about Laura—her mental illness and what led to her death."

Dr. Hartley's expression became more serious. "Laura Harrington was a complex case. When she first arrived, she exhibited symptoms of severe depression and delusions. However, something changed after her admission. The treatments we were using didn't seem to help. In fact, her mental state worsened over time—almost as if she were being... influenced by something outside of her mind."

Emma's heart began to race as she leaned forward. "What kind of influence?"

Dr Hartley paused, carefully choosing her next words. "There was more to her story than just her psychosis."

Emma's curiosity grew, though she could sense an underlying discomfort in Dr. Hartley's tone. "What do you mean?"

Dr Hartley's gaze softened, as if bracing herself for what was to come. "Laura had become a vessel for something darker that wasn't entirely of this world."

Dr. Hartley leaned forward, her voice low but steady. "Laura became deeply involved in black magic. I discovered this only sometime after her admission. Her obsession with it seemed to worsen her condition, driving her into increasingly violent episodes.

She believed she could control or summon forces to help her, but instead, it only fuelled her paranoia and aggression."

Emma's eyes widened. "Black magic?"

"Yes," Dr. Hartley confirmed. "But there was another factor that was even more troubling. Laura had a deep and unrequited love for someone very close to you."

Emma's heart skipped a beat. "Who?" she asked, her voice tightening with anticipation.

"Your father," Dr. Hartley said softly. "Professor Ravenwood. Laura was deeply infatuated with him, but he rejected her."

Emma froze, her mind racing. The connection between Laura's obsession and her father's rejection hit her like a wave.

Dr. Hartley continued, her voice filled with quiet sympathy. "When your father rejected her, Laura's emotional distress turned into something violent. That's when things spiralled out of control. Her obsession with him, combined with her dabbling in black magic, led to a violent outburst. It was this incident that resulted in her being admitted to the asylum."

Emma's breath caught in her throat, but she did not say anything as she looked at Doctor Hartley.

Dr. Hartley met her gaze. "I know all of this because Catherine told me. Your mother knew everything about Laura's involvement in black magic and her obsession with your father."

Emma's mind raced, struggling to process the revelation. The pieces of the puzzle began to fall into place, each one revealing a more complex picture of Laura's torment. How could her father's rejection have triggered such a profound descent into madness? The thought left her reeling. It was almost impossible to reconcile the idea of her father as the object of someone's obsession, the catalyst for their suffering. A wave of confusion and anger washed over her. What had Laura experienced in those moments of desperation? Was her madness rooted in love, or something darker? How had her father's indifference contributed to such a tragedy?

The weight of this newfound knowledge was unbearable. Emma's throat tightened as she asked, her voice barely above a whisper, "So… were her feelings for my father the major factor in her breakdown?"

"Yes," Dr. Hartley replied, her voice sympathetic. "Laura's feelings for your father were intense—consuming, really. When he rejected her, it shattered her completely."

Her expression grew more sombre. "While Laura was at the asylum, I discovered something that deeply concerned me. She had been performing rituals, trying to summon dark forces. I found disturbing items among her belongings—your father's picture, a lock of his hair, and other personal objects. It seemed that her mother, unknowingly, had brought these things in during one of her visits."

Emma's eyes widened in shock as Dr. Hartley's voice grew heavy with concern. "Laura's obsession had turned dangerous. She wanted either revenge on your father or some form of control over him. It was clear she wasn't just mentally unwell—there was something darker at play."

Seeing the growing concern on Emma's face, Dr. Hartley sighed deeply. "I tried to manage the situation, but it became evident that I couldn't do it alone. That's when I reached out to your mother for help."

"My mother?" Emma looked puzzled as she asked.

Dr. Hartley nodded, her gaze solemn. "Yes. Your mother was a gifted psychic, experienced in matters like this. I had hoped she could understand Laura's motivations and put a stop to the dangerous path she was on."

Emma held her breath, waiting for more.

Dr. Hartley's voice softened. "When Catherine arrived, she tried communicating with Laura, but things only worsened. As soon as Laura realised who Catherine was, her rage intensified. Despite Catherine's best efforts to intervene, Laura's violence escalated, and there was nothing more we could do."

Emma's breath caught in her throat as she listened, her heart racing in anticipation.

Dr. Hartley's gaze grew heavier, her voice taking on a sombre tone as she continued, "When your mother confronted Laura and tried to get through to her, something unexpected happened. Catherine suddenly froze, her eyes glazing over as a psychic vision overtook her."

Emma leaned in closer, her pulse quickening.

Dr Hartley lowered her voice to a whisper. "Catherine's vision transported her to a time before Laura's admission to the asylum. It was late at night, and Laura was alone in her room, desperately manipulating an Ouija board. Her fingers moved frantically, summoning dark forces in a desperate, futile attempt to win Adrian's love. The room in the vision was suffocating, thick with a malevolent presence, a tangible embodiment of Laura's twisted desire and the dark power she sought to command."

Dr Hartley took a deep breath, her expression shadowed with sorrow. "Catherine tried everything she could to reach Laura, to pull her back from the brink of darkness. She spoke gently, her voice a thread of hope, trying to cut through the chaos that had overtaken Laura's mind. But the vision made one thing devastatingly clear: Laura was already lost, her thoughts twisted and consumed by the forces she had summoned. The dark magic had taken root, warping her perception and driving her further into madness."

Emma shuddered as Doctor Hartley continued, "Realising the gravity of the situation, Catherine used her psychic abilities in a desperate attempt to break the hold of the malevolent forces.

The disruption of her rituals infuriated Laura beyond reason. In a frenzy, she lashed out at Catherine, her rage almost inhuman, fuelled by the darkness she had courted for so long. Screaming and wild-eyed, Laura bolted from the room. Catherine and I ran after her, but it was too late by the time we reached the rooftop. Laura was already at the edge, and in one heart-stopping moment, she was gone."

Emma looked deeply disturbed, her eyes wide with the weight of everything she had just learned. Dr. Hartley continued, her voice softening with regret and sympathy. "Laura's death was a devastating event," she said. "To protect the privacy of those involved and to spare your family any further distress, I kept Catherine's involvement and Laura's black magic practices a closely guarded secret. The official explanation given was that Laura's death was a consequence of her mental illness."

Dr. Hartley paused, as if the next part was difficult to say. She took a deep breath to steady herself. "But there is one more thing you should know. Six months after Laura's tragic end, your parents were involved in that fatal accident."

Emma's heart sank, the latest information sinking into her like a heavy stone.

"I know this is a lot to take in," said Doctor Hartley, her voice full of compassion. "But I hope that understanding Laura's past—and your mother's role in trying to help her—brings you some clarity. Sometimes, even the darkest truths can illuminate the mysteries that haunt us."

Emma sat silently for a moment, the weight of everything she had just learned pressing down on her. A shiver ran down her spine, and she clenched her hands to steady herself. She took a deep breath and met Dr. Hartley's eyes, her voice strained. "There's something else I need to tell you", she said quietly, the words coming out almost as a whisper.

Dr. Hartley leaned in, her expression filled with concern. "What is it, Emma?"

Emma's throat tightened, but she forced herself to continue. "Laura… she's been haunting me," she said. "It's not just a lingering presence or an uneasy feeling. I've seen her—felt her anger, her desire for revenge. It feels like she is trying to make me pay for what happened, and it is only growing stronger."

Emma took a steadying breath, her voice cracking slightly. "It started when Mrs. Harrington came to me for help. Ever since I took on the case, Laura's spirit has become increasingly aggressive. It's like her anger has been directed at me, and I can't shake the feeling that she's trying to exact revenge."

Dr. Hartley's expression softened, her eyes full of genuine worry. She leaned forward, her voice steady and compassionate. "Emma, I can't begin to imagine how terrifying this must be for you. Laura's pain was immense, and I think her spirit hasn't found peace. But you don't have to face this alone. Understanding her story might be the key to confronting her, but if the haunting intensifies, we may need to explore more spiritual or psychic avenues to protect you. I'll do whatever I can to support you, whether sharing more about Laura's past or your mother."

Emma sat for a moment, absorbing Dr. Hartley's words. A rush of emotion swept through her – grief, fear, and an unexpected comfort in the presence of someone who had known her mother. Tears pricked her eyes, and she swallowed hard, feeling the raw ache of loss all over again. "You knew my mother," she whispered, her voice trembling. "I... I wish I could have gotten to know her."

Dr. Hartley's eyes grew misty, and she reached out, her hand gently covering Emma's. "Your mother was a remarkable woman," she said softly. "Brave, compassionate, and fiercely protective of those she loved. I see that same strength in you. It's difficult to face the darkness, but you're not alone. You carry her spirit within you."

Emma's heart ached at the thought, but it also sparked something fierce within her – a flame of determination to honour her mother's legacy and protect those in need, just as her mother had. As she rose from her chair, she drew in a shaky breath and said, "Thank you, Dr. Hartley. I am grateful for your help and for sharing this with me."

Dr. Hartley, too, got up. Her eyes lingered on Emma with a mix of concern and admiration. "Take care of yourself, Emma. And remember, you're not alone in this."

Emma took a moment to look around Dr. Hartley's cosy study, and with a heavy but grateful heart, she reached out to clasp Dr. Hartley's hand. "I'll be in touch," she promised, her voice steadier now, carrying a note of quiet strength.

Dr. Hartley squeezed her hand, a gesture of silent support, before letting go. She accompanied Emma to the front door and hugged her, conveying the newfound fondness she felt for her friend's daughter.

Stepping out into the cool evening air, Emma paused on the front steps, briefly closing her eyes. Then she walked to her car, her footsteps purposeful. As she drove away from Willow Creek, the early evening sky gradually darkened, and the small town receded into the distance, leaving her alone with her thoughts.

The revelations about Laura's descent into black magic weighed heavily on Emma, painting a haunting picture of desperate rituals and dark energy summoned in an obsessive quest for her father Adrian's love. Emma could almost feel the oppressive presence Laura had invoked—a force that had not only consumed her but had led to her tragic demise.

Reflecting on Laura's obsession, Emma was troubled by the sheer destructiveness of black magic. Laura's attempt to manipulate powers beyond her control had led to devastating consequences, leaving a trail of emotional and spiritual ruin. The true cost of

Laura's choices, and the ripple effect on everyone around her, left Emma deeply unsettled.

With Dr. Hartley's revelations about black magic, Emma's thoughts turned to her mentor Kai.

It was a month after the incident where Emma had cut her wrist, during one of her therapy sessions, that she recounted the experience. Her therapist, recognising the profound nature of the experience, had suggested she seek out Kai—a shaman and professor at Cambridge known for his ability to help those in spiritual turmoil.

When Emma first met Kai, it felt as if the room shifted. Tall and lean, his presence was silent yet overwhelming, as though he carried the knowledge of ages in his calm, steady gaze. His piercing grey eyes seemed to peer past the surface, seeing into the heart of her turmoil. In that moment, Emma understood that this encounter wasn't by chance. There was something fated about it—like the universe had guided her to him for a reason. Without speaking a word, Kai offered her something she hadn't realised she was missing: the assurance that she was not alone in her struggle and that her path, however difficult it seemed, was leading her somewhere important.

Kai had mentored Emma through her psychic awakening, guiding her with patience and profound insight. His presence was a beacon of strength and serenity, and his teachings had equipped Emma with the tools to navigate the spiritual realm. Known for his intuitive abilities and deep connection to the universe's energies, Kai was both a mentor and a trusted ally, someone Emma could always turn to in times of need. He would know how to deal with the malevolent energy tied to Laura's spirit. Kai's experience with such matters would be invaluable, especially considering the dangerous implications of black magic. Emma knew that if she needed help, she could always reach out to him.

She thought of practical ways to fortify her home, including protective rituals and cleansing practices she had relied on in the past. It was time to ensure her sanctuary remained shielded from the darkness unleashed by Laura's vengeance.

Beyond physical safeguards, she knew maintaining balance was crucial, carving out moments for self-care and reflection. Laura's tragic story served as a cautionary reminder of the consequences of wielding power recklessly.

The road stretched ahead, and Emma focused on what needed to be done with each passing mile.

CHAPTER 11

The Weight of Truth

Saturday, 15th October 2024

Emma woke up the next morning, the weight of her conversation with Dr. Hartley still heavy on her mind. As she moved through her morning routine, her thoughts shifted to the work that awaited her. Rose had rescheduled her Thursday and Friday appointments, compressing two days' worth of clients into today. It would be a demanding day but being a psychic and holistic practitioner was not just a career for Emma—it was a calling.

Each session was a chance to offer guidance and healing, to use her abilities to make a meaningful difference. Clients came to her for reassurance, seeking insights into their deepest fears and unanswered questions. Her practice had taught her how to compartmentalise, setting aside her own turmoil to be fully present for those who needed her.

Dressed in a dark grey skirt, black leggings, a black sweater, and ankle-length boots, she completed her look with crystal jewellery. She tied her hair back into a ponytail and applied light makeup. One last glance in the mirror, and Emma knew she was ready to tackle the day ahead.

As she walked towards The Croissant Cottage, memories of her failed relationship with Christian resurfaced—an intense, passionate connection that had ultimately ended in betrayal. The parallels between her own experiences and Laura's story became strikingly clear. Emma had once been consumed by a similar kind of emotional turmoil, her heart aching from unfulfilled promises.

Though her pain was different, the anguish and sense of betrayal she had felt with Christian echoed the despair Laura must have experienced. The profound connection between Laura's torment and her own emotional scars remained at the forefront of her mind as she arrived in front of the bakery.

Michael was behind the counter, arranging pastries. When he saw Emma enter, his expression shifted from friendly to deeply concerned. It was the first time he had seen her since that unsettling night when she had come running out of the woods.

"Emma," he said, his voice filled with genuine worry. "I've been thinking about you since that night. Are you alright?"

Emma offered a faint smile, appreciating his concern. "Morning, Michael. I'm okay."

Michael stepped forward, his concern unwavering. "I'm glad to see you, but really... is there anything I can do?"

Emma hesitated, feeling the sincerity in his gaze. Finally, she nodded, grateful for his kindness. Michael gave her a small, reassuring smile. "If you ever want to talk about what happened, I'm here."

"Thank you, Michael," Emma said, her gaze shifting to the array of pastries. She ordered a croissant, which Michael wrapped in a bag and handed to her.

Michael returned behind the counter and added, "I'm heading to The Obsidian Fog tonight for a drink. Would you like to join me?"

Emma considered his invitation, a hint of warmth touching her expression. "I've got a busy day with appointments, but I'll let you know by evening if I can make it."

Michael's smile was gentle, yet hopeful. Turning to the next customer, he called over his shoulder, "I'll be looking forward to it."

Emma thanked him and left the bakery. As she made her way to the studio, the thought of an evening out with Michael made her feel warm.

When Emma arrived at the studio, she found Rose busy setting up for the day. Upon seeing Emma, she greeted her with a warm smile.

Emma returned the greeting and stepped into her consultation room, where she started preparing for the day ahead. As the morning progressed, she focused on her regular clients, guiding them through their healing sessions and offering advice on their spiritual journeys.

Around mid-morning, Rose approached Emma with a curious look. "Emma, your 11 o'clock appointment is here. She's come all the way from Richmond and seems quite eager for her session."

"All right, send her in," said Emma, standing up as Rose left.

A few moments later, a tall, elegant woman in her early forties entered the room. She carried herself with sophistication, dressed in a chic blazer and trousers. However, there was a flicker of nervousness in her eyes.

"Hello, I'm Emma. How can I help you today?" Emma said, extending her hand.

The woman shook it firmly. "Hello, Emma. My name is Samantha Collins. I've heard wonderful things about you and your work. I'm hoping you can help me."

"Of course, Samantha. Please, sit and tell me what's been troubling you."

Samantha sat down, smoothing her trousers, her posture tense. "I've been feeling this heavy, unsettling weight for a while now. It's affecting everything—my sleep, my work, even my relationships. I've tried therapy, medication, meditation... but nothing seems to help." She paused, her voice wavering slightly. "My husband passed away unexpectedly eight months ago, and I just can't seem to move past it."

Emma's expression softened, her voice gentle. "I'm so sorry for your loss, Samantha. Grief can create a lot of emotional blockages that carry over into every aspect of our lives. Let's see if we can help release some of that today."

Samantha nodded, grateful for Emma's understanding.

"Let's begin with an energy reading," Emma continued. "Let's move to the sofa so you can lie down comfortably, and I'll guide you through the process."

Samantha did as instructed, settling onto the soft sofa. Emma sat on a chair next to the sofa and closed her eyes briefly, centring herself. She extended her hands over Samantha, sensing the energy in her field. It was heavy, tangled with pent-up emotion, and Emma could feel the tumultuous undercurrent of grief and unprocessed feelings.

"There's a lot of tension here," Emma said softly, her voice calm and reassuring. "It's like a storm inside you, unable to find its way out. Have you been able to express these emotions since your husband's passing?"

Tears welled up in Samantha's eyes. "No, not really. I've been overwhelmed and don't know how to cope."

Emma nodded sympathetically. "Grief can often trap our emotions in ways we don't expect. Let's focus on releasing some of that tension today."

She continued the session, guiding Samantha through deep breathing exercises, using crystals and essential oils to help open up the blockages in her energy field. As Emma worked, the room filled with a calming fragrance, the atmosphere soft and serene.

By the end of the session, Samantha's posture had relaxed, her face less burdened. "Thank you, Emma. I feel… lighter, like something has been lifted off me."

Emma smiled reassuringly. "I'm so glad you feel better. Remember, healing is a journey; you don't have to go through it alone."

After the session, Emma recommended some crystals that Samantha could use for ongoing self-healing.

Emma led Samantha over to the crystal display, where the soft glow of various stones filled the space. "These can be powerful tools for maintaining balance. Each one has its own unique energy, and I think a few might be particularly helpful for you."

Samantha listened attentively, a sense of relief in her eyes.

Emma picked up a rose quartz. "This one is wonderful for promoting love and healing. It can help you open your heart and release emotional pain."

Samantha gently held the smooth stone, her fingers tracing its surface. "It's beautiful. I'll take it."

Emma then selected an amethyst. "This one is excellent for calming the mind and enhancing spiritual awareness. It's especially helpful for improving sleep and finding clarity."

Samantha smiled, adding the amethyst to her selection. "This one too, please."

Finally, Emma handed her a black tourmaline. "This is a powerful grounding stone. It can help you feel more secure and protected, especially when dealing with emotional turmoil."

Samantha took the black tourmaline with a grateful smile. "These are perfect. Thank you, Emma."

Once Rose rang up the bill, Samantha paid and offered a final thank you before leaving the studio. Emma watched her go, feeling a quiet sense of fulfilment. She returned to her office, preparing for her next appointment.

After her second appointment, Rose approached Emma, holding her iPhone. "Emma, Mrs. Harrington called earlier. She asked if you could return her call when you have a moment."

Emma's heart skipped a beat. "Thanks, Rose. I'll call her right away."

She quickly dialled Mrs Harrington's number, and after a couple of rings, Mrs Harrington answered.

"Hello, Mrs. Harrington," she said.

"Hello, Emma. Thank you for calling me back," Mrs. Harrington's voice sounded tentative.

"Of course. Is everything alright?" Emma asked, her tone steady and professional.

"I was going through the attic this morning and found some of Laura's things, including her journals. I thought you might want to take a look at them," Mrs. Harrington explained.

Emma's interest was piqued. "Yes, I'd like that."

Mrs Harrington paused before asking, "When would you like to come?"

Emma thought for a moment. "Would 11 a.m. tomorrow be convenient for you?" she asked.

"That works perfectly," Mrs. Harrington replied, sounding relieved. "I'll have everything ready for you."

"Great, I'll see you tomorrow at 11," Emma confirmed. "Have a good day, Mrs. Harrington."

"Thank you, Emma. You too," Mrs. Harrington said before ending the call.

The mention of Laura's journals filled Emma with a mix of anticipation and curiosity. The rest of her day passed in a blur of appointments, but her thoughts kept returning to what she might discover in the journals.

At the end of the day, as Emma sat in her studio, she remembered Michael's invitation to The Obsidian Fog. The thought of a quiet evening out was tempting, but she was simply too tired. She sighed and pulled out her phone, dialling his number.

"Michael," Emma began when he picked up. "I'm really sorry, but I can't make it tonight. I'm exhausted and think it's best to head home early."

Michael's voice was warm and understanding. "I understand. Don't worry about Emma, we'll catch up another time."

"Thanks for being understanding," Emma said, her voice soft. "Have a good night, Michael."

"You too, Emma. Take care," he replied before hanging up.

Emma set the phone down with a quiet sense of relief. The idea of resting in the comfort of her home felt right. As she gathered her things, the pull of solitude was exactly what she needed.

Emma left the studio, leaving Rose to lock up. Once outside, she decided to stop by *The Enchanted Page*, the bookstore next to her studio. It was evening, and a light drizzle was falling, adding a gentle sheen to the streets. The cosy store, known for its eclectic selection and warm ambiance, was a place she often visited.

Emma pushed open the door, greeted by the familiar tinkle of the bell and the comforting scent of old books. Margaret looked up from behind the counter, her face lighting up with a welcoming smile.

"Evening, Emma. How's the day treating you so far?" Margaret asked as she walked over.

Emma returned the smile. "Evening, Margaret. It's been a busy one. I'm hoping to find something on hauntings and psychic phenomena. Something to help me make sense of a few things."

Margaret gave a knowing nod. "The historical hauntings book is in the non-fiction section, right by the windows. And the new release on psychic phenomena just came in today—it's over in the paranormal corner."

Emma nodded gratefully and made her way to the sections. She picked up the haunting book first, then browsed through the paranormal corner, stopping at the book Margaret had mentioned."

With her selections in hand, Emma returned to the counter. "These look perfect," she said, handing them to Margret.

Margaret smiled warmly. "Books provide the clarity we need, even when we're not sure exactly what we're searching for."

Margaret rang up the books and exchanged a few pleasantries about the weather and local news.

As she left the store, the drizzle had intensified slightly, creating a soothing rhythm as it pattered on her umbrella. She walked back to her cottage, feeling a sense of calm and eagerness as she thought about the books in her bag.

Once home, Emma placed the books on the coffee table in the living room, planning to read them later. She moved to the kitchen and brewed a fresh cup of coffee, the rich aroma quickly filling the room. Taking a moment to savour the warmth, she then set a pot of water to boil for pasta and began preparing a quick vegetable sauce. The comforting scents of garlic, herbs, and simmering tomatoes blended together, offering a small sense of peace.

After a few minutes, she decided to call Serena. Reaching for her phone, she dialled her best friend's number and waited for her to answer.

"Emma!" Serena answered, her usually cheerful voice replaced with a concerned tone. "Are you okay? Why haven't you called me after that day?"

Emma sighed softly, feeling the weight of her friend's concern. "It's been tough, honestly. The haunting… it hasn't stopped. Laura was… there's this strange connection to my parents. She was obsessed with my father."

Emma then told Serena about everything that had happened and what she had discovered since their last conversation.

Finally, Emma said, "It's like everything's tangled together, and I don't know what to make of it all."

Serena's tone shifted to one of deep empathy. "I'm really sorry, Emma. I don't know what to make of this either. Is there anything I can do to help? Do you want me to come over?"

Emma paused momentarily, then shook her head, though Serena couldn't see it. "No, I'm okay. I just need to figure out how to protect myself better. But I really appreciate you offering."

"I'm just so worried about you," Serena said softly. "Promise me you'll be careful, okay?"

Emma smiled, touched by her friend's concern. "I promise. I'll take care of myself. Thanks for always being there for me, Serena."

They exchanged a few more words of comfort and ended the call.

Her pasta ready, Emma plated it and sat down to eat. Serena's support gave her a small sense of hope amidst the burden of the haunting. After dinner, she sat at her desk, making notes about Laura—the connection to her father, the dark magic, and Laura's tragic end weighing heavily on her. Curiosity mixed with dread as she wondered what secrets Laura's journals might reveal. She wrote down her thoughts and questions, hoping to find answers in the journals the next day.

Later, Emma moved to the couch in her living room, reached for one of the new books she had picked up earlier—the one on psychic phenomena—and began reading, hoping it might offer some new clarity. She turned the pages mechanically, unable to fully immerse herself in the book.

Suddenly, a cold draft swept through the room, sending a shiver down her spine. Emma's breath fogged slightly in the cooler air, and she froze, listening closely. Then came the sound—a soft, rhythmic tapping from the far side of the room. It was faint, almost like a distant heartbeat, but it was steady, insistent, and unsettling.

Emma's eyes darted around, but she saw nothing unusual. The tapping grew louder, more pronounced, echoing through the quiet space. Her heart began to race as a feeling of dread settled in. She set the book aside and rose from the couch, drawn towards the source of the sound.

Her footsteps were almost inaudible against the creaky floorboards as she moved cautiously toward the noise. As she reached the spot where the tapping seemed to originate, it abruptly stopped, plunging the room into an eerie silence. Emma froze, her pulse quickening, her breath shallow. The absence of sound only deepened her anxiety, and she could almost feel the air growing heavier, thick with unspoken tension.

With a shaky breath, Emma slowly returned to the couch, her nerves taut and her senses alert. She sat there for a moment, trying to steady herself, before grabbing the remote and switching on the TV, hoping some noise might break the stillness. She flicked through channels aimlessly, but nothing held her attention. The quiet was still there, like a weight pressing down on her.

Emma decided to call it a night around midnight, feeling both physically tired and mentally drained. She needed rest before her drive in the morning. She switched off the TV and headed to her bedroom. As she lay down in her bed, she tossed and turned, unable to quiet her mind, before finally falling into a fitful sleep.

At around 3 a.m., Emma was jolted awake by a chilling, eerie sound. Her heart raced as she sat up, the room unnaturally cold. Faint whispers echoed through the air, and objects in her room began to shake. With a sudden crash, a picture frame shattered on the floor.

Emma's breath caught as she searched the room for the source of the disturbance. The air felt thick, oppressive, and the temperature dropped even further. A rustling noise came from her closet, and her heart pounded louder with each step toward it. The whispers grew more insistent, almost mocking.

She swung her legs off the bed and stood, her pulse quickening with each movement. As she reached for the closet door, the noise stopped abruptly. Hesitating, she swung it open, finding the closet empty. An icy draft brushed against her face. Then, with a loud slam, the door shut, making her jump back. Her pulse quickened as she tried to open it again, but it wouldn't budge, as if held shut by an invisible force. Panic began to set in, and she pulled harder, but the door remained locked.

The whispers grew louder, echoing in her ears, making her dizzy. The lights flickered, casting eerie shadows that twisted and contorted, forming ghastly shapes that seemed to reach for her. The temperature dropped even further, and Emma could see her breath misting in the freezing air.

A loud thud behind her made Emma spin around. Her nightstand drawer had slid open on its own, spilling its contents onto the floor. Papers and personal items scattered across the room as if thrown by an unseen hand. Emma backed away, eyes wide with fear, but tripped over a fallen book, sending her crashing to the floor.

Scrambling to her feet, she felt a cold, invisible hand brush her ankle, sending a shiver up her spine. The sensation was unmistakable—icy fingers gripping her skin. She stumbled backward, her heart pounding. The whispers grew louder, almost deafening, and terrifying sounds echoed in her mind.

The lights went out completely, plunging the room into darkness. The only light came from a sliver of moonlight filtering through the curtains, casting an eerie glow. Suddenly, the closet door creaked open slowly, revealing a dark, gaping void. Emma's breath hitched as an unseen force seemed to pull her toward it. She tried to resist, but the force was too strong. Before she knew it, she was yanked inside, the door slamming shut behind her.

Inside the closet, it was pitch black. Emma fumbled for the light switch, but it was useless. The whispers intensified, surrounding her from all sides, as though closing in. A suffocating pressure pressed down on her chest, making it hard to breathe. Panic surged as she realised she was trapped in the dark.

Banging on the door, she shouted for help, though she knew no one would hear. The air grew colder, and she felt something sinister moving closer. The walls seemed to close in, and faint mocking laughter echoed in the confined space.

Fear reached its peak as cold, bony fingers wrapped around her wrists, pinning her against the back wall. She struggled, but the grip was too strong. The whispers morphed into a chorus of malevolent voices, taunting her, feeding off her fear.

Then, the darkness in front of her began to shift and swirl. A shadowy figure slowly materialised, taking shape. Emma's heart pounded as she watched in horror. The figure solidified into the ghostly apparition of Laura. Her face was gaunt and twisted, her eyes hollow, filled with a malevolent glare. The spectral image of Laura's broken body from her fall was horrifying.

Laura's spirit glided closer, her ethereal form flickering like a distorted memory. Emma felt paralysed, unable to move or speak. The whispers grew louder, more insistent, filling the closet with a cacophony of anger and pain.

Then, they formed a distorted, angry chant, repeating Emma's name in an otherworldly tone. "Emma... Emma... Emma..." The temperature plummeted further, and icy fingers brushed against her skin, sending a shiver down her spine. The overwhelming intensity of the haunting made it clear—Laura's spirit was furious and tormented.

Emma's eyes widened in terror as Laura's spirit reached out, her fingers elongated and claw-like. The darkness in Laura's eyes seemed to pull Emma in, a vortex of despair and rage. Emma could feel the weight of Laura's emotions pressing down on her, threatening to suffocate her.

Summoning her strength, Emma barely whispered, "Laura, what do you want?"

For a moment, the whispers ceased, and Laura's spirit locked eyes with her. The look was a mix of rage and pain, and Emma felt the depth of it. The evil emanating from Laura was almost palpable, a dark force wrapping around Emma, squeezing the air from her lungs.

As Laura's spirit floated closer, Emma saw flashes of Laura's past—dark rituals, intense obsession, and despair. The sheer intensity of the haunting left Emma trembling, her mind on the brink of panic.

The spirit vanished before Emma could say anything more, leaving the closet in eerie silence. The door creaked open on its own, releasing Emma from her terrifying confinement.

Stumbling out of the closet, Emma trembled with a mix of fear and adrenaline. She ran out of her bedroom, sank onto the couch, breath coming in short, sharp gasps as she fought to steady her racing heart. The cold of the closet seemed to linger on her skin, a chilling reminder of Laura's spectral presence.

The weight of the night's horrors clung to Emma as she sat in the silence of her living room, the chill of fear still crawling beneath her skin. Laura's spirit had made her intentions clear: this was far from over. Her mind raced, not just with the lingering terror of what she had experienced, but with the unsettling realisation that she had barely scratched the surface of what was happening.

Dawn's light crept slowly into the apartment, offering little relief from the dark thoughts clouding her mind. Emma stood, her limbs stiff and unsteady, her chest still tight from the adrenaline. She needed something to ground herself and shake off the aftereffects of the nightmare. With a deep breath, she moved towards the kitchen to make herself some coffee.

As the coffee brewed, she could still feel the ghostly presence of Laura, the anger in her eyes, the relentless, accusing energy that had been so unnerving.

Emma closed her eyes for a moment, steadying herself. She knew she had to act fast. No longer just a passive observer, she was now in the eye of the storm, and she had to face whatever was coming.

CHAPTER 12

Shattered Reflections

Sunday, 16ᵗʰ October 2024

Sitting in the kitchen, Emma rubbed her temples to ward off the exhaustion that clung to her like a heavy fog. The events of the past night had left her drained, both physically and emotionally. Glancing at the clock, she realised it was already 8:00 a.m. She had promised Mrs. Harrington she would be there by 11.

With a heavy sigh, Emma pushed herself to her feet. She quickly showered, her mind racing with a thousand thoughts, then opened her closet with a sense of dread and grabbed a few items.

Dark jeans, a black sleeveless top, boots, and a jacket provided some sense of armour for the day ahead. She applied a touch of bright lipstick, a small attempt to mask her pale, weary face. But despite her efforts, the haunted look in her eyes remained.

Rain started lashing against the windscreen as Emma drove towards Willow's Creek, distorting the world into a shimmering, shifting blur. Dark clouds loomed overhead, casting shadows across the barren countryside. Her grip on the steering wheel tightened, knuckles pale against the dark leather, as the wipers fought to keep up with the relentless downpour.

The rhythmic swish of the wipers and the steady hiss of the rain filled the car, a dismal backdrop to her troubled thoughts. Occasional flashes of lightning revealed stark, leafless trees and mist-shrouded fields, the storm echoing Emma's inner turmoil and deepening her sense of dread.

Upon arriving at Mrs. Harrington's house, Emma was greeted by the housekeeper who led her down the hallway to the living room.

Mrs Harrington was seated in an armchair by the fireplace, her posture straight, but her eyes softened with a welcoming expression. She immediately rose when she saw Emma.

"Ms. Ravenwood, come and sit. Make yourself comfortable," Mrs. Harrington said, gesturing to the nearby chair. "Would you like some tea or coffee?" she asked, her tone gentle.

Emma hesitated, her throat dry. "Thank you, Mrs. Harrington. I'll just have some water," she replied, her voice low.

Mrs Harrington gave a small nod, signalling the housekeeper to prepare the drink before settling back into her chair. Emma sank into the chair, trying to shake off the fatigue from the restless night.

The housekeeper returned shortly, handing Emma a glass of water, which she accepted gratefully. She took a few sips, the cool liquid offering a brief moment of relief, before placing the glass on a nearby table.

Emma glanced up at Mrs. Harrington, nodding slightly to signal that she was ready for the purpose of her visit – Laura's journals.

"Come with me, Ms. Ravenwood," Mrs. Harrington said, her voice calm but purposeful. "I'll show you to Laura's things."

They walked together through the dimly lit hallway, the house's quiet amplifying the moment's weight. Mrs. Harrington led Emma towards a narrow staircase at the end of the hall, its steep incline looming ahead like a path to some forgotten place.

The stairs creaked beneath their feet as they ascended, each step echoing in the silence. When they finally reached the top, the air was cool and stale, tinged with the musty scent of forgotten memories.

Mrs Harrington flicked on a single overhead lightbulb, casting a weak, flickering glow that barely reached the corners of the attic.

The light revealed cobwebs draped over old wooden beams and trunks, adding to the eerie atmosphere. She gestured towards the boxes and trunks in the corner, their edges worn and weathered—each one filled with remnants of Laura's past, possibly holding the key to understanding her tragic story.

Leaving Emma to go through the boxes, Mrs. Harrington returned to the living room. Emma approached an old trunk first, its leather straps cracked and peeling. Taking a deep breath, she lifted the lid, revealing a mix of old clothes and faded photographs. As her fingers brushed over the brittle fabric and yellowed images, she carefully sorted through the contents. Each photograph was a frozen moment in time, faces staring back at her with a mixture of curiosity and melancholy, a glimpse into lives long past.

Her hands trembled slightly as she moved on to a smaller, more ornate box, its wooden surface etched with intricate carvings. Inside, she found a collection of journals and letters, their pages yellowed with age. One journal caught her attention—its cover was simple, but the name "Laura" was written in elegant script on the inside. As she flipped through the pages, the writing was dense and emotional, filled with Laura's raw, passionate reflections.

Emma's heart raced as she delved deeper into the journals. The words vividly depicted Laura's inner turmoil—her unspoken love for the professor and the growing desperation that seemed to suffocate her. Each entry revealed the extent of Laura's obsession and the mounting pressure that had driven her to the edge of madness.

Emma paused at one journal in particular, its cover worn and tattered. The entries inside were dated from the period just before Laura's breakdown. She scanned the final entry, written the day before Laura's hysterical outburst. In it, Laura spoke of her hope and anxiety about confessing her feelings to the professor. She had planned to reveal her emotions the next day, her words filled with a mix of excitement and dread.

Excerpt from the Journal:

"Tomorrow is the day. I must tell him how I feel, how deeply I have loved him from afar. The pain of hiding it is unbearable. My heart aches with every moment I spend in silence. I am determined to finally confess. I hope he will understand, even if he cannot return my feelings. If only he knew how fervently I adore him, perhaps things could be different. But what if he rejects me? I fear the torment that such a rejection would bring..."

Emma's hands trembled as she closed the journal. The raw emotion in Laura's final entry—the hope of a confession that never came—cut short by the breakdown that led to her being admitted to Ravensbrook Asylum. It became clear to Emma that this emotional intensity, this unrequited love, had been the catalyst for Laura's eventual unravelling.

Determined to learn more, Emma sifted through the letters and mementos. Each one revealed an unspoken love for Professor Adrian, but none had ever been sent. They were private declarations left unread by their intended recipient. As Emma continued her search, each discovery added another layer to Laura's tragic story, shedding light on the events that had driven her to the brink of madness.

Holding the letters in her hands, Emma found herself grappling with an unsettling dilemma. Should she reveal everything she had uncovered about Laura to Mrs. Harrington? The truth was tangled and painful, especially the revelation of Laura's obsessive, unrequited love for Professor Adrian Ravenwood—her father. Added to that was the involvement of Emma's mother, Catherine, and her attempts to stop Laura's dark rituals. It was a connection Emma hadn't anticipated, making the situation feel intensely personal.

But would exposing this buried past bring solace to Mrs. Harrington, or would it deepen her grief? Emma knew the truth could be both healing and wounding. She wasn't sure if

Mrs. Harrington was ready for the full weight of it. Torn between the duty to disclose what she had learned and the instinct to protect both her heart and Mrs. Harrington's from further pain, Emma put the letters back in the box. For now, she decided, she would say nothing. She would speak to her mentor, Kai, about this moral dilemma before deciding how to proceed.

With the final journal clutched in her hands, Emma descended from the attic and found Mrs. Harrington in the living room, sipping hot tea. She offered some to Emma, but Emma politely declined.

With a steady voice but edged with urgency, Emma asked, "Mrs. Harrington, can you tell me more about the day you admitted Laura to the asylum?"

Mrs. Harrington's face grew solemn as she began recounting the events. "Laura came home from school that day in a state of distress. She was soaked to the bone, drenched by the heavy rain. Her hair was a mess, and she seemed agitated—her eyes wild with an emotion we couldn't fully understand then."

Emma listened intently, her heart racing as Mrs. Harrington continued. "Laura began to scream and destroy things around the house, consumed by a sudden, uncontrollable fury. The house staff and I tried to calm her, but we couldn't. Her rage and despair overwhelmed us."

Mrs. Harrington's voice softened, heavy with the memory. "Eventually, we called the family doctor. When he arrived, we had to hold her down while he administered a sedative. He said her condition was so severe, she had to be admitted to Ravensbrook Asylum right away."

Emma nodded, taking in the gravity of Mrs. Harrington's words. The details of Laura's outburst painted a much clearer picture of the intensity of her emotional state than before.

With the journal in hand, Emma stood up and said, "I would like to take this with me," she said gently. "I'd like to see if I can uncover anything further. Perhaps it can help us understand more about what happened."

Mrs Harrington nodded, a look of concern crossing her face but also a hint of relief. Emma could sense that Laura's tragic past burdened her, and uncovering the truth would offer the old woman some closure.

As she approached the door, the rain outside slowed to a drizzle. Getting into her Jeep, Emma decided to drive through Willow's Creek to the school where Laura had studied. She checked her phone for directions and realised it was not too far from the manor.

The streets were quiet as she made her way towards Willow's Creek High School, an old brick building that had been updated over the years. Despite the renovations, it still held an air of faded grandeur. Ivy clung to its historic walls, contrasting sharply with the sleek, modern windows that reflected the passage of time.

The massive wrought-iron gates were locked, as they were every Sunday, leaving Emma staring at the entrance from her car. A sudden wave of dizziness washed over her as she sat there, an unexpected and disorienting sensation that made her grip the steering wheel. Her vision blurred, and the world around her seemed to tilt before she could steady herself.

Closing her eyes in an attempt to steady herself, she was violently pulled into a psychic vision; the images crashed over her like a wave.

As the vision unfolded, Emma could feel the rawness of Laura's heartache and the suffocating weight of rejection. It was as if she were living the moment alongside Laura, her emotions rising with each word spoken.

In the vision, the school hallways were transformed. The modern updates vanished, replaced by the dim, flickering lights of an older, more dilapidated building. Emma saw Laura standing alone in a classroom, her eyes filled with desperation and longing. The classroom was stark and cold, with worn wooden desks and a blackboard smudged with chalk marks.

Professor Adrian Ravenwood faced Laura. His expression was a mix of kindness and firmness. The scene was set in the early afternoon, with the light from the narrow windows casting long shadows across the room.

Laura's voice trembled with emotion. "I have to tell you something. I... I love you. I cannot keep these feelings to myself any longer."

Professor Ravenwood looked shocked and confused, but his face softened with understanding. "Laura, you are a bright and talented student, but this... this is not appropriate. I am your professor, and more importantly, I am a married man with a daughter. I love my family dearly."

Laura's face crumpled with despair. "But I love you so much. Please, can't you see that we are meant to be together? I would do anything for you."

Shaking his head firmly, Professor Ravenwood took a step back. "Laura, this has to stop. Your feelings are not reciprocated. If you continue down this path, I will have no choice but to inform your mother. You need to focus on your studies and move on."

Tears streamed down Laura's face as she begged, "Please, don't do this. I can't bear it. I'll do anything you want me to, just don't push me away."

Professor Ravenwood's voice grew sterner. "This is my final word, Laura. You need to let go of this madness. If you don't, I will have to take action to ensure this does not continue."

Emma felt Laura's heartache and desperation as the scene unfolded. The intensity of Laura's emotions was palpable, and the professor's firm yet compassionate rejection was clear. It was evident that this confrontation had been a turning point for Laura, leading to her eventual breakdown.

The vision faded, and Emma found herself back in her car, a deep sadness settling over her. She paused to collect her thoughts, the weight of Laura's emotional turmoil heavy on her mind.

She felt empathy for both Laura and her father, each trapped in a painful, unspoken conflict. As the rain softly tapped against the car roof, Emma understood that uncovering these truths was crucial to helping Laura find peace.

Needing to regain her strength, Emma noticed the emptiness in her stomach. As she drove back to Hawes, a misty haze lingered on the highway as the rain had finally stopped.

A few minutes into the drive, Emma spotted a small café attached to a gas station along the roadside. It was unassuming, with a simple sign reading "Highway Café." She parked her car and got out.

The interior was basic, with a few plastic tables and chairs, a counter filled with pre-packaged snacks, and a coffee machine humming softly in the corner. The café was nearly empty, save for a trucker sipping coffee and a couple of travellers browsing the shelves.

Emma approached the counter, where a tired-looking barista greeted her. "What can I get for you?"

"A large coffee and a ham and cheese sandwich, please," Emma replied, her stomach growling in anticipation.

She took a seat at a small table by the window and allowed herself a moment of quiet. The past few days had been overwhelming, and she knew she needed to process everything. The conversation with Mrs. Harrington and the discovery of Laura's journals had given her valuable insights, but there was still much more to uncover.

Once her coffee arrived, she took a sip, feeling the caffeine slowly revive her. As she waited for her sandwich, Emma reached into her bag and pulled out Laura's journal, which she had taken from the attic with Mrs. Harrington's permission. Flipping through the pages, her eyes were drawn to the elegant yet chaotic handwriting.

One entry immediately caught her attention:

'Tonight, I performed the spell as instructed by B. It should have drawn him closer, but instead, the darkness seems to close in around me. My heart aches, and I fear I have invited more than just love into my life.'

Emma's mind raced, wondering who 'B' was - who had taught Laura the spell. Her fingers trembled as she turned the page, uncovering a series of notes on black magic. Elaborate spells designed to attract love filled the pages, each more complex and desperate than the last. The ingredients - rare herbs, symbols, and incantations - were meticulously listed, each one carrying a sense of urgency and control.

Another entry was even more unsettling. It described a binding spell meant to make someone fall in love, written in a chilling tone:

'If he does not come to me of his own will, I will make him mine through the power of the ritual. His heart will be bound to mine, forever entwined by forces beyond his understanding.'

Emma's breath caught in her throat. The dark energy seemed to pulse from the pages. Laura's obsession with controlling love— and the desperation behind her spells—revealed a young woman consumed by her own desires and fears.

Emma closed the journal, the weight of Laura's dark intentions pressing down on her. The café's quiet hum of activity seemed to fade into the background, leaving Emma alone with the chilling secrets of Laura's past.

Lost in thought, Emma was jolted by the waitress setting the sandwich on the table. Despite the dark revelations in the journal, her stomach growled with hunger. She took a bite of the simple sandwich, and though modest, it helped settle her nerves. As she ate, she replayed the vision in her mind. Emma pulled out her notebook and began jotting down her thoughts, organising the information she had gathered so far. The journals, the vision, the professor's rejection—it all painted a tragic picture of obsession and despair.

Finishing her meal, Emma felt her strength returning. She slipped the journal back into her bag, paid for her meal, and got back on the road. By late afternoon, she arrived in Hawes. Her first stop was Elysian Threads, a small boutique offering an eclectic mix of vintage and modern clothing and accessories. Nestled on a quiet side street, the shop exuded a mysterious charm. After parking her car, Emma stepped inside.

Inside, Elysian Threads was a kaleidoscope of styles— embroidered jackets hung beside flowing bohemian skirts, while vintage band tees shared space with luxurious silk scarves. Shelves were lined with various accessories, from chunky handcrafted jewellery to delicate lace gloves and vibrant beaded headbands. The store felt like a treasure trove, with each corner offering a new discovery, a blend of old-world elegance and modern flair. Soft lighting and the faint scent of incense filled the air, creating an atmosphere where Emma could lose herself each time she visited.

The young woman behind the counter gave Emma a warm smile, which she returned. Emma moved through the garments, finally choosing a delicate vintage ivory lace blouse with a high collar and pearl buttons, paired with a long, wrap-around skirt in charcoal-grey wool. The skirt featured an asymmetrical hem and a subtle plaid pattern, giving it timeless versatility. Next, she picked out a pair of black leather ankle boots, embroidered with silver and turquoise, and a sleek black leather cuff bracelet with engraved silver studs and an ornate clasp.

After leaving the boutique, Emma drove home. The rain, now intensifying, fell steadily against the windscreen.

Once home, she kicked off her boots and immediately went to the bathroom. She drew a bath, letting the warm water fill the tub as she undressed. She added a handful of lavender bath salts as the water rose, and the soothing scent quickly filled the air. She sank into the water, letting the heat relax her tense muscles and the silence envelop her.

After her soak, she changed into something comfortable – soft leggings and a cosy sweater. Feeling refreshed, Emma headed to the kitchen, where she poured herself a glass of red wine, savouring its rich scent before starting on dinner.

She decided on a simple yet comforting meal—roast chicken, garlic mashed potatoes, and sautéed vegetables. The familiar motions of cooking, accompanied by soft classical music playing in the background, helped ease the tension in her body. The aroma of garlic and roasting chicken soon filled the air, grounding her in the moment.

Once dinner was ready, she set the table and sat down to enjoy her meal. Afterward, she took her wine and curled up on the couch, starting a familiar movie on the TV. With the soothing sounds of the classical music still lingering, she allowed herself to unwind, the gentle glow of the screen offering a welcome distraction.

As the evening wore on, Emma was abruptly jolted from her relaxation. An eerie chill swept through the room, cutting through the warmth, wrapping around her like a cold embrace. The TV screen flickered ominously, its light casting strange, dancing shadows on the walls. Emma's heart began to race, a deep sense of dread washing over her.

The atmosphere grew heavy, the air thick with palpable tension. The once-comforting hum of the television turned into an unsettling background noise, punctuated by the sharp creaking of the floorboards. Emma's instincts screamed that something was wrong, and her fear mounted.

Then came the whispers—soft at first, like the rustling of leaves. They quickly grew louder, more insistent, a cacophony of ghostly murmurs filling the room. Emma's eyes darted around, but the room remained shrouded in darkness and shadow.

A cold gust of wind swept through, swaying the curtains as if caught in an unseen storm. The lights flickered in response, as though the presence that stirred the air also toyed with the electricity. Emma shivered, her breath visible in the sudden chill. She felt a presence—an overwhelming sense of being watched. The feeling was suffocating.

The kitchen door slammed shut with a deafening bang, startling Emma and sending her heart into overdrive. She jumped to her feet, her gaze fixed on the doorway as an eerie silence followed. A sudden crash from the kitchen made her blood run cold—a cabinet had been thrown open, and its contents scattered across the floor.

Emma hesitated, then slowly approached the kitchen, her steps cautious. The room was in disarray, with pots and pans strewn about and a broken dish lying in pieces. Her pulse raced as she steadied her breathing, feeling the oppressive weight of the atmosphere.

It was then she saw Laura's spirit. Her ghostly figure stood in the doorway, its presence unmistakable. Laura's form was twisted and grotesque, her spectral body contorted in a way that made her seem both menacing and heart-wrenching. Her eyes burned with a fierce, malevolent intensity, a stark contrast to the desperation Emma had witnessed earlier.

Laura's voice cut through the air, harsh and filled with anger. "You think you can just come here and uncover my pain? You think you can walk away unscathed?"

Emma's breath caught. Laura's figure flickered, a twisted reflection of the girl she had been. Her eyes blazed with fury, her form shifting as if caught between the living and the dead.

"No," Emma said, her voice trembling. "I don't want to hurt you. I'm here to help, but I cannot do that if you are angry and violent."

Laura's form solidified, her anger directed at Emma with frightening intensity. "Help? You think you can help? You are the daughter of Adrian Ravenwood. The very man who caused me so much pain."

Emma's eyes widened. "What do you mean? My father didn't—"

Laura's voice cut her off, filled with bitter rage. "He turned me away, left me in despair. Your father had the power to help and love me, but he cast me aside. And now, his daughter comes here, thinking she can fix what he left broken?"

Emma struggled to process Laura's words. "My father was married. He had a family. He…"

Laura advanced, her ghostly form flickering and wailing. "What?! He rejected me! And his rejection was my undoing. And now, you, his daughter, must pay for his sins!"

A wave of icy wind slammed into Emma, and she staggered back, her breath coming in sharp, ragged gasps. Laura's spirit loomed over her, her malice palpable. Emma's heart raced, the weight of Laura's rage pressing down on her.

"I'm not my father," Emma cried, her voice trembling. "I don't want to fight you. I want to understand what happened, to help you find peace."

Laura's anger faltered for a moment, her spectral form wavering. "You think your words can change anything? You think you can erase the pain his rejection caused me?"

Emma stood her ground, fear turning into resolve. "I can't undo the past, but I can help you move forward. Let go of your anger. It's consuming you and hurting those who come near."

Laura's spirit hesitated, her rage battling against Emma's plea for peace. The room trembled with the struggle, and Emma focused all her psychic energy to push back against Laura's malevolent presence.

"You have to find peace," Emma said firmly. "For yourself, and for everyone you've hurt."

With a final, piercing wail, Laura's spirit began to fade, her form dissolving into the darkness. The oppressive cold lifted, and the whispers faded into an uneasy silence. Emma slumped against the wall, her entire body shaking from the encounter. The haunting had not ended, but Laura's rage had been quelled for now.

Exhausted and emotionally drained, Emma sank onto the couch. The events of the evening swirled in her mind, a haunting reminder that Laura's story was far from over.

Eventually, she fell into a fitful sleep on the couch.

Whispers of Faith

Monday, 17th October 2024

It was 5 a.m. when Emma woke up on the couch where she had passed out the previous night, overwhelmed by profound physical and emotional exhaustion. The harrowing encounter with Laura's spirit had drained her, and the weight of the night's revelations pressed heavily on her mind. As she looked out of the window, she saw it was raining heavily, casting a sombre mood over the day.

She moved through her morning routine with deliberate calm. First, she made her way to the bathroom and splashed cold water on her face, the refreshing jolt helping to invigorate her and clear away the remnants of sleep.

Next, she headed to the kitchen where she brewed coffee and prepared a simple breakfast of oatmeal with fresh fruit and yogurt.

After breakfast, Emma took a long, hot shower and dressed in comfortable, practical clothes – jeans, a cosy sweater, and sturdy boots – ready for the day ahead.

Determined to find some peace, she decided to visit a secluded clearing she knew, nestled in a small grove about a 20-minute drive from Hawes. With plenty of time before she needed to be at the studio, she hoped the tranquil spot could offer her some respite. She had discovered it during one of her nature walks, and its serene beauty had always helped calm her mind. The drive through the winding roads of the Yorkshire Dales was peaceful, the rain-dappled landscape adding to the contemplative mood of the morning.

Upon reaching the grove, Emma parked her car and walked along a narrow path leading to the clearing. The rain had slowed to a gentle drizzle, and the forest was lush and vibrant. As she entered the clearing, tall, ancient trees formed a natural circle, their canopies creating a protective dome overhead.

Emma found a large, flat stone in the centre and sat down. The earthy smell of the forest floor and the distant sound of dripping water created a soothing atmosphere. The grove's timeless serenity felt sacred, a space where she could completely relax.

She closed her eyes and took deep, measured breaths, letting the calm of the grove wash over her. The connection to nature and the sacredness of the place provided a profound respite.

As she settled into the tranquillity, her thoughts drifted to a powerful shamanic session she had experienced years ago with Professor Kai. The memory unfolded with crystal clarity.

Kai had meticulously prepared the space, arranging sacred objects around the room. Incense burned in a handcrafted vessel, releasing a sweet, calming fragrance that mingled with the flickering shadows cast by candlelight. The room was dim, the atmosphere dense with the energy of ritual and the mysteries of the unseen.

"Close your eyes, Emma," Kai had instructed, his voice gentle yet commanding. "Focus on your breath and allow yourself to relax. We are going to journey inward." Emma had done as he asked, feeling her breath grow deeper, her body surrendering to the rhythm of his words. Kai's shamanic drum began to play, its beats powerful and hypnotic. The drum, crafted with reverence, had a head made from carefully selected deer skin, naturally tanned to a warm, earthy beige. The drumhead was adorned with hand-painted symbols: a spiral at the centre, representing the journey of life, surrounded by sacred patterns that spoke of ancient traditions and the four directions.

The frame of the drum was wrapped in a handwoven band of fabric in rich, earthy tones, embroidered with traditional patterns reflecting Kai's heritage. Feathered talismans, representing spirit guides and protective forces, hung from its edges, swaying gently in time with each beat. The drum's resonance carried the power to alter consciousness, guiding Emma into deeper states of awareness.

In the altered state, Emma experienced a vision so vivid it felt more real than reality itself. A black wolf emerged at the edge of a clearing, its sleek, inky fur shimmering subtly in the dappled light. Each ripple of muscle beneath its coat spoke of latent power, and it exuded an aura of both grace and wildness. Its piercing, vivid blue eyes locked onto Emma's with a penetrating and protective gaze, as though the wolf could peer into her soul and understand her every thought and fear.

This wolf was more than a mere animal; it was her spirit guide, a being of immense wisdom and strength. Emma felt an unspoken connection to it, a bond forged in the depths of her soul and spanning lifetimes. The wolf symbolised her inner resilience and the well of intuitive knowledge she could call upon. It embodied both the light and the shadow, the balance she needed to embrace within herself.

The vision shifted, and Emma found herself following the wolf deeper into a dense forest. They arrived at a circle of ancient stones, emanating an energy that hummed with age-old power. At the centre of the circle, a radiant, mystical figure materialised. It was shrouded in a cloak of shimmering light, and symbols seemed to dance across its surface, changing and shifting as she watched. The figure's presence filled her with awe, yet there was a comfort in it, a familiarity she could not place.

Without speaking, the figure's voice echoed within her mind: "Emma, you have embarked on a journey of great significance. Trust in your inner strength and the wisdom of the spirits that guide you." The words reverberated through her being, igniting a sense of purpose. The black wolf remained by her side, a silent sentinel, as the figure imparted knowledge that transcended words, each insight deepening her understanding of her path.

When the vision began to fade, Emma felt a sense of loss but also a newfound clarity. Kai's voice called her back, gently guiding her to the present. She opened her eyes, forever changed by what she had seen and felt, as if the encounter had unlocked a part of her soul that had been waiting for this moment.

Sitting in the forest clearing, Emma remembered that session with a renewed sense of purpose. A few weeks after returning from the cabin, she had stepped into a small, secluded tattoo parlour in London. The scent of ink and antiseptic lingered in the air, and the buzz of the needle filled the room. The artist had listened quietly as she described the wolf, its vivid blue eyes, and what it meant to her. When the needle touched her skin, she closed her eyes and was transported back to that forest, to the moment when the wolf had first appeared, strong and watchful.

As she gently touched the back of her neck, where the tattoo lay hidden beneath her dark hair, a sense of calm and certainty washed over her. The black wolf with blue eyes had become a part of her, a constant reminder of her journey and the strength she carried within. The ancient stones, the mystical figure, and the spirit animal were not just visions but profound symbols of her inner journey.

The memory of that shamanic session with Kai reminded her that she was never truly alone. She had the guidance of powerful spiritual forces and her own innate wisdom to navigate whatever challenges awaited. Her path was illuminated by a strength she now understood more deeply, woven from the threads of resilience and spirit.

She reached into her bag and pulled out a small, smooth crystal shaped like a wolf. Its surface was cool and comforting against her palm, carved from black onyx with tiny sapphires set into the eyes, catching the light with a subtle gleam. The intricate carving held a powerful energy, and as Emma held it tightly, she felt an immediate connection to her spirit animal—the majestic black wolf with piercing blue eyes that had guided and protected her through her shamanic journey.

She closed her eyes and focused on the crystal's energy, feeling the wolf's strength and wisdom flowing into her. The presence of the spirit animal brought a deep sense of protection and grounding, a reminder that she was never truly alone and could always call upon its guidance when needed. The energy of the wolf, a spirit of grace and resilience, anchored her in the present moment, offering a profound sense of security.

After spending more time in the grove, Emma felt a renewed sense of grounding, her mind clearer and her resolve stronger. The timeless serenity of the place had done its work, restoring her inner balance. As she left the clearing and made her way back to her car, she breathed in the crisp, earthy air, feeling more connected to herself and the world around her.

Driving back to Hawes, the sky remained overcast, but the rain had stopped, at least for now. The heavy clouds seemed to echo the subtle shift in her emotional state, as if even the landscape had paused in quiet acknowledgement of her renewed calm and determination. Ready to face the day's challenges, she felt a growing sense of peace that she carried with her, the black wolf's spirit always present in her heart.

She reached her studio and started with her day's appointments. Around mid-morning, Rose interrupted her, saying that Detective Harris from Willow's Creek Police Department was on the line.

With a puzzled look, Emma took her phone from Rose and said, "Hello."

"Ms Ravenwood, this is Detective Harris from Willow's Creek Police Department. I'm sorry to disturb you, but we have some troubling news. Dr Evelyn Hartley was found lying unconscious at the bottom of her staircase this morning by her housekeeper. The circumstances are suspicious, and we noticed that you were one of her recent calls."

Emma sat up, her mind racing. "Is she...?"

"She's in a critical condition at the hospital," the detective replied. "We need to ask you a few questions regarding your connection with her and any other relevant information."

Emma quickly confirmed with Detective Harris that she would head to the station within the hour. She filled Rose in on the situation and left her studio.

As she drove to Willow's Creek police station, Emma's mind raced with questions about Dr. Hartley's condition. The news unsettled her deeply, and a sense of unease settled in her chest. She could not shake the feeling that something far darker was at play, but what, exactly, was beyond her grasp. It was too soon after her visit to the doctor's home—was it truly an accident, or had Laura's spirit played a role in this?

As she approached Willow's Creek, the streets, slick from the morning rain, glistened beneath the grey sky. Occasional cars passed by, their tyres splashing gently through puddles while the windshield wipers swept away the mist clinging to the glass.

Emma followed the signs directing her to the police station, its utilitarian structure becoming more prominent as she neared. The building was functional and unremarkable, yet its stern presence spoke of its role in law and order. She parked in the visitors' lot, the rhythmic sound of her boots against the pavement echoing her growing apprehension as she made her way to the entrance.

Inside, the station bustled with the quiet hum of activity typical of law enforcement offices. The reception area was straightforward, with a large desk, officers shuffling about, and the distant sound of phones and conversations. Emma approached the front desk, where a middle-aged woman with a no-nonsense demeanour greeted her and directed her to a waiting area.

As Emma settled into a plastic chair that felt hard and uncomfortable, the weight of the situation began to press on her. She knew that what she shared needed to be carefully measured.

Every detail carried weight, and she had to balance answering the detective's questions with safeguarding her own secrets.

After a 15-minute wait, an officer led her to the interview room. It was stark and functional, with a plain table, metal chairs on either side, harsh fluorescent lighting, and a one way mirror on one wall. Two men, both police officers, were seated at the table, reviewing some papers.

As Emma entered, one of the officers stood up. "Ms. Ravenwood, I'm Detective Harris," he said, his voice steady but carrying the weight of the situation. He gestured to the other officer. "This is Officer Parker," he added before offering a polite nod. Officer Parker, a younger woman, held a notebook and watched Emma with a calm, assessing gaze.

"Thank you for coming in, please have a seat," Detective Harris said, gesturing to the empty chair.

Emma sat down, her nerves betraying her calm facade. Detective Harris took a seat across from her, and Officer Parker remained at the side, observing quietly, her notebook ready but unused for the moment.

"I understand this might be an inconvenient time for you," Detective Harris began, his tone steady. "But we need to investigate everyone connected to Dr. Hartley and anyone who has been in contact with her recently. Any information you can provide will be helpful."

Emma nodded but remained silent.

"Ms. Ravenwood, can you tell me how you're connected to Dr. Hartley?" Detective Harris asked, his gaze steady.

Emma nodded, taking a deep breath before answering. "Dr. Hartley was a friend of my mother's. I contacted her because I was seeking information related to a personal matter. There wasn't anything more to it."

The detectives exchanged glances before Officer Parker asked, "Can you tell us more about what you were discussing with Dr. Hartley? Are there any specifics that might be relevant?"

Emma hesitated, choosing her words carefully. "We were discussing some personal history related to my mother. I had never spoken with Dr. Hartley before, but I reached out to her to understand a few things about her connection to my family."

Detective Harris leaned forward, his gaze steady. "Did Dr. Hartley mention anything unusual during your conversation? Did she seem threatened or concerned? Anything that stood out to you?"

Emma shook her head, keeping her tone casual. "No, nothing unusual. It was just a general conversation about my mother and my family history."

The questioning continued, with the detectives probing various aspects of her recent interactions with Dr. Hartley. They inquired about her whereabouts that morning, pressed her again about her reasons for visiting the doctor, and asked whether she had noticed anything out of the ordinary during her visit. Emma maintained her carefully crafted narrative, answering each question without slipping, and she avoided any mention of her discussion with Dr. Hartley about Laura or the supernatural occurrences.

As the questioning drew to a close, Detective Harris reviewed his notes, then looked up at her. "We appreciate your cooperation, Ms. Ravenwood. We may need to follow up with you as the investigation progresses. Please keep us informed if you remember anything else that might be relevant."

Emma nodded and, rising to her feet, she said, "Yes. I'll let you know if I remember anything."

As Emma walked out of the interview room, she felt a brief sense of relief that the questioning was over, but her concern for

Dr. Hartley's condition deepened. She considered going to the hospital to learn more about her condition, but she was not sure which one she had been admitted to.

Standing in the lobby, unsure of how to find out, she spotted Detective Harris walking toward the exit. She quickly approached him. "Detective, could you tell me which hospital Dr. Hartley was taken to?"

He glanced at her and nodded. "Willow's Creek General. It's just a short drive from here."

Emma thanked him, then stepped out of the station and into her Jeep. Pulling up directions to the hospital on her phone, she followed the route through the quiet streets of Willow's Creek.

It was only a ten-minute drive, and soon enough, she pulled into the hospital parking lot. After finding a spot, she made her way towards the entrance, her mind focused on finding out more about Dr. Hartley's condition.

Once inside the hospital, Emma approached the reception desk and inquired about Dr. Hartley. After checking the records, the receptionist directed her to the intensive care unit, where the doctor was being monitored. Emma's pulse quickened as she made her way to the waiting area, hoping to learn more about Dr. Hartley's condition.

After a brief wait, a nurse led her into the ICU waiting room. The sterile environment, punctuated by the quiet hum of medical equipment, cast a sombre mood over the space. A small group of people, presumably Dr. Hartley's family and close friends, were gathered, their faces etched with concern. Emma introduced herself as a friend of the doctor, offering quiet reassurance to the group.

One of them, a man in his mid-thirties, introduced himself as Dr. Hartley's nephew. He explained that the doctor's injuries were minor, and she was in a stable condition. Though they were still awaiting a full assessment, Dr. Hartley seemed out of immediate danger.

After her visit to the hospital, Emma drove back to Hawes, her thoughts lingering on Dr. Hartley's condition. While she was glad to hear the doctor was stable, her concern remained. Upon arriving at the studio, she took a moment to steady herself before stepping inside. The familiar surroundings provided a brief sense of relief, a chance to focus on the appointment ahead.

Rose greeted her with a look of curiosity and concern. Emma returned the greeting and briefly filled her in on the detective's questioning, as well as the update on Dr. Hartley's condition. "She's stable, but still in critical condition," Emma said, her tone distracted.

Then she headed to her consulting room, eager to shift her focus to the work that awaited her.

As the day wore on, Emma moved through her appointments, though her thoughts occasionally wandered back to Dr. Hartley and Laura. She shared a quick lunch with Rose in the back of the studio, taking a brief respite before diving into the rest of her sessions.

By the time the day ended, Emma had finished her appointments and prepared to leave.

The drive back to her cottage was quiet, the evening sky a dull grey after the rain had passed, leaving a crisp chill in the air. Despite the unsettling encounters with Laura's spirit, the calm of her home offered a welcome contrast, soothing the emotional and physical weariness of the day. She parked in the driveway and walked up the path to the front door, the gravel crunching softly beneath her steps.

Inside, Emma kicked off her shoes and shed her damp coat, letting the familiar warmth of the cottage envelop her. She headed to the kitchen and prepared a simple dinner of ham and cheese sandwiches with a side salad.

After dinner, once she had tidied up the kitchen, Emma decided a long, hot shower would help ease the tension in her muscles.

As the water soothed her, the steam surrounding her seemed to clear her mind. She recalled her aunt mentioning a storage unit where she had kept some of Catherine Ravenwood's most cherished belongings. Emma had not given it much thought at the time, but now, the memory resurfaced with new significance.

She knew the keys to the storage unit were among the important papers locked away in a cabinet in the cottage. She wondered if there was something there, among her mother's possessions, that might provide more answers or offer a clue for dealing with the haunting.

Stepping out of the shower, Emma slipped into soft shorts and a camisole before making her way to the living room. The warm glow of the lamps cast gentle shadows that danced across the walls, creating a tranquil atmosphere. She sank onto the couch, sighing with exhaustion, and reached for her journal.

As the night deepened, she finished her final entry and put the journal aside. Preparing for bed, she stood in the centre of her bedroom, closed her eyes, and took a deep, steady breath. In a voice filled with intent and conviction, she recited a protection mantra: "By the light of the moon and the strength of my spirit, I call upon the forces of protection and healing. Shield me from harm and guide me through the darkness."

The words echoed softly around the room, filling the space with a sense of sacred purpose. A gentle wave of reassurance washed over her, easing the tension in her body. She climbed into bed, pulling the covers snugly around herself, and felt a small measure of comfort.

Lying there, Emma's thoughts turned to Professor Kai. She knew she would need his wisdom and experience to confront the darkness that awaited her. With resolve, she decided to call him first thing in the morning. As she closed her eyes, sleep gradually embraced her.

CHAPTER 14

Veil of Protection

Tuesday, 18th October 2024

Emma was finishing breakfast when her phone buzzed, and Kai's name lit up the screen. Her heart skipped a beat. Just last night, she had felt an urgent need for his guidance, and now it seemed as if he had sensed her distress across the distance. The timing was uncanny, almost like a psychic echo of her thoughts. Kai's presence in her life had always brought clarity, and as she picked up the phone, she knew it was no coincidence that he was calling her at this moment.

She answered the call, a wave of relief washing over her, "Kai," she said softly.

"Emma," Kai's voice came through, calm but tinged with an unmistakable depth. "I sensed a disturbance... felt it, deep inside. I knew you needed me. Something's wrong, isn't it? Are you truly alright?"

Emma leaned back, closing her eyes as she let out a slow breath. The relief of hearing his voice made her feel less alone in all this.

"No," she said, her voice barely a whisper, filled with a tremor of uncertainty. "Kai, it's Laura... her spirit... It's... it's haunting me. It started the moment Mrs. Harrington stepped into my office, but now... it's escalating. I can feel it growing stronger every day."

She then proceeded to recount everything that had happened—from the eerie encounters with Laura's spirit, to the unsettling connection between her and Emma's parents, and even Doctor Hartley's accident the day before.

When she finished, there was a long pause on the line. Kai's voice finally broke the silence, serious and concerned.

"This energy you're dealing with is dangerous, Emma. It's not just a restless spirit—there's malevolence behind it. You need extra protection, and you need it immediately."

Emma remained silent, processing the weight of Kai's words. He continued, his tone firm but calm. "You need to shield yourself, both physically and energetically."

He outlined a series of protective measures, advising her to use protective crystals, set up a salt barrier around her home, and perform a cleansing ritual to ward off the malevolent energy.

"Emma, these forces will take any opportunity to slip through. You must act immediately," Kai urged.

"I will, Kai," Emma replied softly, her resolve strengthening. "I'll follow your guidance."

"Emma, you're not alone," he reassured her. "I'm with you, even if not physically. We'll get through this."

Emma thanked and ended the call with Kai and quickly set to work. First, she gathered her protective crystals and placed them around her home. Then, she sprinkled salt at each corner, creating a barrier, and lit sage to cleanse the space. She moved through the rooms, the smoke swirling around her, feeling the energy shift as she worked. Finally, she sealed the doors and windows with salt, forming a protective line.

With the rituals completed, Emma took a deep breath, feeling a sense of calm settle over her. Moving purposefully through her cottage, she retrieved the key to the storage unit from the safe in her bedroom and placed it in her bag. The storage unit was on the outskirts of Maplewood, an hour's drive from Hawes, and she planned to head there straight from work. Locking the front door, she climbed into her Jeep and made her way to the studio.

Emma's day was packed with client appointments, each one demanding her full attention and energy. Yet, one client stood out, exuding a particularly captivating presence.

Emma immediately noticed the ethereal glow surrounding her as she entered the consultation room. At 45, Hayley carried a presence that seemed to light up the space. Her aura shimmered with radiant golds intertwined with vivid emeralds, swirling together in a harmonious dance. The colours pulsed gently, like a heartbeat, filling the room with warmth and calm. The golden hues spoke of deep wisdom and boundless compassion, while the vibrant greens hinted at a heart open to love, healing, and personal growth.

Emma could tell that Hayley had journeyed through darkness and emerged stronger, carrying a light that could uplift others. Her energy felt soothing yet empowering, exuding a resilience that was both tender and unyielding. Emma also sensed Hayley's deep connection to nature, as if the earth itself had blessed her with this luminous energy—a gift meant to guide her path in this life.

As their session unfolded, Emma shared her observations with Hayley, offering insights and guidance tailored to her radiant energy. The two women exchanged words, and as the session came to a close, Hayley thanked Emma and left.

Around noon, Emma took a break for lunch. Rose had picked up a garden salad and a grilled chicken sandwich from the nearby café, the aroma of freshly brewed coffee filling the air as they sat together at the back of the studio.

As they ate, they chatted about work – clients, upcoming appointments, and the latest studio happenings. It was a typical lunch break, offering a brief pause in the flow of their day.

Emma quickly wrapped up her day as her last client left, eager to get to the storage unit. She gathered her things, said goodbye to Rose, and left the studio.

She drove through the fading evening light, heading towards the outskirts of Maplewood. The road wound through tranquil countryside, fields and woodlands stretching on either side. As she drove, she wondered what she would find there. Would it shed light on Catherine's mystical practices or reveal something personal about her experiences?

The countryside gradually gave way to the outskirts of Maplewood. By the time she arrived at the storage facility, around 5:30 pm, the sun was sinking lower in the sky, casting long shadows. The units, a cluster of metal buildings, stood in stark contrast to the soft, natural surroundings.

The facility's entrance was marked by a rusted gate and a weathered sign that had seen better days. The gravel driveway leading to the units was uneven, with patches of overgrown grass encroaching on the edges.

Emma parked her Jeep and walked down the gravel driveway, her footsteps crunching with each step. The units, made of corrugated metal, stood weathered and worn, their paint faded and chipped. Each door was numbered, and the complex carried an air of neglect. The units near the entrance were in slightly better condition, but as Emma made her way toward the far end, where her family's unit, #37, stood, the deterioration became more pronounced. The paint had peeled away, and the metal was covered in grime.

The path leading to her unit was littered with scattered debris and remnants of old packaging. As she walked, the lights above flickered sporadically, casting a dim glow that barely pierced the growing darkness. The area was eerily quiet, broken only by the distant hum of machinery from nearby businesses and the occasional rustle of wind through the grass.

Reaching locker No. 37, Emma felt a shiver run down her spine as she took the key from her bag. The shutter was heavy and rusted, its mechanism sluggish as she turned the key. She rolled the shutter up, revealing the dark, musty interior. The atmosphere inside mirrored the neglect outside. Taking a deep breath, she stepped inside.

Emma's eyes scanned the dark space as she fumbled along the wall for the light switch. Her fingers brushed against the cold metal, and she flicked it on. A single overhead light flickered to life, casting a weak, intermittent glow that barely illuminated the room. The light struggled to stay steady, and the shadows it created stretched long and eerie across the space.

Inside, the unit was a cavernous space packed with a haphazard assortment of old furniture, boxes, and relics of a bygone era. Stacks of dusty boxes were piled high, some with their contents partially visible—faded photographs, brittle papers, and ancient keepsakes. An old wardrobe, its once-polished wood now dulled and scarred, stood in one corner, while a cracked mirror leaned precariously against the wall.

Her aunt, a meticulous woman, had left clear instructions in a note along with the key in her will, indicating the precise location of her parents' belongings. The far end of the unit, where those items were stored, felt particularly unsettling. The shadows there seemed deeper, the atmosphere heavy with abandonment. The faint buzzing of the overhead light combined with the creaks of the metal building, creating an unsettling silence punctuated only by the occasional groan of the structure shifting.

Emma took a steadying breath and stepped forward, each footfall stirring up a thin layer of dust that swirled in the dim light. She carefully navigated around the stacks of boxes and the forgotten relics of another time, her heart thumping steadily in her chest as she made her way toward the far end, where her parents' past lay waiting.

Emma sifted carefully through the dusty boxes, her fingers grazing over faded labels that offered only vague hints of what lay inside. Her heart thudded with anticipation as she uncovered a beautifully ornate box, its surface adorned with intricately carved floral patterns. With deliberate care, she lifted the lid, the hinges creaking softly as it opened to reveal a collection of delicate trinkets. Nestled among them were several journals, their leather covers worn but well-preserved.

Her hands trembled slightly as she reached for one. The cover felt smooth yet sturdy beneath her touch, a testament to years of careful use. Opening the first page, she saw her mother's name, "Catherine," elegantly written in familiar, flowing script. The date inscribed beneath made her stomach clench – it was the same year Laura had died.

Emma settled onto a nearby box, her mind racing as she began to read. The journal entries detailed her mother's growing unease and the turbulent atmosphere surrounding Laura's last days. One entry, in particular, struck Emma deeply:

"Laura's obsession with Adrian had reached a dangerous point. Her anger and desperation had twisted into something dark and unsettling. The night of her death, I watched in horror as Laura, consumed by her madness, climbed to the roof of the asylum. I saw her standing on the edge, and then she jumped. In the days that followed, I could feel the change - the air grew heavy, and shadows seemed to move where they shouldn't. Laura's spirit lingers, a vengeful presence that haunts me even in my dreams. I have begun to sense her growing malevolence, directed at Adrian and anyone connected to him. I am especially worried for little Emma, my baby girl. Her rage has become a shadow over my life, and I fear what she might be capable of."

Emma's breath caught in her throat as she read the words. Her eyes misted, her mother's love and fear for her so tangible in the lines. Catherine's concerns, woven with the undeniable presence of Laura's restless and vengeful spirit, felt like a weight on her chest. Catherine had been haunted, not just by the memory of that night but by the very essence of Laura's twisted obsession.

She closed the journal and placed it inside her bag to read more thoroughly later. As she continued sifting through the boxes, the atmosphere in the storage unit took on a more ominous tone. The air grew uncomfortably cold, and Emma could see her breath misting in front of her. The single overhead bulb flickered erratically, casting eerie shadows on the walls.

Emma's unease deepened when a sudden chill seemed to envelop her, making her skin crawl. The temperature plummeted further, and she felt an oppressive and suffocating weight settle in the space. Then, the dim bulb above her flickered once more and went out completely, plunging the storage unit into darkness.

Panicking slightly, Emma fumbled for her phone, using its flashlight to illuminate the space. But the beam was weak—her phone's battery was low, and the vastness of the unit swallowed the light, leaving only faint, scattered patches of visibility. As she moved the phone around, the shadows seemed to shift unnaturally, and the silence was unnerving.

Suddenly, an unnerving chill swept through the unit, like an invisible hand brushed past her. The temperature dropped further, and Emma could see her breath hanging in front of her. Her skin prickled with fear as an invisible weight pressed down on her shoulders, making each movement feel laboured and heavy.

The weak beam from her phone's flashlight illuminated an old mirror, its surface cracked and clouded with age. The fractured reflections twisted into a chaotic pattern, and Emma caught fleeting glimpses of shadowy figures moving behind her, their forms shifting in and out of focus. Then, a faint whisper broke the silence, growing louder with each passing second as if it were clawing its way into her mind.

A sudden, sharp sound shattered the silence – a loud crash echoed through the unit, followed by the rattle of metal and the clatter of old boxes spilling their contents across the floor. Emma swung her phone towards the noise, but the darkness seemed to conspire against her, casting erratic, ghostly patterns on the walls.

The air grew colder still, and a gust of icy wind swept through the unit, further plummeting the temperature. Her phone's flashlight flickered once, then went completely dark. Next, the entire screen went blank, leaving her in utter darkness. Emma's heart raced as she fumbled to turn it back on, but no matter how she pressed the buttons, the phone remained unresponsive, its battery seemingly drained or malfunctioning.

As she scrambled in the dark, a figure began to materialise in the shadows, flickering in and out of focus. Suddenly, her phone's screen lit up, flickering weakly, the light casting a dim, wavering glow. Her breath caught in her throat as the ghostly outline of a woman slowly took shape—hollow eyes filled with fury, a twisted face contorted in rage and despair. It was Laura! The figure drifted closer, its movement unnatural, like a shadow floating through the air, its malevolent presence pressing in on Emma, suffocating the space around her.

A piercing wail echoed through the unit, rising from a mournful cry to a cacophony of anguish and rage. The sound reverberated off the metal walls, creating an almost physical sensation of being trapped in a storm of emotional torment. The phone's screen flickered uncontrollably, casting fleeting, distorted images of Laura's menacing spirit.

The temperature continued to drop, and gusts of icy wind became violent, slamming against the walls and rattling the boxes. Emma felt an unseen, icy hand grab her arm, sending a jolt of terror through her body. Fear and desperation surged through Emma as she stumbled backward.

With a desperate cry, Emma turned and sprinted towards the front of the unit. She stumbled as her feet tangled in the scattered boxes, sending their contents crashing to the floor. She barely regained her balance, her breath coming in ragged gasps as she reached the entrance. With trembling hands, she pulled the shutter down, and just as it neared the ground, she heard a loud slam from the inside, as if something—or someone—had thrown itself against it. The noise reverberated through the metal, sending a jolt of terror through her body. She struggled to lock it, but somehow managed, the sound of the lock echoing in the silent night.

Shaken and breathless, she bolted from the unit and ran to the far side of the parking lot where her Jeep was parked. Her hands shook as she fumbled through her bag, each second feeling like an eternity. She kept glancing over her shoulder, fearing she might see Laura's spectral form creeping closer. Finally, she found the keys, unlocked the Jeep, and jumped inside, slamming the door shut. As the engine roared to life, she sped away, her mind reeling from the terror she had just escaped.

Emma's drive back to Hawes was consumed by a heavy silence. A little after she left the storage unit, the rain began to fall, steadily at first, then intensifying into a downpour. The heavy rain blurred the road ahead, and the only light came from the erratic flicker of her car's headlights. The rain created a watery veil over the landscape, distorting the world outside and making it difficult to see beyond a few feet.

Her hands gripped the steering wheel so tightly that her fingers ached, each turn of the wheel feeling like a struggle to keep control. Her thoughts churned with a mixture of fear and disbelief, her mind trapped in the terror of the storage unit. Laura's hollow, vengeful eyes, the suffocating weight of the darkness—everything clung to her, even as the rain continued its rhythmic drumming against the windshield.

The road was slick, the visibility poor, and every sound, every twist in the path made her heart race. She could not shake the feeling that the night itself had turned against her, that every shadow lurking outside the car was a potential threat. But whether it was the storm or her mind playing tricks on her, Emma could not tell. She kept her focus on the road, desperate to get home, the encounter replaying in her head like an unrelenting nightmare.

The intensity of the haunting had left Emma physically and emotionally drained. Her breath came in shallow gasps, her pulse racing, as if trying to escape the terror that had consumed her.

As she drove, Emma struggled to process the chilling experience. The chaos of the storage unit, the darkness, and Laura's overwhelming presence seemed to transcend the physical realm, suffocating her in a way she had never felt before.

Her thoughts kept returning to her mother's journal, which had revealed the depth of Laura's obsession and the darkness that had consumed her. One particular entry stood out—the one where her mother had written about sensing Laura's spirit long before Emma uncovered the full truth. The entries were a sobering reminder of the danger still lingering, and Emma couldn't shake the feeling that Laura's malevolence had been waiting for her to uncover the truth—now intent on revenge.

As she neared Hawes, the storm lightened, and the familiar lights of her town came into view. Emma felt a mix of relief and dread as she drove straight home, parking the Jeep in her driveway before stepping out. As she entered her cottage, she breathed a sigh of relief.

Once inside, Emma reached for her phone, relieved to see that it seemed normal now, no longer malfunctioning as it had at the storage unit. Her fingers trembled slightly as she dialled Kai's number. The phone rang several times before going to voicemail. Taking a deep breath, Emma left a brief voicemail, her voice wavering as she recounted the terrifying encounter and the intense malevolence she had felt. She ended with a quiet plea for Kai to call her back as soon as possible.

Feeling drained, Emma slipped out of her rain-soaked clothes and took a quick, hot shower, hoping the warmth would wash away the lingering chill of fear from her encounter. The steam enveloped her, providing a momentary sense of calm, but her mind remained consumed by the day's events. Afterward, she dressed in comfortable clothes and made her way to the kitchen. Mechanically, she prepared a bowl of oatmeal for dinner. As she ate, she hardly registered the taste of the food. The process felt automatic, a stark contrast to the fear she had experienced.

Emma decided to go to bed early. In the bedroom, she carefully placed her mother's journal on her desk, intending to examine it further in the morning. Exhausted, she climbed into bed, but sleep was elusive. Her thoughts circled back to the storage unit as she lay there in the darkness. Her psychic senses, honed through years of practice, remained on high alert. A feeling gnawed at her—a sense that something of immense importance had been left behind, hidden deep within the cluttered space. Maybe Laura had not wanted her to find it and had attacked to prevent its discovery.

She closed her eyes and drifted off to sleep, the darkness of the room wrapping around her like a heavy blanket. Hours passed as she slept, and just before dawn, the dream began.

Emma found herself standing outside the now-familiar storage unit. She wanted to turn and run, but suddenly she saw something coming towards her from inside the unit - it was the black wolf, her spirit animal; its piercing blue eyes glowed softly as it gazed at her.

Its presence felt like a silent command. Without a sound, it turned and walked back into the storage unit, its tail swishing as it glanced back to ensure she was following. The wolf moved with purpose, as if it knew exactly where they were going. Compelled, Emma stepped forward, her feet moving automatically as the wolf guided her.

The wolf stopped in front of a small, ornate box glowing faintly in the dim light. The soft pulse of the glow was mesmerising, as if the box itself were alive with energy. Emma felt an undeniable pull towards it, as though it held the answers to questions she had not even dared to ask.

Just as she reached out to touch the box, the air shifted—heavy and oppressive. Laura's spirit emerged from the shadows, her form flickering like a fading flame, but her eyes burned with an intense, malevolent light. Emma's heart skipped a beat. The box was not just hidden—Laura was fiercely protecting it.

The black wolf stepped forward, placing itself between Emma and the ghostly figure. Its low growl vibrated through the air, a warning to the dark force that loomed in front of them. Laura's form seemed to flicker and waver, but the wolf stood firm, its protective presence unwavering.

Emma reached for the box, but before she could touch it, the scene shifted, the dream unravelling around her as if pulled apart by an unseen force. With a jolt, Emma was awake, her heart pounding in her chest. The dream had left her breathless, but she knew one thing for certain: the box held a truth she could not ignore. She had to return to the storage unit—there was something in that box that Laura was desperate to keep hidden.

Unearthing Shadows

Wednesday, 19th October 2024

A steady rain drumming against the window, Emma picked up her phone and saw that it was 6:00 a.m. She quickly checked for any messages from Kai, but there was nothing. Her thumb hovered over the screen for a moment as she recalled the voice message she had left him the night before, detailing what had happened at the storage unit. Hoping he would reply soon, she pulled herself from beneath the covers and got out of bed.

Moving through her morning routine, she stepped into the shower. Warm water cascaded over her, washing away the remnants of fatigue. The steam enveloped her in a cocoon of heat, melting away the morning chill.

She dressed in a knee-length deep brown suede skirt, its texture soft and familiar, paired with a beige halter top that complemented her warm complexion. She slid into her sleek black long boots, and a fitted jacket completed the ensemble, snug and protective against her skin. She applied light makeup and let her long dark hair fall in loose waves.

In the kitchen, Emma grabbed a banana from the fruit bowl and ate it as the coffee maker beeped, signalling her coffee was ready. She poured a steaming mug and took a moment to enjoy the warmth and aroma, savouring the simple start to her day.

Feeling more grounded, Emma gathered her bag and keys, ready to step out into the rain-soaked world.

Emma pulled her jacket tighter around her and hurried to her Jeep, slipping inside. She drove through the rain-soaked streets of Hawes, the town shrouded in a muted, sombre haze. The wipers beat a steady rhythm, the rain drumming on the roof creating a calming, almost hypnotic sound.

When she arrived at her studio, she parked and paused for a moment, gathering herself. Grabbing her bag, she pulled her jacket close, then dashed into the building.

Rose looked up from her desk with a warm smile.

"Good morning, Emma," she greeted, her voice friendly and inviting.

Emma smiled back as she made her way over. "Morning, Rose," she replied, her tone matching Rose's warmth.

Rose handed her the clipboard with the day's appointments, organised as always. Emma glanced over the schedule, noting that her first client would arrive in about fifteen minutes.

She moved into the consultation room, took a deep breath, and centred herself for the session ahead. The soft glow of a few candles she had lit added to the serene ambiance, settling her into the peaceful space.

A few moments later, Rose knocked gently before opening the door to let in the first client. Emma stood, ready to guide them through the session.

At around 11:30, Emma sat back in her chair, taking a brief break as she sipped her coffee. The day had been steady, and she welcomed the quiet moment to collect her thoughts. Just as she relaxed, her phone rang. She glanced at the caller ID and froze. It was Dr Evelyn Hartley.

Her heart skipped a beat, and Emma's hand trembled slightly as she answered the call.

"Dr. Hartley! How are you?" Emma's voice betrayed the concern she felt.

"Emma," Dr Hartley said, pausing before continuing, "I'm still in hospital but recovering well." Her tone was warm but weary.

"I'm glad to hear that. I was worried," Emma replied, relief flooding her as she exhaled.

"My nephew told me you came by to see me while I was here. That was very kind of you," Dr. Hartley added.

"I wanted to check on you," Emma replied softly.

Then, in a more serious tone, Dr. Hartley asked, "Emma, Laura... the haunting... it's becoming more intense, isn't it?"

Emma's breath hitched. "Yes, it is. Yesterday... it was terrifying. She's not just angry; she wants to hurt me."

Emma recounted the frightening encounter at the storage unit and the unsettling discoveries in her mother Catherine's journal.

There was a long pause on the other end before Dr. Hartley spoke again, her voice low and urgent. "I suspected as much. I need to tell you what happened before I fell. Can you visit me in the hospital tomorrow? There are things we need to discuss in person."

"Of course," Emma agreed quickly, her voice tight with concern. "I'll be there. Thank you, Dr. Hartley."

"Take care, Emma," Dr. Hartley said, her voice now softer. "And be careful."

Emma hung up the phone, her thoughts on what Dr. Hartley wanted to say the next day. She took a slow breath and returned to her desk, preparing for her next client.

The day continued without incident. Emma guided each client through their sessions, offering support with her usual calm and practiced demeanour.

It was around 6.00 p.m. when the last client of the day left, the door clicking shut behind them. Emma exhaled, stretching her shoulders, finally feeling a moment of quiet. She took a sip of water from her bottle when Rose appeared in the doorway, her expression unreadable.

"Emma," she said, her tone slightly hesitant, "there's a man here who wants to see you. His name is Blackwood. He didn't have an appointment but insists it's urgent."

Emma's heart skipped a beat. The mention of urgency brought a tightening in her chest.

"Mr. Blackwood?" Emma repeated, her brow furrowing. "What does he want?"

"He didn't say," Rose replied, her voice cautious. "Just that it couldn't wait."

Emma paused, a cold prickle of unease creeping down her spine. Her instincts were always sharp, and something about the situation didn't sit right.

"All right," Emma said, standing up slowly. "Send him in."

Rose gave her a quick nod and turned to fetch Mr. Blackwood. Emma's stomach churned. Instinctively, she reached into her bag and pulled out the black onyx wolf crystal, clutching it tightly in her hand. A sense of foreboding settled over her as she waited for him.

Moments later, Mr. Blackwood entered, his presence almost immediately filling the room with an air of discomfort. The man was in his late seventies, dressed in a dark, worn suit that didn't seem to fit the light, tranquil environment in the room. His eyes were sunken, his expression hard to read, but there was something undeniably unsettling about him.

"Ms. Ravenwood," he greeted her, his voice raspy and low, as though it had been strained through years of disuse.

"Mr. Blackwood," Emma replied, her voice steady but cautious. She gestured towards the chair. "Please, take a seat."

Once seated, the atmosphere in the room shifted. The air felt heavier somehow, as though the space had become darker. Mr. Blackwood's energy was intense—his aura impenetrable, heavy with something she couldn't identify but instinctively feared.

He began speaking, recounting a recurring nightmare that had plagued him for months. The imagery he described was vivid, filled with shadowy figures and a sense of dread. But there was an odd calmness to his tone, as though the terror in his words had already become a constant companion, something he had long accepted.

Emma listened carefully, trying to read between the lines. His story felt oddly familiar, and the darkness he described seemed to echo the malevolence she had recently faced with Laura's spirit.

Once he finished, there was a long pause before either of them said anything.

"Is there anything else you'd like to share?" Emma asked, her voice tinged with caution, a subtle but clear desire to bring the session to a close.

Mr Blackwood's gaze locked onto hers with unnerving intensity. "Just that I have a feeling our paths will cross again soon, Ms Ravenwood."

It was almost like a whisper, and for a few seconds, Emma wondered if she had imagined it. But a chill ran down Emma's spine, and she sensed an underlying threat, something she couldn't fully understand but knew was dangerous. She clutched her wolf crystal tighter.

Then she heard Mr. Blackwood's raspy voice say, "This nightmare... it feels like more than just a dream."

Emma hesitated, her unease growing stronger. "It's getting late," she said carefully. "Perhaps it would be best if we rescheduled for another appointment, so we can give this the attention it deserves."

Mr Blackwood's expression remained inscrutable, but he nodded slowly as if acknowledging the end of their meeting. Without another word, he got up and left.

Emma sat for some time, feeling the dark, almost tangible force that lingered even after Blackwood had left. The words, *"our paths will cross again soon" echoed in her mind.* She wondered if she had really heard it. But deep down, she feared it was not a warning, but a certainty.

Then, without knowing why, Emma reached for her phone and dialled Michael's number.

The phone rang a few times before he picked up, his warm voice breaking through. "Hello, Emma."

"Hi, Michael," she replied. "I know I couldn't join you the other day, but... I could really use a drink tonight if you're interested."

Without hesitation, Michael's voice came on the other end. "Of course. Where would you like to go?"

Emma let out a small sigh of relief. "How about 'The Obsidian Fog'?"

"Sounds perfect," Michael responded. "If you're at home, would you like me to pick you up?"

"No, I'm at The Soul Sanctuary," Emma replied. "I can walk from here."

After confirming they would meet in about half an hour, Emma ended the call, feeling a little lighter than she had in a long time.

Emma stepped into the washroom and quickly touched up her makeup, smoothing out the smudged eyeliner and adding a little more colour to her lips. She adjusted her suede skirt and blouse, ensuring they sat neatly over her frame. After brushing her hair and spritzing on a light perfume, she gave herself one last glance in the mirror before heading to the front of the studio.

Emma left the studio with a quick goodbye to Rose and stepped into the cool evening air. She had decided to leave her car behind, not wanting the responsibility of driving tonight.

As she made her way towards The Obsidian Fog, she felt a lighter sense of relief – this evening with Michael was exactly what she needed.

Once she arrived at the pub, Emma stepped into the warm, inviting atmosphere. The dimly lit space, with its cosy booths and the gentle hum of conversation, felt welcoming. She immediately spotted Michael seated at a booth near the back, his eyes lighting up as she approached.

"Hey, Emma," he greeted, standing up to give her a warm hug.

Emma hugged him back with a smile. "Hi, Michael," she replied as she slid into the seat opposite him.

Almost immediately, a waiter approached their table and handed them a menu. Michael looked at Emma and asked, "What would you like to drink?" he asked with a smile.

Emma thought for a moment before deciding on bourbon on the rocks. Michael placed their order, and as the waiter departed, he leaned back in his seat, a hint of curiosity flickering across his expression. Their conversation soon turned to work and the latest happenings in Hawes, flowing effortlessly between them as they awaited their drinks.

When the drinks arrived, Emma took a sip of her bourbon, setting the glass down gently before meeting Michael's gaze.

Michael set his glass aside, his expression full of concern. "Emma, what happened in the woods that night? What were you doing out there at that hour? Please, tell me. I've been worried."

Emma exhaled slowly, her gaze drifting to the glass in front of her. She hesitated, the weight of everything pressing on her. "I'm dealing with something… it's hard to explain," she said quietly, her voice barely above a whisper.

Michael's brow furrowed, his concern deepening. "You can tell me, Emma. You can trust me."

She shook her head softly. "It's not about trust. I do trust you, Michael. More than I've trusted anyone in a long time," she replied, her voice soft but steady.

She paused, searching for the right words, her fingers absentmindedly tracing the rim of her glass. "It's… a presence. Something… something is haunting me. The things I've been seeing, what's been happening… it's getting worse," she continued, the weight of her words hanging between them.

Michael leaned forward, his expression growing more serious. "What kind of things?" he asked, his voice low and tense.

Emma took a steadying breath and began to explain—about Laura and her connection to Emma's parents, how the spirit had become more persistent and aggressive with each encounter. As she spoke, Michael listened intently, absorbing every detail. His expression shifted from concern to fear, his worry for her now unmistakable.

For a moment, Emma met his gaze, feeling the weight of his concern settle deep within her. Her heart skipped a beat as she saw the depth of his emotion reflected in his eyes. The sincerity of his feelings seemed to echo in the quiet space between them.

As her gaze faltered, Emma's eyes welled up, the fear and vulnerability she had kept hidden now breaking free. The sting of her emotions flooded her chest, and for the first time in a long while, she allowed herself to feel it all.

Without a word, Michael stood, the movement quiet but purposeful, and walked over to her. He sat beside her, his presence a comforting anchor. Gently, he placed his hand over hers, offering the kind of solace she had not realised she needed until that moment.

Emma turned to face him, her breath catching in her throat. The air between them seemed to shift, charged with something unspoken. In that instant, Michael leaned in, his hand still resting softly over hers, and their lips met in a kiss that felt like everything.

The touch was tender at first, as if he were trying to convey all the words he could not say. But as the seconds stretched on, the kiss deepened, soft and slow, each movement stirring something in both of them. It was a kiss that spoke of unspoken promises, of longing and comfort wrapped into one. Emma felt the warmth of his lips against hers, the gentle pressure of his kiss growing more insistent as his hand, now caressing the back of her neck, drew her closer.

The world outside them seemed to disappear, leaving only the connection between them, undeniable and consuming. Every part of Emma's being *vibrated* with the sweetness of the kiss— gentle but passionate, beautiful in its vulnerability. It was a kiss that spoke of unspoken emotions, wrapping them both in a moment of pure, heartfelt intimacy.

A rush of emotions flooded her — desire, tenderness, and an inexplicable sense of belonging. As they pulled apart, breathless, Emma's eyes fluttered open to find Michael gazing at her with an intensity that matched her own. She knew then that something had shifted between them, opening the door to a new and uncertain chapter.

Their eyes lingered on each other for a beat, the charged silence speaking volumes. Michael broke it with a soft smile, and though he tried to lighten the mood by asking if she would like another drink, Emma gently shook her head. "No, Michael," she whispered. "I'd like to go home."

Understanding her completely, Michael signalled for the bill. After paying, he stood and offered his hand. "Let me take you home," he said, his voice filled with quiet sincerity.

Emma slipped her hand into his, and together they left The Obsidian Fog. The drive back to her place was tranquil, filled with an unspoken understanding, their emotions swirling in the shared silence. When they arrived, Emma turned to him, a soft smile playing on her lips. "Would you like to come in for a drink?"

Michael nodded, and they stepped inside her cottage, the warmth of the space welcoming them. Emma poured them each a glass of bourbon, and they settled into the living room, the atmosphere between them growing even more intimate. The earlier tension melted away, replaced by a shared sense of comfort and something deeper.

Their conversation ebbed and flowed, punctuated by quiet moments where their gazes met, full of unspoken desire. Emma's hand brushed against Michael's, a subtle yet electrifying touch. In response, he gently reached out, cupping her face in his hands. Their eyes held for a moment before he drew her in for another kiss. This one was deeper, more deliberate, as they surrendered to the pull between them, their connection deepening with every breath they shared.

The kiss became a catalyst, their passion quickly escalating. Michael stood, his hand still clasping Emma's, and she rose to her feet, their movements perfectly in sync. She led him to her bedroom, the warmth between them intensifying with every step.

In the dim light of the room, Michael's eyes roamed over Emma with a mixture of reverence and desire. He took his time, his fingers tracing along her jawline, her neck, and down to her shoulders. Each touch was gentle, almost worshipful, as if he were memorising every curve and contour. Emma responded with equal tenderness, her hands exploring the planes of his chest, feeling the steady beat of his heart beneath her fingertips. Their movements were slow and deliberate, a dance of intimacy that spoke of trust and unspoken emotion.

As they undressed each other, the air between them crackled with anticipation.

Michael's hands were warm, each touch anchoring Emma in the present moment. In his embrace, she felt safe.

Their lovemaking was a blend of passion and gentleness, each movement a testament to the connection they were discovering. Emma's breath deepened as Michael's lips traced along her collarbone, his touch sending shivers through her. She responded by weaving her hands into his hair, pulling him closer. The rhythm of their bodies moved in harmony, driven by mutual desire. Michael's gaze never left hers, his eyes filled with adoration and awe, as if seeing the rawest parts of her and embracing them fully.

As they lay together afterwards, the soft glow of the bedside lamp cast gentle shadows across the room. Emma felt a stillness envelop her, a deep sense of peace. The intimacy they had shared left her both physically content and emotionally stirred, a sensation she had not experienced in years.

Her mind drifted briefly to the scars left by Christian's betrayal. She had sought comfort in others before, but nothing had felt this profound. Where past connections had left her feeling empty, Michael's presence had ignited something real - an awakening of desires and hopes she had buried long ago.

The contrast was striking: with Michael, there was a rawness and authenticity she had not felt before. It was not just about the physical closeness but the emotional vulnerability he inspired. As she nestled closer to him, a flicker of hope warmed her heart. For the first time in a long while, she allowed herself to believe in the possibility of something meaningful, something genuine.

As Emma drifted into a peaceful slumber beside Michael, the tranquillity in the room wrapped around them like a soft, protective cocoon. But outside the cottage, the night was anything but serene. Shadows thickened, twisting into unnatural shapes, and the moon's light struggled to pierce the oppressive darkness that had gathered.

In that darkness, Mr. Blackwood stood, his gaunt figure almost blending into the void. His eyes glinted, cold and malevolent, as he muttered incantations that carried the weight of ancient curses. Each word seeped into the wind, poisoning the air with a dark energy that made the very ground beneath him tremble. The shadows seemed to pulse in rhythm with his chants, bending to his will as if feeding off his malice.

Blackwood was not just any client from Emma's past; he was the malevolent force behind Laura's descent into madness, the psychic who had introduced her to forbidden, soul-corrupting arts. His teachings had left an indelible mark on Laura, dragging her down a path from which there had been no return. Now, his presence here was more than ominous—it was a promise of unfinished business, a harbinger of old horrors rekindled.

His rage simmered beneath the surface, like an inferno barely contained. Years ago, Catherine Ravenwood had shattered his grip on Laura, thwarting his black magic and derailing his insidious plans. The hatred he harboured for Catherine had festered and grown, and now, as he stood outside her daughter's home, he burned with a desire for revenge that felt nearly tangible.

Inside, Emma's dreams began to shift, invaded by the faint echo of Blackwood's dark energy. Unsettling images whispered through her subconscious, shadows that hinted at danger waiting in the wings. The storm Blackwood had conjured loomed ever closer, and with each whispered incantation, the night seemed to pulse with a sinister heartbeat, a warning of the darkness yet to be unleashed.

CHAPTER 16

Edge of Darkness

Thursday, 20ᵗʰ October 2024

Emma woke up at 7 a.m. to find a sweet note from Michael. The note explained that he had to leave early to open the bakery but promised to call her later. A smile tugged at her lips, and for the first time in a while, warmth spread through her chest, lifting her spirits.

She stretched languidly as she rose from bed, her body still pleasantly heavy from the night before. Moving through her morning routine, she practiced yoga with an ease that felt new, her body awakening gently with each stretch. The comforting aroma of fresh coffee brewing in the kitchen greeted her, filling the cottage with warmth and familiarity. She prepared a simple breakfast of scrambled eggs, savouring each bite as it fuelled her, the quiet of the morning adding to the calm.

After a long, relaxing shower, Emma dressed in dark jeans, a red sleeveless halter top, a black jacket, and heels. She applied a touch of makeup, accentuating her eyes with a subtle smoky effect, completing the look with a confident, effortless grace.

On her drive to work, Emma's thoughts wandered to her upcoming visit to Dr. Hartley later that afternoon. She could not stop thinking about the doctor's cryptic words on the phone: "The fall wasn't just an accident." Dr. Hartley had fallen down the stairs recently, and Emma had assumed it was just a mishap, but the way the doctor had said it had made her wonder if there was something more to it.

Her thoughts, however, soon shifted back to the previous night - Michael's touch, the way he held her, the intimacy they shared. Reliving the tenderness of their lovemaking, she smiled to herself, the warmth of the memory filling her with a sense of peace and contentment that stayed with her throughout the drive.

When Emma arrived at The Soul Sanctuary, she parked the Jeep and made her way inside. The familiar scent of incense and calming energy greeted her as she stepped through the door. She smiled as she approached Rose, who was already busy at her desk.

"Morning, Rose," Emma said, her voice warm.

"Morning, Emma," Rose replied, looking up with a warm smile. We've got a really packed day ahead. Let me fill you in on today's appointments."

"By the way, Emma," Rose began, tapping away at her keyboard. "There was an unusual email this morning. A woman named Charlotte from London. I haven't had the chance to look into it yet, but the subject line indicated it's urgent."

Emma's pulse quickened at the mention of the name. A sudden shift in the energy around her told her that this wasn't just any ordinary message. The hairs on the back of her neck stood up as a wave of unease washed over her, confirming what she had already suspected. There was something important—and unsettling—about this email.

"Urgent?" Emma asked, her voice steady but with a subtle undercurrent of tension.

Looking at the computer screen, Rose replied, "The subject line says, 'Need help urgently.' I was going to read it after we finished the morning appointments."

Emma closed her eyes for a moment, allowing her intuitive senses to sift through the feeling that lingered. There was a deeper pull here, something that beckoned her attention, and it was not just a request for help – it felt like a warning.

"We'll look into it later," Emma replied, masking the sudden surge of urgency in her chest. "For now, let's focus on today's schedule."

But as she said the words, she could not shake the feeling that this email was more than just an ordinary cry for help. The path ahead had just subtly shifted, and she knew that whatever this was, it was going to lead to something very dangerous.

Emma completed her first two appointments, each session blending seamlessly into the next. At 1 p.m., she had lunch—tuna salad and a croissant Rose had picked up from the café next door.

After lunch, Emma headed to Willow's Creek. The drive was quiet, her mind focused on the upcoming meeting with Dr. Hartley.

When she arrived at the hospital, Emma parked and took a deep breath before heading inside. She made her way to Dr. Hartley's room, where the doctor had been moved from the ICU. As Emma entered, Dr. Hartley looked up from her bed, a mixture of fatigue and relief on her face.

"Emma! It's so good to see you," Dr. Hartley said, her voice still a bit strained but filled with genuine warmth. Her tired eyes softened as they met Emma's, a look of comfort and relief in them.

Without hesitation, Emma crossed the room and wrapped Dr. Hartley in a warm, reassuring hug. "I'm so glad you're okay, Doctor Hartley, I've been thinking about you," Emma murmured, her tone filled with sincerity.

Dr Hartley leaned into the embrace for a moment, clearly grateful for the gesture. When they pulled apart, she smiled, her face softening. "Thank you, Emma. My injuries were minor, and they're almost healed."

Emma settled into the chair beside the bed, her concern still evident. "I'm relieved you're recovering, but... you seem... you said the fall was not an accident."

Dr. Hartley's expression shifted. She seemed to weigh her words carefully, her brow furrowing as she spoke. "There's something I need to tell you about that day. Something I didn't understand fully until now. It's more than just the fall... I can't shake the feeling that there's something else at play here." Her voice dropped to a whisper, as if the very words were heavy on her chest.

Emma leaned in, sensing the gravity in Dr. Hartley's voice. There was something in the way she spoke that sent a chill down Emma's spine.

As Dr Hartley recounted her experience, her voice wavered with the tremors of fear she could no longer contain.

"There was this overwhelming chill," she said, her voice dropping to a whisper. "It crept up my spine and wrapped around me, like an icy hand." Her eyes widened as if the scene replayed before her, her gaze haunted. "I felt... watched. Like something unseen was there, something with a will of its own."

Her breath quickened as she described the sensation of being pushed. "The air itself turned hostile. One moment, I was walking down the stairs, and the next... I was thrown. Hurled into the abyss." She paused, her face growing pale. "I remember the terror in my chest, the helplessness."

Her voice faltered, and she inhaled sharply, trying to steady herself. "The pain... it was sharp and immediate. But it was the fear, Emma. The fear that consumed me. The knowledge that this wasn't just an accident – it was something far darker, something far more sinister."

Dr Hartley's eyes glistened with a haunted look as she continued, her voice barely audible. "It was Laura. I've tried to make sense of it, but the truth is clear now... She was the one who pushed me." Her voice cracked. "And Emma, the intent behind it... I'm scared. Scared for myself, and for you."

Her words left a heavy silence hanging in the air, one that seemed to press on Emma's chest.

Emma's heart raced as she listened, the weight of the revelation sinking in.

Dr Hartley's face grew more solemn. "Her rage, her anguish - it's as if she's trying to drag everyone connected to her into her torment."

Emma listened intently, her mind racing through everything that had happened recently. She began, her voice steady but underlined with unease. "After what happened to you, things have only escalated."

She recounted her recent encounters, her voice capturing the gravity of her experiences. "Laura's spirit hasn't given me a moment's peace. I've had visions, encounters - she's so angry, so desperate, and her face twisted in pure agony. I could feel the cold grip of her rage."

Emma paused, taking a deep breath as she steadied herself. "And it's not just me. I found in my mother's old journal that she, too, felt haunted by Laura's spirit before she died. Laura's wrath isn't just directed at me—it seems to consume anyone who was ever connected to her."

Dr Hartley's expression grew grave. "We have to find a way to stop this. What can we do?"

Emma nodded, her eyes narrowing with determination. "Dr. Hartley," she asked carefully, "do you remember anything specific my mother did that night at the asylum? Did she say or do anything unusual? Was there something she used to counter Laura's black magic?"

Dr Hartley's gaze turned pensive as she searched her memory. "Yes," she said slowly. "Catherine held something that night – a pendant, or maybe an amulet. It was small, intricately crafted from silver, and I think it had a gemstone embedded in it. She clutched it so tightly, but I never got the chance to ask what it was or what it meant."

Emma's heart skipped a beat. "Do you have any idea what kind of amulet it was, or what it might have been used for?"

Dr Hartley shook her head, regret shadowing her features. "I'm afraid I don't. I only know that it seemed deeply significant to her."

Emma's thoughts whirled, a sense of urgency blooming within her. "Then I need to go back to the storage unit. If that amulet is still there, it might hold the key to stopping Laura—or maybe give us some kind of protection."

Dr Hartley nodded, understanding the importance of Emma's search. "I hope you find what you need. If your mother held onto that amulet, it must have mattered greatly."

Emma managed a grateful smile, reaching over to give Dr. Hartley a gentle hug. "Thank you, Doctor. I'll keep you updated on what I discover. Please take care of yourself."

Dr. Hartley squeezed Emma's hand, her eyes filled with a mixture of fear and hope. "Be careful, Emma. Whatever happens, don't underestimate Laura's wrath."

As she stepped out of the hospital room, Emma's decision was immediate—she needed to go directly to the storage unit. The amulet, if it was even there, could be the key to understanding why her mother had used it and how it might help her confront Laura's spirit. She had no idea if it would be waiting for her, but she couldn't afford to ignore any possibility.

Sliding into the driver's seat of her Jeep, she barely registered the steady drizzle tapping against the roof. The windshield wipers swiped furiously, struggling to clear the rain from the glass. Outside, the darkening sky pressed in, and the thickening rain seemed to amplify the unease settling over her.

The streets ahead shimmered with water, slick and treacherous, as she drove towards the outskirts of Maplewood. Each streetlight bled into the mist, casting weak halos on the pavement, making everything seem distorted, surreal. Her thoughts drifted back to the encounter with Laura's spirit just days ago, the memory clinging to her like a second skin, heightening the tension in her chest.

The drive dragged on, each mile stretching longer than the last, every sound magnified in the quiet of the car. The wipers fought against the relentless rain, but it was as if nothing could clear the fog of dread that seemed to settle with the storm. Her knuckles were white against the steering wheel, her eyes darting to the rear-view mirror and the side windows, half-expecting to see something—anything—move in the darkness behind her.

When she finally neared the storage unit, the tension had built to an unbearable point. The parking lot was deserted, shrouded in shadows that seemed to stretch unnaturally long under the dim light of the streetlamps. Emma sat in the Jeep for a moment, the engine idling, her heart hammering in her chest.

After a few moments, Emma took a steadying breath, opened the door, and stepped out. The rain hit her face, cold and insistent, but she kept walking, each step deliberate. Her footsteps splashed softly through the shallow puddles, the sound unnervingly loud in the silence. The shadows around her seemed to move, stretching and shifting in the corner of her vision, heightening the feeling that something unseen was lurking, watching.

When she reached her unit, her fingers curled around the cold metal handle of the shutters, a sharp jolt of electricity racing up her arm. For a moment, she hesitated, as if the shutters themselves might push back against her touch.

Taking a deep breath, Emma opened the shutters; the sound of the hinges groaning in the silence was almost deafening. Inside, the air was thick and damp, heavy with the scent of decay, and something else—a faint, almost imperceptible energy that made the hairs on the back of her neck rise. The weak light from the overhead bulb barely reached into the corners, casting long, unsettling shadows across the rows of boxes.

Then, as the hesitation passed, her mind drifted to the black wolf. She remembered how it had guided her towards the boxes in her dream, its unwavering presence cutting through her fear. Its silent strength gave her the courage to face whatever lay beyond the shutters.

As Emma moved towards the boxes containing Catherine's belongings, a heavy sense of apprehension settled over her. The relentless rain drumming on the building's exterior seemed to mirror the storm inside her. Every creak and distant echo deepened the unease that clung to the air.

She carefully opened the delicate box where she had found her mother's journal and sifted through its contents—silver trinkets, pendants, bracelets, and a few exquisite charms. Some had crystals embedded in them, but none seemed to match the amulet her mother had used the night she encountered Laura.

Her fingers paused over a bracelet, its metal cold and smooth to the touch, when suddenly she heard a faint sound – a soft scrape or rustle, barely perceptible. It was as if something had shifted in the dark corners of the storage unit. Her heart skipped, and for a moment, the room seemed to close in around her. She froze, waiting for another sound, but there was nothing. The silence pressed in even heavier, making the air feel thick, as though the very walls were holding their breath.

Shaking off the eerie feeling, Emma continued to sift through the items, her fingers brushing against each one with careful precision. The box was filled with trinkets that felt insignificant compared to what she was hoping to find. But then, as her hand skimmed the bottom of the box, something strange happened. A subtle vibration pulsed against her fingertips—soft but unmistakable. It felt almost as though the object was alive, reacting to her touch.

Instinctively, she paused and turned her attention to what she had just found. Her hand closed around a deep blue velvet pouch. It was small but distinctly different from the other items, its texture smooth and familiar as if it had been waiting for her to notice it. Emma's heart raced, an inexplicable sense of recognition sweeping over her.

With trembling hands, she withdrew the pouch, her fingers slipping over its soft surface. The faint vibration was still there, pulsing gently in her palm. She opened it and nestled inside, she found a small, ornate box.

She withdrew the box slowly, her breath catching. It was a work of art, crafted from dark mahogany with intricate carvings of scrolls and floral motifs that shimmered faintly in the low light. The polished wood gleamed subtly, as if the carvings might come to life with just a touch. The brass clasp, engraved with fine patterns, clicked open, revealing a plush interior lined with deep, midnight-blue velvet. A reverence filled the air, as though the box held something sacred.

There, nestled within the velvet, was the amulet – an exquisite silver pendant shaped like a teardrop. The swirling patterns etched into its surface seemed to shift with the light, hinting at hidden depths. At its centre, a polished amethyst glowed softly, capturing the light with an ethereal radiance. The silver chain was fine, its elegance understated but undeniably enchanting.

When Emma touched the amulet, an overwhelming sense of energy pulsed through her fingertips. The cool silver was solid and reassuring, yet it seemed to vibrate with an inner hum that felt strangely familiar. As she held it, the patterns etched into the metal seemed to stir with life, almost as though they resonated with her own soul.

The amethyst at the centre glowed with a rich violet hue, its light soft, yet profoundly mesmerising. As Emma held it closer, a warmth seeped from the stone, gently unfurling like the touch of a hand she hadn't realised she'd been longing for. It wasn't just warmth—It was as if the amethyst carried a fragment of her mother's spirit, a presence that soothed her in a way nothing else ever had.

The sensation was unlike anything Emma had ever felt. Overcome by the rush of emotions, Emma closed her eyes, letting the amulet ground her. In that moment, it wasn't just a piece of jewellery—it was a conduit to a bond she thought was lost forever, bringing her mother's love back to her in a way that felt almost real.

With a deep breath, Emma gathered herself, letting the amulet's energy settle within her, reinforcing her resolve. The fear that had tightened her chest moments before began to fade, replaced by a quiet strength. Gently, she placed the amulet back in the box and closed the lid, carefully slipping it back into the velvet pouch. She placed it inside her handbag, its presence now a source of quiet power she could carry with her.

As she drove back to Hawes, the rain had softened to a light drizzle, its gentle tapping on the windscreen steady and calming. The amulet, tucked inside her bag on the passenger seat, felt like a quiet source of comfort. Even though it was out of sight, Emma could still sense its presence, a warmth that settled in her chest and brought her a deep sense of peace.

When she turned onto the path to her cottage, a wave of contentment washed over her. The day, once filled with unease, now seemed distant. She parked the car and stepped out into the cool night air. The rain's gentle fall matched the quiet of the evening as Emma walked toward her cottage, eager to settle in for the night.

Once inside, before she allowed herself to unwind, Emma took out her phone and snapped a few clear pictures of the amulet. She sent them to Dr. Hartley with a message: "Dr. Hartley, I found it. When I touched it, I felt an undeniable connection, like it's been waiting for me. Isn't this what you saw my mother holding?"

Dr Hartley's response arrived almost immediately: "Yes, Emma, that's the same amulet I saw Catherine holding."

Emma's heart raced, a mix of tension and release flooding her chest. "When I touched it, I felt an overwhelming energy, like it's been waiting for me—like it's been charged with something ancient."

"Keep it very safe, Emma," came Dr. Hartley's reply.

Once Emma replied to her, assuring that she would indeed keep it very safe, she placed the box containing the amulet in a safe spot in the living room, feeling its reassuring presence even from a distance.

As she headed to the kitchen to start preparing dinner, Emma's phone rang. It was Michael, just as he had promised in his note that morning. She smiled, feeling warmth spread through her at the sight of his name on the screen.

"Hello, Michael," she answered, her voice light.

"Emma," Michael said, his tone warm. "How's your day been? Are you back from seeing Dr. Hartley?"

Emma paused for a second, remembering the text she had sent him earlier about her visit. "It's been a bit of a day, to be honest. I found something... important. Something that could help with everything."

Michael's concern deepened. "Do you want to talk about it? I can come over."

Emma bit her lip, considering. She wanted to see him, but her body was begging for rest. "I'd love for you to come over," she said softly, "but I'm really tired. It's been a long day. I think I'm just going to settle in early tonight."

There was a quiet pause before Michael's voice softened, understanding. "I get it. Rest up, Emma. But if you change your mind, I'll be here."

"I know," she replied, a small smile in her voice.

Michael continued, his voice soft with sincerity, "And Emma, I just wanted to say that last night was really beautiful. I've been thinking about it all day."

Emma smiled shyly, a warmth spreading through her chest. "Yes, it was," she said, her voice soft but full of meaning.

Michael's tone deepened with warmth. "I can't wait to see you again."

Emma's heart fluttered, her smile widening. "Neither can I," she said, the words almost a whisper.

There was a pause before Michael suggested, "Why don't you drop by the bakery tomorrow morning?"

Emma considered it for a moment, then nodded. "Okay. I'll stop by on my way to the studio."

"Take care, Emma. Good night," Michael said softly, his affection clear in his voice.

"Good night, Michael," she replied softly before the call ended, a sense of contentment lingering in her heart.

After ending her call with Michael, Emma turned her focus to preparing dinner. The kitchen filled with the comforting aromas of garlic and herbs as she chopped vegetables and stirred the simmering pasta. The steady rhythm of chopping and stirring helped ground her, offering a brief respite from the weight of the day.

Once the pasta was ready, she plated it, the simple meal a small but welcome pause. As she sat down to eat, her mind wandered back to Michael's voice, warm and sincere, still echoing in her thoughts. The connection they had shared felt unexpected, yet right, and it made her smile softly to herself. But just as quickly, her thoughts turned to the amulet—the weight of it still in her fingers, the quiet energy that had filled her when she held it. She couldn't help but wonder what it all meant, and what else lay hidden within it, waiting to be discovered.

After finishing her meal, Emma cleaned up the kitchen, her movements slow and deliberate. She placed the empty dishes in the sink and wiped down the countertops, her thoughts drifting back to the amulet. She walked over to her living room and picked it up from where she had kept it earlier.

She gently held it in her hands. The cool metal felt solid, comforting, as she carefully cleansed it, passing it through the smoke of the sage stick she had lit. The earthy, warm, and slightly sharp aroma of sage filled the air as she focused on the task, clearing any lingering energies from it.

Once she was done, she held the amulet in both hands, closing her eyes. Almost instantly, she felt a wave of warmth wash over her. The energy of the amulet seemed to resonate with her, its power growing stronger with each breath. She again felt her mother's presence surround her, a quiet but unmistakable force that filled her heart with a sense of peace.

In that moment, Emma felt the comforting embrace of her mother's love. The feeling was both tender and powerful, like a familiar melody she had almost forgotten, now playing softly in her soul.

She stayed still, letting the energy flow through her, grounding her and wrapping around her like a protective shield, soothing her mind and heart.

When she finally opened her eyes, the room felt different, lighter. The connection with her mother lingered, and she realised the amulet had become more than just an object; it was a bridge to something deeper—deeper than anything she had ever known.

In the bedroom, Emma gently placed the amulet on her bedside table, changed into her pyjamas, and climbed into bed. As she settled under the covers, a deep sense of gratitude washed over her, knowing the connection to the amulet would guide her through whatever lay ahead.

She fell into a deep sleep almost instantly, unaware that the ancient power within the amulet began to stir, quietly preparing to shield her from the darkness that was drawing near.

At 3:00 a.m., the cottage was wrapped in an eerie stillness, the only sound the soft rhythm of Emma's steady breathing. Yet in the darkness, something sinister stirred – an unsettling presence that seemed to weigh down the air itself.

Laura's spirit materialised at the foot of Emma's bed, a swirling mass of shadow and resentment. The ghostly form hovered, its features twisted in a grotesque mockery of pain and fury. The malevolent energy it radiated filled the room like a cold wind, seeping into every corner, suffocating the space with its toxic presence.

It drifted closer, its form growing more defined, intent on reaching Emma. Its hollow eyes gleamed with a thirst for vengeance. But as the spirit drew near, something shifted. A faint warmth, barely noticeable at first, began to pulse from the bedside table. The amulet—small, yet imbued with an ancient power— stirred, its energy vibrating with a quiet intensity.

A shimmering, invisible barrier formed in the air around Emma, as if the amulet itself was rising to her defence. The spirit halted, its malevolent energy recoiling as the barrier expanded. The power within the amulet was ancient, deeply rooted in forces beyond comprehension, and it created a shield that could not be breached.

Laura's spirit writhed in frustration, her dark form flickering, trying to push through the invisible force. The room, once filled with oppressive cold, now pulsed with an unyielding energy that seemed to grow stronger with each failed attempt. The spirit's eyes burned with fury, fixated on the amulet, recognising the ancient force emanating from it – a power that no shadow could overcome.

The spirit circled in growing agitation, its energy weakening with each try, but the amulet's strength only intensified. With every attempt to break through, the force from the amulet pushed back harder, repelling the spirit, forcing it into retreat.

In the silence of the room, the spirit's power continued to diminish, unable to breach the shield woven from the amulet's ancient energy. At last, with a final, inaudible wail, Laura's spirit dissipated, fading back into the shadows from which it came, its presence utterly diminished by the amulet's impenetrable force.

The room fell back into its peaceful stillness. The amulet's protective energy lingered in the air, its ancient power unwavering and steadfast. Emma slept on, unaware of the silent battle that had just unfolded around her. The barrier held firm, ensuring that her rest remained unbroken and her sanctuary untouched.

CHAPTER 17

The Edge of Darkness

Friday, 21ˢᵗ October 2024

Emma jolted awake, her heart racing and her breath coming in short, panicked gasps. She sat up in bed, drenched in sweat, the remnants of the nightmare clinging to her mind like dark tendrils.

Though the amulet's protective energy still lingered in the air, its power had not reached the dream world. There, she had been vulnerable, trapped in the nightmare's grip.

She glanced at the clock. It was 4:30 a.m., the stillness of early morning wrapping around her. Despite the warmth of her bed, a cold shiver seeped into her bones. Hugging her knees to her chest, she tried to shake off the residual fear from the dream. The amulet rested on her nightstand, its gentle glow a small comfort in the darkness of her room.

In the dream, she had been running through a dense, fog-shrouded forest, the moonlight barely piercing the thick canopy of twisted branches overhead. The forest floor was littered with decaying leaves and tangled roots that seemed to grab at her feet. The trees seemed to close in around her, their gnarled limbs reaching out like skeletal hands.

Behind her, she could hear the relentless pursuit of Laura's spirit, her eerie laughter echoing through the trees. Every time Emma glanced back, she caught glimpses of Laura's twisted form, her eyes glowing with malevolent fire. Emma's lungs burned, her legs aching as she pushed herself to run faster, but the forest seemed endless—a labyrinth of shadows and fear.

Suddenly, she stumbled and fell, the ground giving way to a steep, muddy slope. She tumbled down, branches and rocks tearing at her skin. When she finally came to a stop, she found herself at the entrance of an old, decrepit storage unit. Its metal doors were rusted, hanging off their hinges. The air was thick with the stench of decay, and a dismal atmosphere clung to the place.

Emma hesitated, but the sound of Laura's approaching footsteps urged her forward. She stumbled inside, the dim light barely illuminating the narrow aisles lined with rows of lockers. Each one seemed to vibrate with a dark energy, their doors rattling as if something evil was trapped within.

As she moved deeper, the walls seemed to close in around her, shadows writhing like living entities. Whispers and faint cries echoed from the lockers, sending a chill through her. At the end of the aisle, she stopped in front of a large, ornate locker, its door slightly ajar. A deep, guttural growl came from within.

Emma's hand trembled as she pushed the door open with a creak. Inside, she saw Laura—grotesque, her body contorted in unnatural ways, her eyes burning with hatred. Before Emma could react, Laura lunged at her, her hands clawing at Emma's throat. Emma tried to scream, but no sound came out. The locker unit dissolved around her, and she found herself back in the forest, the trees closing in, shadows suffocating her. Laura's grip tightened, dragging her deeper into the darkness.

Emma fought and clawed at the gnarled hands, and finally, with a surge of strength, she tore herself free and ran. The forest transformed, the trees morphing into towering walls of the locker unit, the ground shifting beneath her feet. She was trapped in a nightmarish maze, the boundaries between the forest and the locker unit blurring. Laura's laughter echoed from all directions, Emma's breath coming in ragged gasps.

Stumbling into a clearing, she found a solitary tree bathed in eerie moonlight. From its branches hung dozens of amulets, their crystals glowing faintly. Emma was drawn to the tree, its presence both comforting and unsettling. She reached out to touch one, but as her fingers brushed the crystal, the ground beneath her feet opened up. Darkness swallowed her.

She fell through a void, air rushing past her, her screams consumed by the abyss. When she finally landed, she was back in the locker unit. This time, the walls were covered in thick, pulsating vines. The air reeked of decay, and the lockers were smeared with dark, oozing stains.

She pushed herself to her feet, her body aching. Laura's presence grew stronger, the air crackling with malevolent energy. Fear surged through Emma as she stumbled through the aisles, her heart pounding. Finally, at the end of a narrow corridor, she saw a door covered in intricate carvings of protective symbols. Her breath came in shallow gasps as she reached out, her trembling hands brushing against the cold surface. With a quiet, tentative push, she opened the door and stepped into a small room bathed in golden light.

In the centre of the room stood her mother, Catherine. The light that radiated from her filled the space around her, casting a gentle glow across the entire room. In her hands, Emma saw the amulet pulsing with a steady, protective light, its brilliance mirroring the strength and love in Catherine's gaze.

"Emma," she said, her voice loving yet powerful. "You have the power to end this. Trust in the amulet's power and have faith in your own."

Sitting on her bed, Emma now knew that the amulet was not just a relic but a powerful tool to protect herself and defeat Laura's spirit. Though the nightmare had left her shaken, her mother's presence and what she had revealed at the end had given her courage. She would confront Laura, channel the power of the amulet, and finally put an end to the haunting.

Emma took a deep breath, got out of bed, and moved through her morning routine, albeit with a sense of unease. Once she was dressed, she glanced at the amulet, now safely tucked away in her purse, and felt a small surge of determination. Whatever lay ahead, she was ready to face it.

She decided to walk to the studio, making The Croissant Cottage her first stop. The drizzle that had been falling all morning dampened the streets, and the cool, misty air clung to her skin as she made her way through the grey morning. Despite the gloom, the bakery's warm light glowed through the windows, offering a welcome escape from the dreariness of the day.

As she pushed open the door, a wave of warmth greeted her, instantly melting away the chill from the damp air.

She saw Michael standing behind the counter, arranging fresh pastries. His eyes brightened when he saw her, a smile spreading across his face, making everything feel a little lighter.

"Emma," he greeted, his voice not only warm but conveying the depth of his feelings for her.

Her gaze softened as she met his eyes. Without a word, she walked towards him, her steps easy. She leaned in and kissed him gently, the kiss tender, but with a sweetness that said everything they hadn't yet said aloud. It was a simple moment, yet it felt grounding.

When they finally pulled away, her eyes met his, carrying both warmth and a flicker of something more.

"I found something important yesterday," she said, her voice steady, but a hint of seriousness still there. "It's an amulet... that belonged to my mother."

Michael's smile faded, his expression shifting to one of concern.

Then, without a word, he walked over to where she was standing and pulled her into a close embrace, his arms wrapping around her as if offering comfort without needing to say anything. She let herself settle into the safety of his presence.

"I'll explain everything to you soon," Emma murmured, her voice soft and steady.

He pulled back just enough to look at her, his hands cupping her face with a tenderness that spoke volumes. "I'm here for you, Emma. Whatever it is, we'll face it together."

Her heart warmed at his words. She gave him a small, grateful smile before stepping back, but his gaze lingered on her.

"Have you eaten breakfast?" he asked, his voice gentle but insistent.

She shook her head, admitting without saying much that she hadn't felt like it.

With a soft sigh, Michael moved back to the counter. He quickly prepared a cup of black coffee and grabbed a fresh croissant, sliding both towards her with a small, caring smile. "You need this," he said quietly.

Emma took them with a grateful nod. "Thank you, Michael." She wrapped her arms around him again, holding him just a little longer, appreciating the warmth and simplicity of the moment.

Before pulling away, she kissed him again, this time with a little more urgency, a reminder of the connection they shared. She lingered for a moment, savouring the taste of him, before pulling back.

With a final smile, she stepped back into the misty morning, the warmth of The Croissant Cottage lingering with her, the comfort of their exchange helping to steady her for what lay ahead. Though the rain still fell, the small moments of connection with Michael were all she needed to face whatever came next.

At the studio, Emma settled into her work routine, focusing on writing client reports. It was a quiet day, with no appointments scheduled, allowing her to fully immerse herself in the tasks at hand. Rose stopped by briefly to discuss the inventory of crystals, potential client enquiries, and talk about potential new suppliers before heading off.

Once their discussion ended, Emma turned her attention back to the journals—her mother's and Laura's. She spread the pages out before her, flipping through the entries. She read every single word, hoping to find something that would give her a clue on how to deal with Laura's spirit.

Her eyes lingered on her mother's journal, rereading the passages about the amulet and the haunting incidents. The words seemed to pulse with a hidden meaning, but Emma couldn't quite grasp it.

Then, without warning, the air in the room shifted. A coldness crept up her spine, and the world around her blurred. Her breath caught as her surroundings began to fade, swallowed by an overwhelming sense of displacement. In an instant, she was no longer in her studio—she was standing in the cold, sterile corridor of Ravensbrook Asylum.

The corridor was dimly lit by flickering bulbs, their erratic light casting long, twisted shadows against the cold, sterile walls. The air was thick with a suffocating chill, as though the very atmosphere was soaked in unease. Every step Emma took felt heavier, the weight of the place sinking deep into her bones. And then, she saw Catherine Ravenwood—her mother—standing just outside a door that seemed to pulse with an ominous energy at the end of the hall.

Her face was pale, drawn tight with strain, and in her hand she was gripping the amethyst amulet that was glowing. Its soft, golden light cast an ethereal aura of warmth around her, a beacon in the suffocating darkness. Her lips moved soundlessly, her expression one of fierce concentration and fear as she recited an incantation, her voice a whisper barely audible above the eerie silence.

Then, Catherine stepped towards the door, and the darkness around her seemed to congeal, pressing in like a living, breathing thing. The temperature dropped sharply, and an icy chill swept through the corridor. Emma could almost feel the chill even though it was only a vision.

The door to Laura's room creaked open, its sound unnervingly loud in the stillness. Inside, the shadows were thick, as if the room itself was drowning in darkness. Laura sat in the far corner, her eyes glowing like embers of fire. The room felt alive with a palpable evil, as if it were a living entity, breathing and waiting.

Catherine stepped inside, the amulet casting weak beams of light that barely touched the edges of the room. The darkness pushed against her, a weight so heavy it seemed to crush her. But with each step, she recited the words louder, her voice shaking but laced with a fierce, desperate determination.

Then, Laura's eyes locked onto Catherine's. The shadows seemed to pulse and writhe in response, and a cold, cruel smile twisted across Laura's face. The force Laura had unleashed was as violent as it was overwhelming, reacting to Catherine's efforts with a savage fury that sent the room into chaos. The air crackled with tension, charged with a power too dark to understand, and for a brief moment, it felt as though the very walls were closing in.

The force Laura had unleashed flared to life with an intensity that shook the very air, its power surging and thrashing like a beast freed from its cage. It clashed violently with Catherine's protective efforts, sending tremors through the room and ripping through the fragile barrier Catherine had fought to maintain. The air thickened with an intense and menacing energy, a pressure that felt like it could crush everything in its path, and for a fleeting moment, it seemed as though the walls themselves were closing in on them both.

The vision began to blur, the edges of the scene darkening as Catherine's struggle reached its peak. Emma's heart raced, her pulse echoing in her ears as she was yanked back into the present moment. The studio materialised around her, but the weight of what she had witnessed lingered, a suffocating urgency pressing down on her chest.

Her mother's desperate battle against the dark forces burned brightly in her mind. Emma now understood the amulet's true significance – it was not just a relic, but a potent weapon that her mother had used against the black magic Laura had unleashed.

With newfound resolve, she turned to her computer, determined to unlock the amulet's full potential. Though she had knowledge about amulets and their powers, she wanted to know more about how to use them to banish evil entities.

She began typing frantically, her fingers moving faster than her thoughts could keep up. Her screen quickly filled with search results, each click bringing her closer to the knowledge she needed. "How to use amulets to banish dark forces," she typed, then immediately followed with, "Protective amulets against spirits."

As the minutes went by, the glow of the screen became a blur as she sifted through countless articles, obscure forums, and mystical websites. Her mind swirled with information about ancient rituals, protective symbols, and the arcane history of amulets used in spiritual warfare. The weight of her task pressed on her, but she knew she was on the verge of finding the answers she needed.

One article caught her attention: it detailed the historical and magical significance of amulets across cultures. The piece explained how amulets could create protective barriers, repel dark forces, and provide spiritual strength. It highlighted that amulets, especially those with personal significance or passed down through generations, carried a unique potency.

The article also mentioned that the effectiveness of an amulet in banishing dark forces was often enhanced by a specific ritual, which typically involved cleansing the amulet, setting intentions, and performing a ceremonial invocation to activate its power.

Another source spoke of combining amulets with meditation and visualisation techniques to amplify their effect. Focusing on the amulet's power and visualising a protective shield around oneself was said to strengthen its protective qualities.

Emma refined her search to find specific instances where amulets were used in rituals. She found herself engrossed in stories spanning centuries, each recounting the power of crystal amulets in banishing evil.

One tale from a village in Eastern Europe spoke of a blacksmith who forged an amulet from black obsidian to protect his family from a malevolent spirit. The village had been plagued by illness and fear, but the blacksmith's ritual with the amulet, performed in a protective circle, had banished the spirit, leaving the village safe again.

Another story, from the American Southwest, told of a medicine woman who used smoky quartz to lift a curse that had brought drought and sickness to her tribe. After crafting an amulet and focusing her energy during a ritual, the skies opened, and rain poured down, restoring health and hope to her people.

As Emma read on, a deep connection stirred within her – these stories seemed to guide her towards something significant.

Leaning back in her chair, she absorbed the narratives, sensing the underlying truths in the power these amulets were said to hold, even beneath their mythic layers. The patterns of energy described in the tales aligned with her own understanding of the universe's currents—how intention, ritual, and the earth's energies could be harnessed to shift the balance. The idea of using her mother's amulet, imbued with such energy, resonated with her deeply.

Emma compiled a list of steps and methods that seemed most useful, planning to combine them with the ritual Kai had taught her. She was confident that integrating the amulet's power with her shamanic practices could give her an edge in confronting Laura's malevolent spirit.

With renewed purpose, Emma gathered the information she had found, preparing for the next steps. She knew she'd need to consult with Kai to integrate the amulet's power into her ritual and ensure she was fully prepared for the confrontation ahead.

After locking up the studio with Rose, Emma walked home, her mind preoccupied with the details she had uncovered and the vision of her mother's struggle.

Once Emma arrived home, she took a deep breath, settling into the quiet of her surroundings. With a steady hand, she pulled out her phone and dialled Kai's number. He answered almost immediately, his voice calm and steady.

"Emma, I was just listening to the voice message you sent earlier. Sorry for the delay—I had to take care of something for a friend. My phone was off," Kai explained.

Emma understood. Kai often had to withdraw to protect himself—and others—from the potent energies he worked with. She then recounted her unsettling experiences with the amulet, the visions it had triggered, and the persistent hauntings of Laura. Kai listened intently, his attention unwavering. When she mentioned the amulet, his breath caught.

"Amulets like that are powerful tools against dark forces," he explained. "But they need to be used with intention and clarity. For the ritual, you'll need to create a sacred space and use the amulet to draw the energy needed for the ritual. And the most important thing is, you need to connect deeply with your own inner strength during the process."

Kai then provided detailed instructions for the ritual, guiding Emma step by step.

She would need to be in a place free from distractions, then create a sacred space filled with protective symbols. Once the space was prepared, she would focus on her intentions, visualising a strong protective barrier surrounding her. The final step would be to place the amulet at the centre of the space and chant an invocation to activate its power. Drawing on her inner strength and spiritual focus, Emma would reinforce the barrier, ensuring it shielded her from Laura's malevolent influence.

Emma quickly scribbled notes, absorbing every detail.

Kai's tone became more urgent as he added, "And Emma. Tomorrow night's a full moon. The moon's energy will amplify your power, so it's crucial you perform the ritual then."

At the end of the conversation, she said, "Thank you, Kai," her voice steady but filled with a renewed sense of purpose.

"Be careful, Emma. Trust your intuition, stay grounded and focused," Kai said, his voice filled with concern.

After the call, Emma moved to the kitchen in her cottage, quickly making a sandwich and eating in silence, her mind already focused on the next steps.

At around 10 p.m., feeling exhausted yet restless, Emma finally decided to go to bed. She placed the amulet on her nightstand, hoping its energy would offer her some sense of security, and prepared herself for sleep.

But as the clock struck 3 a.m., the peace of the night shattered.

Emma was wrenched from sleep by a blast of frigid air, her breath misting in the freezing darkness. The room seemed unnaturally still, but the icy chill hinted that something had gone horribly wrong. A sudden, heavy thud echoed from somewhere beyond her bedroom, breaking the silence and sending a jolt of fear through her. The unease she felt wasn't just in her mind; the entire cottage seemed to hold its breath, bracing for something sinister.

Heart pounding, she got out of bed and moved cautiously into the living room. Her footsteps echoed through the thick, cold air. Shadows in the corners of the room seemed to shift and twist as if watching her. Her pulse quickened, and she sensed a growing presence around her.

The silence was abruptly broken by a piercing scream — a sound filled with pain and fury. The walls seemed to shake, and Emma felt a pressure building, making it hard to breathe. Her vision blurred as the temperature dropped further, leaving her shivering.

From the centre of the room, a dense black fog began to take shape, swirling and solidifying into Laura's spirit. No longer a vague apparition, Laura was now a twisted figure of shadows, her eyes glowing with an unnatural intensity. The energy she emanated felt stronger, almost as if something was fuelling her rage.

Emma's breath caught in her throat as the dark tendrils around Laura whipped through the air, reaching for her. The room became a battleground, the darkness pressing in from all sides. In a desperate bid for protection, Emma raced back to her bedroom, her heart pounding. She grabbed the amulet from the nightstand with trembling hands, feeling the faint warmth it emitted. It wasn't much, but it was her only hope. The moment she clasped the amulet, she felt its protective energy wrap around her like a shield, pushing back the suffocating presence surrounding her.

She ran back into the living room, clutching the amulet tightly. Its glow cast long beams of golden light, pushing back some of the darkness, but the shadows didn't retreat easily. Laura's spirit, now more powerful than ever, surged forward with a roar.

Emma began chanting the ancient words Kai had taught her, her voice quivering but steady. The amulet's light flared, cutting through the dark, yet Laura's form resisted, her screams echoing with a newfound strength. The shadows writhed and lashed out, fighting back against the protective light.

Emma's determination grew as she focused her energy, pouring every ounce of her will into the chant. Slowly, the light from the amulet intensified, piercing through Laura's form. The shadowy figure started to waver, and despite the invisible force keeping her strong, Laura's energy began to fracture. With a final, earsplitting scream, her spirit fragmented and dissolved into nothingness.

The cold in the room began to recede, and Emma stood, breathless and exhausted. Even though the immediate danger had passed, the battle left a deep impression. She realised the encounter had taken more out of her than she expected. The thought that something was amplifying Laura's power, fuelling her rage, made her uneasy. The fight was far from over.

CHAPTER 18

The Final Encounter

Saturday, 22ⁿᵈ October 2024

After the encounter, Emma had spent the rest of the night wide awake, clutching the amulet tightly. Her mind raced with the intensity of what had just happened. Every creak of the cottage, every flicker of shadow, seemed to whisper of something darker lurking just beyond the veil. Her body ached with exhaustion, but her mind refused to let go of the fear that had gripped her so violently.

At one point, she had almost picked up the phone to call Michael, but had stopped. She didn't know if the danger had passed or if it was just waiting, simmering beneath the surface. She couldn't risk putting him in harm's way, not when she wasn't sure what would happen next.

At 6 a.m., she forced herself out of bed. The weight of the day's significance pressed down on her, and though she longed for rest, she pushed through the exhaustion. After a quick cup of black coffee, she turned her attention to the task at hand.

In the kitchen, the usually comforting space felt more like a battleground against the dark force she was preparing to confront tonight.

"Tomorrow night's a full moon" - she could still hear Kai's words in her mind. The full moon. He had told her it was the perfect time for the ritual, when the moon's energy would amplify her own. She knew that the full moon was a powerful force in rituals, a time when energy peaked, and the veil between worlds thinned. It was the natural cycle of release and renewal that made the full moon ideal for tonight's ritual.

She had studied the old practices, the ancient rites that called upon the moon's energy to clear away malevolent forces. The full moon wasn't just a symbol of completion – it was a time of letting go, of banishing what no longer served. With every phase, the moon waxed and waned, but at its fullest, it was a potent tool for sending dark spirits back to where they belonged.

As the grey light filtered through the rain-streaked windows, making everything seem dim and shadowy, Emma moved with quiet determination as she cleaned the counters and set out her ritual items. She first took out the amulet from its pouch and carefully placed it on the kitchen table. Its dark hue blended with the sombre tones of the day. She then cleansed it with salt water, rinsed it in fresh water, and smudged it with sage. Emma ran her fingers over its surface, feeling its coolness and drawing a small measure of reassurance from it. This amulet would be her anchor in the coming confrontation. She gently placed it back in the pouch.

Turning to the sacred herbs—sage, rosemary, and lavender—Emma picked them up one by one, the dried leaves brittle but still potent. She ground them together in a mortar and pestle, the earthy, pungent scents filling the kitchen, mingling with the damp air outside. The heavy aroma seemed to settle in the room, heightening her focus. Once they were ground, she placed the powder in an airtight container and set it aside.

The black candles came next. She chose four, one each for the four directions: North, South, East, and West. The candles were not just symbols of protection; they were also for banishment. Each was carefully placed alongside the herbs, their dark waxes waiting for the flame that would ignite them.

Next, Emma filled a clean glass jar with fresh water, an essential element for purification. The water was clear but shimmered in the dim light, mirroring the dark clouds outside. She placed it next to the candles and then selected a ritual bowl from her collection, ensuring every item was in its proper place. She reviewed everything one last time, then packed them into a bag.

Her stomach growled as the afternoon dragged on, and she quickly grabbed a sandwich, knowing she'd need the energy for what lay ahead. Suddenly, the sound of her phone vibrating on the counter broke the quiet. Michael's name flashed across the screen, but she hesitated, staring at it for a moment. He couldn't be involved in this.

With a sigh, she typed out a quick message: "Busy with work. I'll talk to you soon." She hit send and turned her attention back to the ritual. Almost immediately, there was a reply from him: "Emma, I had to come to Richmond for some work. I'll be back tonight. Call me once you're free."

Emma read the message, relief washing over her. Richmond was a four-hour drive, and it was already late afternoon. He would not be back for hours. She was glad he was not here. Otherwise, what if he had stopped by on his way back from the bakery? She did not want him to get dragged into any of this. It was too dangerous.

As the evening approached, the gloom outside deepened, and the drizzle turned into a steady rain, pattering relentlessly against the windows. She reviewed her notes and skimmed through the ancient texts that had become so familiar to her over the years. The chants and invocations Kai had taught her were written in a language she barely understood but had practiced tirelessly.

As evening settled in, Emma's phone buzzed with a call from Kai. She answered quickly, feeling a rush of reassurance just hearing his calm voice.

"Emma, I know this is a powerful ritual, and I know you've never done anything like it before, but I want you to understand the danger involved. The energy you're tapping into is strong, and the forces you're facing are real. But you've prepared well. Trust yourself. The moon's power will amplify your strength, but remember—stay grounded. The ritual will work as long as you stay focused, clear in your intentions."

His words settled over her like a blanket of calm, reminding her that despite the darkness she was facing, she had the strength to overcome it. She was ready.

Emma carefully chose her outfit for the evening—a black t-shirt, jeans, and a black hooded jacket—practical for both the ritual and the cool night air. The rain had turned into a light drizzle, the soft tapping against the windows adding to the growing sense of urgency. She glanced at the clock in the kitchen: 8:00 p.m. She quickly brewed a strong cup of black coffee, drinking it down and managing to nibble on a few biscuits for some sustenance.

The final hours before midnight passed in a quiet yet restless contemplation. Emma sat in her living room, the dim, grey light of the overcast sky casting a muted glow across the room. The weight of the coming ritual pressed on her as she could feel the energy of the night building, a subtle vibration resonating deep in her bones. The moon, with its ancient power, was now an ally in this battle. It was the force of completion, of endings, and of new beginnings. And tonight, it would help her close a chapter long overdue for closure.

For one last time, Emma mentally rehearsed the ritual steps. She went over every detail, the weight of her preparation and the looming confrontation pressing heavily on her mind. Then, taking a deep breath, she rose from her seat; it was almost midnight.

She went to her altar, said a short prayer, and picked up the black wolf crystal she had placed there earlier, slipping it into the pocket of her jacket. Then, gathering the bag with the ritual items, she walked out of the cottage into the cool, quiet night. The path to the woods was dark and winding, the drizzle having completely stopped. The air felt thick with anticipation as she made her way toward the trees.

A few minutes before midnight, Emma stood in the centre of the clearing, her breath shallow and quick, mixing with the biting cold air. The forest around her seemed to close in, the trees standing like silent sentinels in the thickening gloom. Dark, swollen clouds loomed overhead, their presence a warning. The moon, barely visible behind the heavy clouds, cast only faint silver glimmers on the ground. But Emma knew its energy would still guide her, its ancient light piercing through the shadows of the night, even if unseen.

Her pulse raced in her ears as she began to draw a large circle in the earth, carefully sprinkling salt to mark the boundary. The circle was wide enough to encompass her completely, a sacred space that would protect her from the forces she was about to face. With each movement of her hand, the salt shimmered in the dim light, the energy of the circle building with the drawn lines.

Once the boundary was set, she placed the four candles, one in each direction around her. Next, she set the amulet – its deep amethyst hue gleaming faintly – at the very centre of the circle, a beacon for the forces she was about to confront. Beside the amulet, she placed the powdered herbs and a bowl of water, the ingredients for the ritual. The dark energy from Laura's spirit had to be faced head-on, and Emma's determination burned brighter than the cold fear gnawing at the edges of her mind. This was no ordinary ritual. She was about to face a powerful, malevolent force that would test her limits.

Emma's hand trembled slightly as she lit the candles, their flames flickering and dancing like fragile whispers of light. The woods seemed to watch her, the shadows closing in, eager for what was to come. Then she began the chant, her voice steady but filled with the weight of the ritual. The ancient words escaped her lips, their resonance cutting through the heavy silence, pulling the power of the night into the clearing. The wind picked up, pushing through the trees in sharp bursts, carrying with it the threat of an approaching storm. The trees creaked and groaned, as if in response to her words.

Suddenly, a twig snapped behind her, sharp and loud, causing Emma to spin around. The forest seemed to stir, the wind hissing through the leaves like a warning. The darkness thickened, swallowing the faint moonlight, and a chill swept through the clearing. Emma's heart pounded in her chest as her senses went on high alert. The hairs on the back of her neck stood up, each rustle in the trees now a potential threat. Every crack, every shift in the forest seemed amplified in the heavy silence.

Then it came – a low, eerie groan that echoed through the trees, followed by a series of sharp, cracking noises as branches snapped and fell to the ground. The fog, which had begun to gather around her feet, thickened rapidly, coiling and swirling with a malevolent energy, as if it had a life of its own. The temperature plummeted, the air turning frigid, biting at her exposed skin. Emma's breath came in visible puffs, the cold sinking into her bones.

The shadows between the trees twisted unnaturally, like dark fingers reaching out to grab her. The air grew dense, thick with an oppressive presence that seemed to press against her chest. The ground beneath her feet seemed to tremble slightly, an unsettling sensation that rippled through her. She could feel it now, the powerful force gathering around her, something ancient and hungry, lurking just beyond the veil.

The fog closed in tighter, and with it came a sound that made Emma's blood run cold—a faint whisper, growing louder with each passing second. The whispers seemed to come from everywhere at once, filling the air with incoherent voices, murmurs of torment and rage. Her pulse quickened as the air grew heavier, the ground trembling more violently beneath her. She could feel the presence now, unmistakable and crushing, like an invisible weight pressing down on her chest.

Then, from the swirling fog, a figure emerged. It was Laura's spirit, but she was no longer the faint, translucent apparition Emma had seen before. This time, the spirit was something darker, more twisted. The ghostly form that once appeared as a shadow now seemed to have substance, her features distorted into something grotesque. Her eyes were hollow, empty pits of blackness that swallowed the faint light around them. Her mouth stretched unnaturally wide, a twisted grin of sharp, broken teeth that gleamed in the fog, her expression contorted in pure malice.

Emma froze, her chant faltering as the horror of the sight rooted her to the spot. Laura's spirit opened her mouth and let out a guttural, inhuman scream, a sound that shattered the night and echoed through the forest with bone-rattling force. The ground beneath Emma's feet seemed to shake violently, as though the very earth was responding to the scream. The air felt like it was being sucked out of her lungs, leaving her gasping for breath.

The clearing seemed to warp, the edges of reality blurring as the spirit's power surged. Emma's heart hammered in her chest, her voice trembling as she struggled to continue the chant. Laura's form seemed to shift, her body undulating in unnatural ways, growing larger, more menacing with each passing second. The clearing felt like it was closing in around her, the trees leaning inward, their branches creaking as if alive.

Laura's spirit reached out, her cold, decaying fingers lingering just beyond the boundary of the circle. A wave of pure terror crashed over Emma, almost knocking the air from her lungs. Emma's vision blurred as the force of the spirit's power washed over her, and she could feel herself struggling to maintain her grip on the ritual.

The air grew thick with malevolent energy, and the ground beneath her feet trembled once more, a subtle but undeniable sign that the battle was just beginning. Laura howled again, her voice filled with a raw, guttural fury that vibrated through Emma's very bones. The trees around her groaned, their branches twisting and swaying violently, as if reaching for the edges of the circle, desperate to breach the boundary that protected Emma from the spirit's wrath.

Emma's blood ran cold as she tried to hold her ground, her heart racing and her mind struggling to keep focus. The clearing was no longer just a place in the woods—it had become a battleground, the spirit's power threatening to consume everything in its path. Emma picked up the amulet and gripped it tightly, her only source of strength in the face of the nightmare unfolding before her.

She knew - it was now or never. Closing her eyes, she began to chant.

Suddenly, a voice sliced through the air: "Emma!"

It was Michael.

Her heart skipped a beat as she heard his desperate cry. He must have got back from Richmond and stopped at her cottage on the way to his home. Her sense of dread deepened as she saw him standing at the edge of the clearing.

"Emma!" Michael shouted again, his voice cracking with panic as he saw the dark, twisted scene before him.

She had no time to warn him.

He rushed forward, driven by fear for her, but as he crossed into the clearing, Laura's fury was unleashed. Emma gasped as invisible chains lashed out, striking Michael with brutal force. His body was violently thrown to the ground, the impact sending a ripple of shock through the air. She could feel it—feel him— struggling to breathe, as though the very earth beneath him had come alive to trap him.

Laura's presence reached for him, a suffocating, shadowy cloud that seemed to fill the very air. Emma's heart pounded, but she remained in the circle, knowing she couldn't break the protective barrier without weakening herself. She clenched her fists, watching helplessly as Michael struggled beneath the weight of the malevolent force. The ground beneath him seemed to shift and writhe, pulling him further into the earth, as if it wanted to swallow him whole.

The trees around them began to groan and bend, their branches snapping and twisting like whips, lashing out at him with dangerous intent. She could hear Michael's breath, laboured and frantic, as the suffocating energy pressed down harder, the air thick with malice.

A sickening cry escaped his lips as an invisible pain tore through him, a sharp, searing agony that made Emma wince. She could almost feel it herself, as if his pain was her own. She watched in horror as he struggled to rise, his limbs heavy and unresponsive. The weight of the spirit's fury was too much—too powerful. His vision blurred, his body quaking under the pressure, and Emma could hear the unearthly noise that filled the clearing, the wail of Laura's wrath reverberating in every bone.

His body was buckling, his chest rising and falling erratically as if he could no longer hold on. Emma's breath hitched in her throat, but she did not move. She had to finish the ritual—no matter how desperately she wanted to rush to him, she could not break the circle.

The forest around them began to tremble, the ground shaking violently, as if it wanted to tear itself apart. Michael's form disappeared beneath the overwhelming force of the spirit's attack, and Emma's hands clenched into fists, the raw terror bubbling up from within her. She could see him. Could feel him, but she could not do anything.

The fear of seeing Laura attack Michael pushed Emma beyond the limits of her terror. It ignited something deep within her—something fierce, desperate. She couldn't let him be consumed. She couldn't lose him.

Her pulse raced as the air grew thicker with malice. She knew there was only one way to save them both.

She had to finish the ritual.

Her breath came in ragged gasps as she summoned every ounce of focus she had, her body trembling with the weight of the power around her. Reaching out, her fingers closed around the amulet, its surface now cold but steady in her palm. The faint pulse of light that emanated from it seemed to call to her, urging her forward.

With every ounce of strength left—physical, emotional, and mental—Emma poured her will into the amulet, her mind a tunnel of concentrated focus.

The amulet began to pulse with life, its glow faint at first, a mere whisper of light in the overwhelming darkness. But with each beat of Emma's heart, the light grew, gradually pushing against the suffocating shadows. The darkness that had been pressing in on her writhed, recoiling from the light as if it were being burned, its dark tendrils trying to retreat, but the amulet's radiance was relentless, chasing them back.

Laura's shriek echoed through the clearing—so raw, so full of rage, that it felt like the very trees trembled in fear. Emma's heart pounded in her chest as she tightened her grip on the amulet. The power within her flared in response, and the amulet's light surged outward, clashing violently with the dark force that was still torturing Michael.

"Laura!" she cried out, her voice more powerful than she could have imagined. "This ends now! Leave him alone!"

The scream that followed from Laura sent a shockwave through Emma's mind. But she didn't falter. She couldn't. She kept chanting.

With every word she chanted, her voice grew stronger, her command unwavering. The amulet's light burned brighter, the clash between light and darkness an almost tangible force in the air. Laura's spirit writhed, her form shifting and twisting, her face contorted in fury as the blinding light began to tear at the very core of her existence. It was as if the light itself was burning through her, stripping away the shadows that clung to her like a second skin.

Then, with a final, primal scream, Laura's form began to distort violently, the darkness recoiling as if the very fabric of the spirit's being was being torn apart. Emma's chant reached its peak, her voice a force of nature, a blade cutting through the malevolent energy that sought to tear them all apart.

The air exploded with light.

It was as if the entire clearing had been swallowed by a blinding star, a burst of pure energy that shattered the night. Laura's spirit writhed one last time, her form dissolving into the nothingness from which she had come. The wail that escaped her faded slowly, leaving only silence in its wake.

As the light from the amulet began to fade, the clearing fell eerily still. The darkness lifted, and the world seemed to exhale with relief. Emma collapsed to her knees, every muscle in her body screaming in exhaustion. It was over.

The moment Michael stirred in her peripheral vision, Emma's heart skipped. He was alright—shaken, but alright. He slowly pushed himself to his feet, his body trembling from the attack, but there was something else in his eyes—worry, yes, but also admiration. A flicker of fear passed through his gaze, but as their eyes locked, admiration took hold. A silent acknowledgement of the battle they'd just fought.

His voice cracked as he called out to her, "Emma..."

She could barely respond, her voice barely a whisper, as the last of her energy drained away. But she felt it. The weight of the fear and the tension melting away, leaving only the quiet, soothing stillness that followed the storm.

He moved towards her, his steps slow but steady. He knelt beside her, taking her trembling hands in his. "Emma," he said softly, his voice thick with emotion.

Emma could only nod, her breath ragged. She was too exhausted to speak, too drained to move. But as Michael gently lifted her to her feet, she felt his strength steadying her. She was safe now. It was finally over.

As Michael steadied her, Emma leaned into him, the weight of the last few hours crashing over her like a wave. She had not realised how much she had been holding in until now.

Taking a deep, shuddering breath, Emma whispered, "It's over. Laura is gone."

Michael's hand found hers, offering a quiet, comforting squeeze. "Let's get out of here," he said, his voice low, filled with a tenderness she hadn't expected.

She nodded, leaning into him as they slowly made their way out of the clearing, the quiet woods now feeling like a different world—one that had been torn apart and reborn, both terrifying and beautiful in its quiet aftermath.

Once they reached the cottage, Emma's exhaustion seemed to amplify in the warmth and familiarity of her home. She sank into the couch, feeling the weight of the night's events settling heavily on her shoulders.

Michael moved with a sense of purpose, heading to the small bar cabinet in the corner of the living room. He poured two generous servings of whisky, the amber liquid glinting in the soft light. He handed one glass to Emma, who accepted it with a tired but grateful nod.

The first sip of whisky burned, but the warmth that followed was a welcome contrast to the chill of the night. As the alcohol began to work its way through her system, Emma felt some of the tension ease from her body. Michael sat next to her on the couch, his own glass of whisky cradled in his hands.

In the quiet of the living room, Emma began to recount the story of Laura. She started from the beginning, detailing how she first came to know about Laura's troubled spirit. She explained the connection to her mother, Catherine, and the dark forces that had been at play for so many years. Laura's unrequited love for Adrian, her anger, the malevolent energy—all of it had culminated in Laura's haunting, a spectre of unresolved pain and fury.

Emma's mind wandered through the sequence of events that had led to this final confrontation. She recalled the initial encounters with Laura's spirit, each more terrifying and intense than the last. She told Michael about the guidance from Kai, the rituals, and the protective amulet that had ultimately played a crucial role in their victory.

Michael listened intently, absorbing the gravity of the story without interrupting. His eyes, though still reflecting the shock of the night, showed a deep empathy and understanding. He had witnessed firsthand the power of the supernatural, and Emma's recounting of the events provided a context that made the whole ordeal even more harrowing.

The whisky provided a welcome buffer against the raw edges of the night's terror. As Emma continued narrating the whole story, she felt the therapeutic release of finally laying bare the entire story. The recounting was not just for Michael's benefit but also for her own—a way to process and make sense of the extraordinary events that had transpired.

By the time she reached the end of the story, the room was filled with a profound sense of calm. The intensity of the night had been replaced by a quiet, reflective atmosphere. Emma felt lighter, sharing her story with Michael had lifted some of the intensity of the ordeal.

Michael finished his whisky and set the glass down gently. The silence between them was comfortable, filled with the mutual understanding of having faced something truly extraordinary together. The bond forged in the crucible of fear and triumph was strong, and it provided a foundation for the friendship that had grown between them.

As the first light of dawn began to filter through the windows, Emma felt a renewed sense of hope and purpose. The final encounter with Laura had tested her limits, but it had also revealed her inner strength and resilience. The darkness had been pierced by the light of resolution, and now it was time to look towards the future.

Emma and Michael shared a quiet moment as the world outside began to stir. Michael gently pulled Emma into a hug and kissed her, his lips lingering on hers for a moment before he stepped back and looked into her eyes.

"I have to go now to open the bakery, but I'll see you tonight," he whispered, kissing her again before turning and leaving.

Emma stood in the doorway, the cool morning air brushing against her skin as she watched him walk to his car. She watched him drive away and closed the door softly, the latch clicking into place with a sense of finality.

With a deep breath, Emma made her way to the bathroom, undressing and stepping into the shower. The hot water cascaded over her, washing away the dirt from the woods and the remnants of the energy she had confronted.

Once she finished showering, she slipped into a pair of shorts and a t-shirt, then made her way to the kitchen.

She prepared a light breakfast of eggs and toast, savouring each bite as her mind replayed the victorious events of the night. As she ate, she picked up her phone and sent a brief message to Kai, Serena, and Doctor Hartley, sharing the good news of the ritual's success and promising a call later.

With a deep sense of fulfilment and contentment, she made her way to her bedroom, slipping into bed. The cool sheets welcomed her tired body, offering comfort and peace. Reaching over to her nightstand, she took the amulet from its box—where she had carefully placed it after returning from the ritual—and held it gently in her hand. She admired the intricate design, feeling a deep sense of gratitude and connection to her mother, Catherine.

She had faced the darkness and emerged victorious. The amulet's power was a reminder of her strength and the forces that guided her.

Placing it back in its box, she set it on the nightstand and snuggled deeper into her pillow. With a heart full of peace and a mind at ease, she closed her eyes, knowing the darkness had been banished, and drifted into a dreamless sleep.

CHAPTER 19

The Renewal

Sunday, 23rd October to Monday 24th October 2024

In the evening, as the first shadows of twilight gathered outside her window, Emma picked up her phone and called Dr. Hartley. The call was brief, filled with a mix of relief and fatigue. Laura's spirit had been banished, and the haunting that had loomed over her life was finally over. Emma quickly explained the success of the ritual and the sense of closure she now felt.

After ending the call, Emma took a deep breath, savouring the quiet victory. Her next call was to Kai, her spiritual mentor. She shared the details of the ritual, how the energy had shifted, and the finality of the banishment. She thanked him for his unwavering support, knowing his guidance had been crucial.

Emma then called Serena, filling her in on everything that had happened. Serena's voice was warm and filled with relief, sharing in Emma's sense of peace.

After the calls, Emma felt a profound sense of release. She ran a bath, adding lavender salts to the water, and let herself sink into the soothing warmth. The calming scent filled the air, and the heat melted away the last remnants of tension.

After a long soak, she dried off, feeling renewed and lighter. She dressed and began preparing a simple dinner. Michael had called earlier to say he would be stopping by once the bakery closed, and she had invited him to stay for dinner.

As she set the table, she looked forward to a peaceful evening with him, the quiet satisfaction of the day settling in her chest.

On Monday morning, the sky outside her window was overcast, and a pleasant chill hung in the air. Michael had just left, and Emma sat at the dining table, a smile on her face as she sipped her coffee. The serene weather mirrored the tranquillity she felt after resolving the haunting with Laura's spirit and the new connection she was building with Michael.

She dressed thoughtfully in a long black dress with delicate straps, paired with sturdy boots and a jacket. Her makeup was simple yet elegant, enhancing her natural beauty. Before leaving for work, she placed the amulet on her crystal altar, where it rested quietly, its presence a comforting reminder of her strength and recent triumph.

At the studio, Emma greeted Rose and they got to work on the day's appointments.

After her morning sessions, Emma and Rose took a break and headed to a nearby café. The town was already gearing up for Halloween, with festive decorations brightening the streets. Over lunch, Rose reminded Emma about the email they had received from someone new, with the subject line "Urgent." Emma made a mental note to follow up on it.

Returning to the studio, Emma sat at her desk and opened the email:

The subject line read: "Urgent. Please help."

Dear Ms Emma Ravenwood,

I hope this message finds you in good spirits. My name is Charlotte Thompson, and I was referred to you by a trusted friend who is aware of your esteemed expertise in dealing with supernatural phenomena.

I am reaching out to you with a sense of urgency and hope. A close friend of mine, Emily Carter, who resides in Harper's Mill, has been experiencing a series of extremely troubling and bizarre occurrences in her home over the past several weeks. The situation also involves her daughter, who has been exhibiting some strange behaviour, and it has now escalated to a point where it has become unbearable for Emily and her family.

The disturbances began subtly but quickly intensified. Emily began hearing unexplained noises, seeing shadowy figures, and feeling sudden, inexplicable drops in temperature throughout her home. These unsettling occurrences have caused significant emotional distress, leaving the family anxious, fearful, and struggling to cope with the constant state of dread that now shadows their daily lives.

The disturbances began subtly but quickly intensified. Emily is hearing unexplained noises, seeing shadowy figures, and feeling sudden, inexplicable drops in temperature throughout their home. These occurrences have caused significant emotional distress, leaving the family anxious and fearful, struggling to cope with the constant state of dread that has disrupted their daily lives.

Emily is deeply concerned for her family's well-being and safety, and the severity of the events has reached a point where immediate intervention seems crucial.

I am hopeful that you might be able to offer guidance or support to Emily and her family. They are in dire need of someone with your skills and experience to address and hopefully resolve the disturbances that are plaguing their home.

Below, I have provided Emily's contact details so you can reach out to her directly. I understand that this request may come at short notice, but any help or advice you can provide would be greatly appreciated.

Contact Information:

Emily Carter

78 Millstone Road, Harper's Mill,

North Yorkshire, DL8,

United Kingdom.

Phone: +44 7901 234567

Email: emily.carter78@gmail.com

Thank you very much for considering this urgent request. Your assistance could make a significant difference for Emily and her family during this difficult time. Please let me know if you require any additional information or if there is anything further I can do to facilitate this process.

Best regards,

Charlotte Thornton.

Emma felt a wave of concern wash over her. She had barely settled the situation with Laura, and now another urgent plea for help had landed in her inbox. She looked at the contact details for Emily Carter and made a mental note to reach out as soon as she could. For now, she quickly replied to Charlotte Thornton and shifted her focus back to work.

At 6 p.m., Emma and Rose locked up the studio, said their goodbyes, and went their separate ways. As Emma walked home, she passed by The Croissant Cottage, where charming Halloween displays of witches stirring cauldrons and black cats perched on broomsticks decorated the windows. Through the glass, she noticed Michael attending to a customer, and she smiled to herself. In a couple of hours, he would be picking her up for dinner and a movie.

As she admired the festive decorations, Emma realised how deeply absorbed she had been in dealing with Laura's haunting. The gradual transformation of the town for Halloween had nearly gone unnoticed amid the chaos. She made a mental note to ask Rose about decorating the studio and reminded herself to bring up her own decorations from the basement, where she had carefully stored them after last year's Halloween.

Meanwhile, in Harper's Mill, the Carter family house was engulfed in an unsettling stillness, broken only by the intermittent whispers of rain. The house seemed to hold its breath, as if aware of the sinister presence that had begun to make itself known.

Emily Carter was in the living room, desperately trying to maintain a semblance of normalcy despite the growing sense of dread that had plagued her family for weeks. She moved about the room, attempting to tidy up, her hands trembling as she rearranged objects that seemed to have a mind of their own. The oppressive atmosphere weighed heavily on her, a constant reminder of the unseen terror lurking just out of sight.

Suddenly, a loud crash shattered the fragile calm. Emily's heart raced as she turned to find the source of the noise. A lamp had fallen from its place on the side table, its glass shattered into a million pieces across the floor. The room was plunged into darkness, the only light coming from the occasional flash of lightning that illuminated the space in stark, ghostly contrasts.

A bone-chilling draught swept through the room, and Emily's breath became visible in the icy air. The temperature seemed to plummet as a deep, unsettling growl reverberated through the walls. Shadows twisted and stretched, taking on unnatural shapes that writhed and coiled in the corners of the room. The fireplace crackled erratically, sending flickering, grotesque shadows dancing across the walls.

Emily's fear intensified as she heard a sudden, desperate scream from the hallway. It was her daughter, Megan. The young girl's voice, usually full of innocence and joy, was now a harrowing cry for help. Emily rushed towards Megan's room, her footsteps echoing ominously in the eerily quiet house. The pounding of her heart was almost drowned out by the frantic sounds of the house around her.

As Emily reached Megan's bedroom, the door swung open with a violent bang, revealing a scene of chaos. The room was dimly lit by a single flickering lightbulb, and the air was thick with an oppressive energy. Megan stood in the centre of the room, her normally bright eyes now clouded with an unnatural darkness. Her small frame was rigid, her body convulsing as though in the throes of an unseen force.

Emily's breath caught in her throat as she watched in horror. The room was alive with malevolent energy. The walls seemed to pulse with an eerie glow, and the temperature dropped even further, causing Emily to shiver uncontrollably. Objects flew off the shelves, their trajectories erratic and violent. Books and toys tumbled through the air, crashing into walls and each other with bone-jarring force.

Megan's voice, distorted and unnatural, echoed through the room. It was as though multiple voices were speaking through her, their tones a horrifying mix of anger and sorrow. The words were fragmented and incomprehensible, but the malice behind them was unmistakable.

Emily tried to approach her daughter, but an invisible barrier seemed to prevent her from getting closer. She could see Megan's face contorted in a mix of pain and rage, her eyes glowing with a sickly, red light that pierced the dimness of the room. The growling from earlier had intensified, becoming a cacophony of disembodied voices that filled the air with a palpable sense of dread.

In a moment of sheer terror, Emily watched as the lights flickered and dimmed, casting grotesque, shifting shadows across the walls. The shadows seemed to come alive, stretching and morphing into nightmarish shapes that danced menacingly around Megan. The room's temperature continued to plummet, and the air grew so cold that Emily could see her breath misting in front of her face.

Desperate, Emily reached out to Megan, her voice breaking as she called her daughter's name. But the presence within Megan was too powerful, too entrenched in its malevolence. The entity's grip on Megan tightened, and the girl's body jerked violently, as if wrestling with an unseen force.

The house seemed to groan and shudder, the walls vibrating with the intensity of the supernatural struggle taking place within them. Emily's fear escalated as she realised that the demonic presence was not only tormenting her daughter but was intent on possessing her entirely. The possession was not a mere haunting; it was a violent, consuming darkness that sought to claim Megan as its own.

Emily's pleas for help grew more frantic, her voice a raw, desperate cry that seemed to echo into the void. The once-familiar room had transformed into a nightmarish battleground, and Emily was powerless to intervene. The shadows around Megan seemed to close in, their whispers growing louder, promising horrors beyond imagination.

The final chilling moment came as the oppressive silence settled over the room once more, the only sound the ragged breaths of Emily and the eerie, guttural growls emanating from Megan. The malevolent presence had made its intentions clear: it was not only haunting the house but was determined to consume Megan's very soul.

As Emily sank to her knees, tears streaming down her face, she could only hope that help would come in time. The horrifying reality of the demonic possession was now fully manifest, and the true extent of the terror that awaited her family had only just begun.

"Help! Somebody, please help me!" Emily screamed, her voice trembling. Her eyes darted around as the lights flickered ominously, casting eerie shadows that danced across the walls.

The terror was palpable as a vase shattered on the floor and a book flew off the shelf, landing with a heavy thud near her feet. The house seemed to pulse with an eerie, suffocating force, and Emily's desperation was clear.

Back at the cottage in Hawes, Emma sat quietly, the amulet resting in her palm. She was lost in thought when, without warning, the amulet began to turn warm, and she felt it vibrate. She stiffened; the air around her felt charged by an unseen force. Then she heard Catherine's voice: "Emily Carter is in danger… she needs you right now!"

Emma's heart raced as she realised that her next encounter with the unknown was about to begin sooner than she had expected. She quickly picked up her phone and dialled the number she had stored earlier that day.

On the second ring, a woman's terrified voice answered, "Help…"

Before Emma could say anything, a loud, blood-curdling scream erupted from the other end—one that sounded as if it was coming straight from hell...

To be continued...